I had been prepared for fear. Perhaps even terror.

My mother had been a powerful witch, my aunt had often told me that, and to summon such a spirit was always dangerous, even for her own child.

What I had not expected was to feel overwhelmed by love.

My mother had died when I was a young child, and I had little memory of her alive. A haunting scent, laughing blue eyes and a pair of warm enveloping arms about me, that was all I could remember. Catherine Canley had always been just a name to me, a myth, a ghost from my past. Yet here she was before us, a beautiful woman with long fair hair and the same striking blue eyes I remembered.

She floated just beyond the reach of my arms, watching me intently. I had been warned not to look too deeply into the eyes of the dead, and knew not to touch any part of the apparition. But indeed it was hard not to stare, for her face was my own. It was like looking into a mirror.

"M-Mother," I stammered. "Catherine Canley."

The ghost of my mother drifted closer, stretching out slender arms, but stopped just short of the circle.

"Meg, my dearest child." Her voice, like that of the dead Queen Anne, was as dry as the rustle of leaves on the wind. But her clear eyes held a warning. "Do not touch me. Or you, too, will be drawn into the land of the dead."

**Books by Victoria Lamb
available from Harlequin TEEN**

The Tudor Witch trilogy

*WITCHSTRUCK
WITCHFALL
WITCHRISE*

THE TUDOR WITCH TRILOGY

WITCHRISE

VICTORIA LAMB

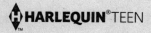

Recycling programs
for this product may
not exist in your area.

ISBN-13: 978-0-373-21102-9

WITCHRISE

A Harlequin TEEN novel/October 2014

First published in Great Britain by Corgi Books, an imprint of Random House Children's Books

A Random House Group Company

www.HarlequinTEEN.com

Printed in U.S.A.

For Gary Abbott.

O the mind,
mind has mountains;
cliffs of fall
Frightful, sheer,
no-man-fathomed.

NO WORST, THERE IS NONE
GERARD MANLEY HOPKINS

Part ONE

LYTTON PARK
CHRISTMASTIDE
1555

THE SUMMONING

Lytton Park, Oxfordshire

"Face north."

Slowly I obeyed, shuffling round on bare feet. The fire had burnt low and I could see only the faintest glimmer of light through the blindfold. But the spell was familiar to me from my training as a witch.

Set four candles about the summoning circle. Four black candles for the four points of the compass.

I shivered, for despite the chill December evening I wore nothing but a simple shift. Yet I was too excited to notice the cold, my heart beating hard, my fingertips already tingling with power.

Pungent smells filled my narrow, low-ceilinged bedchamber: myrrh, juniper berries, scorched yew, and a sickly scent I did not recognize. The preparations were almost complete.

The spirits may be conjured by bell and black candle, and by the burning of churchyard yew and crow's feather.

I ought to have been afraid.

The last time I had tried this spell, I had almost destroyed everything in my world. My mistress, the Lady Elizabeth, sister to Queen Mary, had insisted on seeking advice from her dead mother, Anne Boleyn. I had managed to conjure the executed Queen's spirit, but the timing of the spell had not been auspicious. Something else had come through with her from the underworld: a cruel, dark spirit, which had threatened not only our lives with its malice, but also the whole of England.

Tonight, though, my friend Richard would be my guide, to lessen the chances of our spell going wrong again.

Besides, this time I was summoning up a spirit for my own reasons. My mistress had banished me from Hatfield House, on the advice of her old governess, Kat Ashley. The Queen had reluctantly dropped the charge of treason against her younger sister, but Elizabeth was still out of favour, and now convinced that the presence of a witch in her household—however secret—would get her arrested again. I was back with my father at our family home in Oxfordshire, but I felt certain my destiny would lead me back to the Lady Elizabeth in the future. And to stand against my enemies, to learn best how to use my powers, I needed help—a magickal help that could only come from the world of the spirits.

"Take two steps forward. Enough. You are now almost at the edge of the circle." I heard the rustle of his conjuror's robe as he rose from his knees behind me. "Wait for my word."

The bare flesh on my arms grew goose-pimpled as I waited, and not just from the cold.

I had no doubt that this summoning would succeed. Richard was apprentice to Master John Dee, the Queen's astrologer, a man famed as a conjuror and magician, and had learned the craft from his master. But this was still a dangerous spell.

Richard struck the bell three times with his athame, then

raised his voice. "Hear us, spirit winds of the north! We ask that you heed our call, by the power of fire, and by the power of sacrifice."

He paused, and I guessed he must be pouring a dollop of thick, dark blood from the altar cup into his palm.

"And by the power of this blood."

His wet finger brushed first my forehead and chin, then stroked from one cheek to the other, completing the sign of the cross in blood.

"May the stars look kindly on our enterprise," Richard continued in a ringing voice. "May the dead hear us and obey. By the sacred time, by the dark of the moon, by these spells and this circle, I ask that the spirit be subdued to our will and appear before us."

A thrill ran through me as Dee's apprentice turned away, beginning to chant the ninefold charm. My breathing shallow, I struggled to contain my excitement as the spell came to completion. From behind my blindfold I caught a brief flicker—the candles all dipping together—then the room grew abruptly cold, as though the spirits were approaching.

I lifted my arms in an age-old gesture of welcome, waiting for Richard to finish.

At last he leaned close to my ear, and his breath scorched my cheek. "Call her," he whispered, and I opened my mouth to obey.

But at that moment I felt a chill draught on my bare feet, then heard Richard growl under his breath in frustration.

"What do *you* want, Spaniard?" he demanded. "This is no place for you."

Impatiently I tore at my blindfold.

Alejandro stood framed in the doorway, his face dark with tension, raising a lantern to illuminate the room.

"What are you doing up here, Meg?" Alejandro stared

first at me, then the magickal paraphernalia scattered about the chalk-drawn circle. His gaze flicked to the young man by my side. To the long shift I wore—perhaps a little scanty to be wearing when alone with another man. "And with *him?*"

Oh, Alejandro. What a pest you are, I thought. Yet my heart flooded with tenderness at the sight of him. My Spanish betrothed, so passionate and intense: dark-haired, dark-eyed, graceful as a dancer, both on foot and on horseback. He was strong too, muscular and broad-shouldered, skilled with a long sword, a born soldier. And glaring at Dee's apprentice with undisguised jealousy as though he intended to draw that dagger at his belt and use it.

There was no doubt in my heart that Alejandro loved me, nor that I loved him. Whether we could spend our lives together was less certain. The military priesthood he still hoped to join might permit their priests to marry, but I was convinced his masters would not extend that courtesy to a *witch*.

But he had still risked disrupting this spell, and I could not help my flicker of irritation.

"Working a spell," I told him, "as you can plainly see. Why have you interrupted us?"

Alejandro set his lantern on the table and looked at me broodingly. "What manner of spell?"

He only wants to protect me, I reminded myself, counting slowly to ten before answering.

Richard put a hand on my arm as I drew breath. "Wait," he said urgently. "Don't tell the priest. It's too dangerous."

"Keep out of this, boy," Alejandro snarled, though in fact the two young men were about the same age. Richard was a head shorter though, and lean as a greyhound, so he always appeared younger. And I could see from Richard's tightening expression how much that jibe irked him. But he should not have called Alejandro "priest," when he knew perfectly well that he was still only a novice.

I held up a hand, silencing them. "I am attempting to conjure the spirit of my mother, Catherine Canley, and speak with her."

Alejandro stared from me to Richard. "Are you mad? Or have you forgotten what happened when you summoned Anne Boleyn? You conjured a creature out of Hell along with the dead Queen."

"I have not forgotten. This time will be different."

"Why?" he demanded, his dark brows twitching together in disbelief. "Because you have Master Dee's errand boy at your side?"

I saw the love and concern in Alejandro's tortured face, and longed to smooth away his frown. But he was right, at least in part. The spell was dangerous, and possibly foolhardy. But we had to try. There were still questions I needed to answer, not just about my enemy Marcus Dent, but about myself and the extent of my own power.

"John Dee himself was unable to lay that malevolent spirit to rest," he continued, watching me closely. "It nearly led to your *death*, Meg! Do you seriously believe his apprentice will know what to do if a demon comes out of the void instead of your mother's ghost?"

"You don't understand, Alejandro. There are things my mother may be able to tell us," I muttered, folding my arms tightly across my chest. "Important things."

Much as I loved him, I did not like my betrothed interfering with my magick. He did not understand how much it meant to me.

And how *could* he understand? He had grown up wishing to enter the Catholic priesthood, while at the same time I had been training to be a witch. He was Spanish, I was English. We were complete opposites.

But we had one thing in common. Alejandro never gave up easily either.

"Promise me you will wait until Master Dee can come in person and work the spell for you. If you must raise your mother's spirit, I would trust the conjuror before his apprentice to keep you safe."

Richard snarled, "My master works for Bishop Bonner in London now, as well you know. He cannot be spared from his work."

"His *work?*" Alejandro threw back at him. "Is that what you call it, sniffing out heretics for the bonfire?"

"Master Dee had no choice but to accept Bonner's invitation to work for him. Even the Lady Elizabeth agreed that he must, for it was either that or lose his own life." Richard was openly hostile now, as ready for a fight as Alejandro. "And he may sniff them out, but it is the Spanish Inquisition, your unholy Catholic priests, who light the bonfires under them."

For a moment there was silence, both of them glaring at each other. Then Alejandro turned his head to look at me. His gaze moved over my face, no doubt noting the dried streaks of blood. His mouth tightened.

"You insist on continuing with this spell, *mi querida?*"

"Yes," I said uncomfortably.

His eyes flickered hotly, but to my surprise he did not continue to argue. "You are a stubborn wretch, Meg Lytton, you know that?" His voice grew husky, his Spanish accent very pronounced. "*Muy bien,* if I cannot persuade you to stop, then I shall stay and keep guard over you myself." To my dismay, he closed the door and stood in front of it, crossing his arms. "Proceed."

Richard and I exchanged wry glances. This was not exactly how we had planned the spell to go.

"Oh, very well." I knew it would be impossible to shift him.

"Unless you wish to stop, Richard, and try again another night?"

"What, and miss the best alignment of planets?"

Impatiently Richard gestured me to step back into place, then replaced the blindfold so that I was once more in darkness. "The circle has not been broken. We shall continue." His voice grew curt.

"Extinguish that lantern, priest. And do not interrupt us again, whatever you may see or hear."

Blindfolded, I listened to Richard's rhythmic chanting as he slipped back through the ninefold charm, weaving it about the circle once more.

At first I was very much aware of Alejandro in the room, but then my witch's mind settled into the melodic words and actions of the spell, and I began to sway to their dancelike rhythm, my fingers once more tingling with power. It was like falling into a dream, except that all my senses were on fire at the same time, conscious of everything around me, the creaks and shifts of the old house where I had been born and grew up, birds calling to each other outside in the gathering dusk, the thin whistle of wind under the eaves…

"Call her," Richard whispered in my ear, just as he had done before our spell was interrupted.

"Let the curtain be parted twixt life and death!" I lifted my arms in welcome. "O spirits of the departed, hear me! Catherine Canley, hear me! I who am thy daughter call thee out from the shades of the other world. Come, spirit of my mother, and stand before thy living flesh and blood."

The room grew chill and my voice faltered, forgetting the words Richard had taught me.

It was hard not to recall the last time I had summoned the spirit of the dead in this way. Inexperienced in the ways of dark magick, I had dared to call forth the Princess Elizabeth's executed mother, Anne Boleyn, and she had come to us in the darkness at Hampton Court, a silvery floating lady with sad eyes. But then a terrible storm had descended upon the circle, whipping violently at us, threatening to tear apart the palace brick by brick, the wind howling in our faces...

My senses were suddenly assailed by the powerful scent of burning rosemary; Richard kneeling behind me within the safety of the circle, chanting under his breath, had scorched the dry sprig in the candle flame.

I staggered slightly under a sense of weight, and heard Alejandro draw a sharp breath.

"She is here," Richard breathed.

I had known before he spoke, my flesh goose-pimpled with cold once more, my heart beating thunderously in the silence. There was indeed a presence in the room with us, and it was watching me. The tiny hairs lifted on the back of my neck and my scalp tingled. It was like smelling smoke on a dry afternoon, but not knowing from which direction it came.

"*Madre di Dios,*" Alejandro muttered, and I guessed he must be making the sign of the cross.

Triumph licked like fire along my veins. I dragged off my blindfold and glanced about, my eyes adjusting to the glimmer of candlelight.

I had been prepared for fear. Perhaps even terror. My mother had been a powerful witch, my aunt had often told me that, and to summon such a spirit was always dangerous, even for her own child.

What I had not expected was to feel overwhelmed by love.

My mother had died when I was a young child, and I had little memory of her alive. A haunting scent, laughing blue

eyes and a pair of warm enveloping arms about me, that was
all I could remember. Catherine Canley had always been just
a name to me, a myth, a ghost from my past. Yet here she was
before us, a beautiful woman with long fair hair and the same
striking blue eyes I remembered.

She floated just beyond the reach of my arms, watching me
intently. I had been warned not to look too deeply into the
eyes of the dead, and knew not to touch any part of the apparition. But indeed it was hard not to stare, for her face was
my own. It was like looking into a mirror.

"M-Mother," I stammered. "Catherine Canley."

The ghost of my mother drifted closer, stretching out slender arms, but stopped just short of the circle.

"Meg, my dearest child." Her voice, like that of the dead
Queen Anne, was as dry as the rustle of leaves on the wind.
But her clear eyes held a warning. "Do not touch me. Or you
too will be drawn into the land of the dead."

I nodded, my eyes filling with tears. My mother was so
beautiful and ethereal, her skin as pale as marble, even her
lips, parting now in a smile. It was so cruel that we had been
parted when I had been only five years old. She could have
taught me so much....

"My sister, Jane, taught you all you needed to know," my
mother said softly, reading my thoughts as though I had spoken them aloud.

"Do not grieve for me, Meg. It was my time to leave this
earth. And your time will come too. But not yet. And not
until you have accomplished those deeds which you are destined to do."

It was hard to know if she was speaking aloud or inside my
head, nor even if the other two in the room could hear her. I
was entranced by the rustling whisper of her voice and could
not seem to tear my gaze from hers.

Richard cleared his throat behind me, and abruptly I was able to look away. We did not have much time to gather the information I needed, he was reminding me with that cough. These apparitions rarely lasted more than a few moments.

I struggled to shake off the cloying spell of her presence, trying to recall my mission. "Mother, I need to...to ask you something."

"You want to know about the witchfinder called Marcus Dent."

I swallowed. "Yes."

Marcus Dent. Witchfinder. The man who had condemned Aunt Jane to the stake. Once my suitor, now my mortal enemy...

I wondered if the others were cold too, but did not dare look at Alejandro, a shadowy figure to my left in the darkness. He was standing outside the safety of our circle, I suddenly realized. If my mother's spirit chose to approach Alejandro, perhaps even to touch him, it was possible she could kill him. And although she was my mother, I knew the spirits of the dead could never be entirely trusted.

"The man Dent is dangerous, my child."

"He wants me dead," I whispered. "It was prophesied—some years ago in Germany, by a sorceress he had condemned— that a witch would kill him, and Marcus believes that witch to be me. Is he right?"

"I cannot tell you that." She paused, half closing her eyes as though listening to voices from the shadows about us. "But I can tell you that when you sent Marcus Dent into the void that lies beyond this world, he ripped away some of your own magick. And he is learning all he can about the craft so that his magick will grow in power. Soon it will surpass your own if you do not stop him."

I winced, though we had half suspected as much already

about my enemy. To hear it from my mother's lips was terrible, but I did not have time to examine that information now.

"Is he right? *Is* the prophecy about me?" I asked her.

"I do not have an answer for you."

Frustration built in me. It was almost as though she were deliberately blocking me.

But this was my mother. I looked into her eyes and saw a flicker of sympathy there. Sympathy and sadness. I knew instinctively that she would answer if she could, but something was holding her back. Some obscure rule of the spirit world, perhaps. Then I remembered how John Dee had taught me the correct way to question a spirit and interpret the answers. There were indeed distinct rules to the summoning of a spirit, and I had not been following them.

Or perhaps I had not asked the right question yet.

"Mother," I began carefully, "is there any way you can help me to find the answer for myself?"

Her look grew keen, her blue eyes suddenly glowing. "Do you have the book?"

I stared, then shot a quick glance at Richard. *Book?*

Dee's apprentice shrugged, his face blank.

"Which book?" I asked.

"My journal." The spirit of my mother moved closer, her intense blue gaze locked on mine. "My book of spells."

I held her gaze, so excited by this information that I could barely respond at first. My fingers were tingling furiously, my body prickling with a sudden violent cold. Outside the house I could hear the whine of the wind rising. There was a storm coming.

"Y-you left behind a spell book?" I tried to contain my agitation. "Where is it hidden? Can you tell me, Mother?"

Her smile seemed strained. "I have already said too much. It is hidden. The place will be revealed to you. Watch and see."

"But is it here at Lytton Park? Can you at least tell me that?"

But my mother was fading, growing ever more silvery and spectrelike. "Watch and see," she repeated faintly. Already I could see the wall through her body.

Panic filled me as I realized we were losing her. "Wait, please." My voice faltered. "I—I love you...."

Her smiling look reached my heart. But it turned swiftly back to sadness. "You will be asked to make a hard choice, Meg." Her voice was barely audible against the growing roar of the wind. "Let your heart guide you. Now Queen Mary's husband has left England, leaving her bed empty, her malice towards her sister grows. For she knows King Philip desires the princess in her place."

I stared, wondering what my mother could possibly know of King Philip, the handsome Spanish King who had married Mary Tudor last year, then deserted her to wage war against the French.

"When I was still living on this earth," my mother continued, "I served the princess's mother, the beautiful Anne Boleyn, yet could not save her from King Henry's cruelty. Now Elizabeth's enemies threaten her with false accusation too. But we Canley women are powerful. Never forget that, Meg. Do not be afraid to use your gift, as I once was...."

I felt tears in my eyes. My mother had failed to save Queen Anne from execution. Now it felt as though I had failed Queen Anne's daughter by allowing myself to be dismissed from her side.

Her body was fading to a silvery vapour. The visitation was almost over. My mother turned at the last moment and looked directly at Alejandro. Her eyes seemed to widen.

"Such a bright light..." she whispered.

Alejandro had been frozen throughout the summoning, his gaze fixed on my mother, a curious intensity in his face.

I wanted to shout a warning, but could not seem to speak. It was dangerous to touch a spirit. I had been drawn out of the protective circle during my last summoning, and died a magickal death. Alejandro was not even within the circle.

But as her hands stretched out towards him, Alejandro took a cautious step backward. He bowed, courteous even to a ghost, murmuring in Spanish even as he remained just out of her reach.

Then my mother was gone.

The four candles about the circle flickered and were still. The noise of the wind fell sharply away.

It was over.

My body was trembling, the raw power of the spell still throbbing and coursing through me.

I swayed there, head bowed, eyes closed, trying to shake off the dizzying effects of the spell. My feet seem to be floating like the spirit's. It felt as though I had been drenched in ice-water, wrung out like a cloth, then tipped upside down to dry. It was not a comfortable sensation.

Gradually I became aware of a cold draught.

I looked up and promptly wished I had kept my eyes closed, my heart beginning to race.

My bedchamber had disappeared, Alejandro and Richard along with it.

I was soaring like a bird through the chill mid-winter night, snow whitening the track leading away from Lytton Park, the dark air humming and alive with strange power.

2

MARCUS DENT

I was still clad in my thin white shift. A mercifully long garment, it flapped about my ankles as I was dragged above the treetops, struggling in vain against the spell that had wrenched me away from my friends. I would have seemed to any observer like a great white owl haunting the night, though in truth I felt more like the sorrowful ghost I had summoned. Now I knew how it must feel to be tugged from eternal sleep to stand again in the world of the living, forced to obey a greater power.

This being a vision though, there was no one about to observe my undignified flight. Not until I circled the broken roof of an old hayloft and realized where the spell was taking me.

Home Farm.

The site was a desolate ruin now: a collection of empty and tumbledown buildings a few acres past the wood, their fallen stones overgrown with long grass and brambles. Once though it had been a thriving farm, attached to the big house and providing for our family's needs. But my great-grandfather had allied himself to some minor uprising, and though he had been spared execution, our family fell out of favour at court. So Home Farm had been abandoned, our coffers not deep enough to pay for its upkeep, and now the livestock was kept at the big house instead, and vegetables grown in our own gardens.

The night was very still here, almost expectant. I glanced down, and saw a fair-haired man below me, looking up.

It was Marcus Dent.

Witchfinder, would-be friend to the all-powerful Spanish Inquisition, and my aunt's murderer.

I felt raw terror for a moment, then deliberately slowed my breathing, trying to control my fear. I did not want Marcus to think he had any advantage over me.

This was the man who had once asked me to marry him, claiming he loved me, yet now wished solely for my destruction. My mother's spirit had told me he was dangerous. And probably more witch than witchfinder now.

That much I had already known for myself.

Last time we had met, Marcus Dent had tricked me into climbing his magickal tower, and there attempted to separate my head from my body. When I managed to escape, he shifted shape, pursuing me first as a hawk, then scuttling away in the form of a black rat. I had always suspected that Marcus had taken on some of my power while in the void, and my mother's words tonight had confirmed that. But how such a transfer of power could have happened, and what it might signify for the future, I still did not understand.

The darkness shifted, jolting sideways.

Suddenly I was on the ground, standing in front of him. Beyond him stood the old pigsty, its crumbling timbers whitened by frost and overgrown with brambles, its door half hanging off its hinges.

How on earth had Marcus managed to break my protective spells and get me here?

Perhaps we had created a weakness in our barrier of spells with the summoning. After all, my mother's spirit had got in past those spells. Perhaps Marcus had brought me out the same way.

Unless this was all happening in my head. But how to be sure?

The stars hung far above, cold and vaguely threatening in their majesty, and for a moment the moon peeked out from its hood of cloud, watching us with a doleful face. I could not see the wintry ground but felt the cold strike up through my feet, and shivered.

Marcus studied me in silence, then smiled. "Meg Lytton," he said with heavy emphasis at last, as though my name were some kind of charm.

"Master Dent."

He was dressed all in black, hands clasped behind his back, sleek fair head—no cap—which was tilted to one side as he considered me.

I searched for the scars he had received when I sent him spinning into the void, but his face was unclear, as though there was a mist across it, shimmering whenever he moved or spoke, like a watery reflection being stirred.

He was not really there, I realized. And neither was I.

I was hugely relieved to know this was a vision, not truth. But it was still a shock to be looking directly at Marcus Dent. He looked real enough, I thought. Too frighteningly real.

Beware a traveller who comes over water, over land.

My late aunt, also a witch and the woman who had trained me to follow in her footsteps, had warned me to beware such a man. We had initially feared her prophecy was about Alejandro de Castillo, fresh come from Spain, but now I knew it had concerned this villain, Marcus Dent, who had recently returned from Germany at the time.

How long it seemed since Aunt Jane had been my tutor, and we had lived in peace together in this very house, secretly practising our craft under the full moon each month.

But then my father had forced me into the disgraced Lady Elizabeth's service, and Dent had burnt Aunt Jane at the stake as a witch. Only last spring he had accused me of witchcraft too, condemning me to face trial by water. I had found the strength to escape my bonds that day and turn my skill against the witchfinder. I had opened a gate into the void beyond our world and Marcus Dent had been sucked into darkness.

He had returned, of course. Many times more powerful, not quite human, and now intent on my death.

Nothing was ever simple with dark magick.

"Very well, Marcus, you have my attention." I looked at my tormentor boldly. "What do you want? Why are you in my dreams again?"

"Is this a dream, Meg?"

The air was cold against my cheek, the icy track beneath my feet solid, and I could hear the faint rustling of some wild creature in the overgrown ruins.

He was right. It did not feel like a dream.

"A waking vision, then. What do you want, Marcus?"

There was a flicker of rage in his face, hurriedly suppressed.

"I want you to know that you will fail."

"Fail at what?"

"The quest I am setting you."

"Go away, Marcus. I'm not interested in your games."

"You will be."

I looked at him, distrusting his smile. "You can forget your quest. And keep your distance from Alejandro," I told him. "Or I'll make you sorry you came back from the void."

"Threatening me, Meg?" The witchfinder's confidence infuriated me as always. "You are hardly in a position to be threatening anyone, my dear. But perhaps you mistakenly believe it will not be long before your mistress inherits the throne, and your fortune changes with hers."

I raised my eyebrows, not answering.

He showed white teeth, shaking his head as though I had spoken.

"Wrong again, Meg. Your mistress is no closer the throne than she was, for the wayward princess has been making the most unfortunate friends in your absence. And when the Queen hears of this latest scandal, Elizabeth will be thrown back in the Tower of London, where she belongs." He smiled with satisfaction—Marcus Dent was no friend to the Lady Elizabeth. And that was partly my fault....

"I no longer serve the Lady Elizabeth. And I'm serious about Alejandro. Stay away from him, do you hear?" I struggled to keep my voice level, my hands clenched into fists by my side. I did not know what he was trying to say about the Lady Elizabeth, but it sounded like mere nonsense, designed to distract me from his intentions towards my betrothed. "You can stay away from me too, while you're at it. I've had enough of your foul company to last me into Hell itself."

Behind him the outline of the pigsty wavered, and I caught again that odd rustling sound, more muffled now, like some unseen animal was digging in the ruins.

"Come, Meg, you don't mean that. We were so close once. And I like to think you might come to love me if we met in Hell."

"Not a chance."

"That remains to be seen." His gaze moved slowly down my body, and I felt my skin crawl under that scrutiny. "Would you not rather spend your days and nights with a man you are destined to kill than a man who is destined to kill *you?*"

The witchfinder was speaking of the two prophecies that touched me. First that Marcus Dent would be killed by a witch with the power to summon a dead King—a feat I had already achieved that spring when I raised Henry Tudor from his grave. And second, that Alejandro's wife would die in childbirth, a curse laid on him by a dying witch he had mistakenly betrayed.

"Who can you trust in this business?" Marcus continued smoothly when I did not reply. "That is the question you will have to answer."

"I don't have to answer any question of yours, Marcus Dent," I said hotly, losing my slender grip on my temper. "You are nothing to me. You are a shadow in the darkness."

"Of course," the witchfinder murmured, watching me with raised eyebrows. "I am a shadow. I am what you made me, in fact."

"I thought I made you *dead*."

He was smiling again, the thin curve of his lips malevolent.

"Death is life's mirror, only the glass is kept dark. A lesson you should have learned by now, my young witch."

He took a step backwards, and I realized that his outline was fading, just as my mother's spirit had faded in my chamber as the summoning-spell wore off. Already I could see snow-covered brambles and the timber ruins of the old pigsty more sharply through his body.

The place was silent again now, the wild creature I had heard vanished into the night, though above our heads a brilliant single star was shining, bright and clear in the heavens.

His ghostly smile lingered in the darkness a moment after his body had disappeared, taunting me.

"When you are ready to face me again, Meg Lytton, you

will easily find me." Then the last trace of Marcus Dent was gone, only a thin echo of his voice floating back to me on the chilly air. "Unless I find you first."

The room was dark, suffocatingly so. I swam slowly up out of the vision, my head aching. Someone had wrapped me in a warming cloak or blanket, and was tilting a cup of something spicy to my lips. A fiery liquid burnt my throat and I struggled, pushing the cup away.

"Faugh!" I spluttered. "What is that stuff?"

"She's awake," Richard said drily, and straightened up, smiling down at me. "Thank God. I was beginning to think we would never get you back, Meg. Your father is coming up the stairs to see what all the commotion is about. I'd better head him off before he bursts in here and has a fit. You know how little he likes your Spanish priest, and if he should catch the two of you like *that*..."

Richard vanished through the door, and a few seconds later I heard him talking on the stairs in a soothing voice, using his own not insubstantial magickal powers to persuade my father back down to his study.

I frowned, still light-headed, not quite understanding what Richard had meant.

If he should catch the two of you like that...

That was when I realized I was lying on the floor in my bedchamber, my shift rucked up about my bare knees in a most undignified fashion, my head on Alejandro's lap. My face flushed with embarrassment and I struggled to sit up, dragging my shift down to cover my legs.

"What on earth...?"

"Hush," Alejandro insisted, holding me by the shoulders. He did not sound upset but his smile was strained. "It's awkward, I agree, but I don't think you should move yet. You're very pale. Have another sip of Richard's concoction. I don't know what's in it, and it smells and probably tastes foul too, but it brought you back to us."

"What happened?"

"You tell me." His gaze searched my face upside down. "Your mother's ghost vanished and you collapsed. You lay still for a moment, then gave a dreadful shriek and started drumming your heels on the floor and waving your arms about like a lunatic."

I blinked, considering that information, and my face grew hotter than ever.

Richard came limping back into the room. He had been beaten by his drunken father as a child, one leg broken so cruelly it had never quite recovered. His bad leg was what made him sharp with Alejandro, I felt sure of it, for where Richard was physically awkward, Alejandro was tall, handsome, and startlingly graceful at times.

Besides, Richard was in love with me. He had told me so himself only a few weeks ago when trying to stop me pursuing Marcus Dent. So to see me with my head in Alejandro's lap must have hurt.

Richard closed the door behind him with a quiet click. "No need to fret, I told your father you had suffered a nightmare," he told me, seeing my worried face. "I assured him that I had only come up to check you were all right, and to administer a sleeping draught. Your father seemed to believe me. Though you never know. Perhaps he thinks there's something going on between us."

Above me, Alejandro said nothing in response to this but ground his teeth audibly.

"Don't even joke about that," I warned Richard.

"Very well. I can do a straight face when required. Though I suspect your father would be ecstatic if he thought Alejandro was no longer your betrothed." Richard looked at me, dropping the act. "Some kind of vision, was it?"

I nodded.

"That's not uncommon following the raising of a spirit. I should have warned you before we started, but I didn't want to frighten you."

"Thanks."

"You're welcome." Richard rekindled the lantern and hung it from a hook on the wall. Then he knelt to examine me, his face shuttered as though he did not want me to suspect how worried he had been. But I could tell from the prickly manner in which he spoke that my seizure had frightened him. "Now to check what harm has been done to you, if any. Then you can tell me all about what you saw. Hands first."

I held out my hands, but squinted in pain. The light from that lantern was too bright. Or else I was feverish. My head was throbbing. A memory was straining to be let through, squeezing between the darkness of that other world and the brightness of this harsh new one.

Then I remembered.

"Pigs…"

Richard looked up from studying my palms, frowning. "I beg your pardon?"

"It's in the pigsty." I smiled up at Alejandro, his face still upside down above me, though my head felt like it was cracking in two.

"That's what the vision was trying to tell me. Marcus Dent was there to distract me. To stop me seeing where it was hidden. But he failed. My heart knew the truth."

Alejandro stared down at me, not bothering to hide his bewilderment. "What on earth are you talking about, *mi querida?*"

"My mother's spell book," I explained, glancing from one

to the other with a smile on my face. "You heard my mother say she would show me where it was, and she did. Only she did it in a vision."

"So where is it?" Richard demanded, still holding my hand, his gaze intent on my face.

"It's buried under the old pigsty at Home Farm," I said simply.

"And I'm willing to bet it's been there since she died."

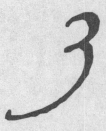

SNOW-STILL

The next morning, sleepily descending the stairs with Ale-jandro, I found my father waiting for me in the doorway to his study. I had to admit, it felt good to be living at home again after a year and a half in the Lady Elizabeth's service. There were so many memories here, crowding about my head. But much as I loved Lytton Park, this was not where I belonged any more.

I had lived at the royal court now, under the shadow of fear, and discovered my power as a witch, sensing where it might take me in the future. This lovely green parkland in the depths of Oxfordshire was easy on the eyes and the heart. But it could no longer contain me. My destiny lay elsewhere, as my mother had made clear when I summoned her.

"Good morning, Meg."

"Father."

I curtseyed, and Alejandro bowed his head beside me. When my father held my gaze, unsmiling, I guessed there was something wrong.

"You wish to speak with me, Father?"

"Just for a few moments," he agreed, stepping aside. "Come into my study, would you?"

I had seen my father's sharp gaze take in our linked hands, and realized that this was the first time Alejandro had indicated his love for me so openly. It was a daring move, considering that he had not asked my father's permission to court me, and was Spanish, a people for whom my father had little love.

My father did not comment on it though, waving me inside his study as though he had other things on his mind.

"What happened last night, Meg?" he asked, frowning. "I heard you shouting. That boy Richard persuaded me to go back to bed, but I know when magick is being worked under my roof. And I do not like it."

He shuffled into his study after me, for his hip had been troubling him this winter. Richard had offered to try and heal his aching bones, but my father had refused to discuss it, a dark frown on his face. He seemed to regard Richard with some tolerance, perhaps sympathizing with his own limping gait, but was easily angered by anything that sounded like witchcraft.

"Come and sit beside the fire with me," my father continued, "and let us talk without pretence for once."

I glanced at Alejandro, worried what this might mean. His face was tense too, but he said nothing.

I settled myself on the broad wooden seat by the fireside. Alejandro did not enter but hesitated on the threshold of my father's study, perhaps sensing that my father did not quite approve of our friendship. Nor was my father alone in that, I thought, for I had often caught the same disapproving look on Richard's face. It seemed no one wanted me to be with Alejandro.

No one but Alejandro himself, that was.

"May I come in too, sir?"

My father frowned, not quite looking at him. "I have no wish to cause you any offence, *señor,* but..."

"But you wish to speak with your daughter alone." Alejandro bowed, but looked at me with chagrin. It was clear he did not want to leave me alone with a man who might be my father but who we both knew was not quite trustworthy. "Of course, sir. I will wait outside."

When the door had closed behind Alejandro, my father stood a moment in brooding silence, looking down at me. Then he demanded, "You intend to marry that Spaniard?"

I open my mouth to reply and abruptly closed it again.

Part of me had intended to say yes, and that realization shook me. I had thought my feelings unchanged since the spring when Alejandro asked me to marry him, on the river walk outside Richmond Palace. But clearly something was different now, for my answer was not so simply given.

Was I so close to accepting Alejandro's proposal, after all?

"I have not yet decided," I managed to say, not particularly willing to discuss the workings of my heart with my father.

"But he has asked for your hand?" he persisted.

I hesitated, then gave a reluctant nod. Why bother to hide the depth of our involvement? My father must have seen our affection for each other. Alejandro had been living under his roof for the past few weeks, albeit sharing a room with my brother William. My father was many things, but he was not a fool.

"And you have not yet given him a reply. So you do not want him, then?" His eyes narrowed on my face, striving to understand. "You seem very thick with him for a girl who is not betrothed."

His questions flustered me. We were secretly betrothed, but only until the spring, when I must give Alejandro my final answer—at my request, he had allowed me a year and day to

answer his proposal, and the time was drawing near when I
needed to decide.

Yes or no.

I did want Alejandro. Of course I did. I loved him with all
my heart and soul. Indeed, I loved him more completely than
I had ever loved any other living creature. But that did not
mean I should seek to bind him to me for ever.

Being in love with someone did not mean you were perfect
for that person, or vice versa. Sometimes the universe played
cruel tricks, pushing two people into marriage who had no
business being together. And I had no wish to become a cos-
mic joke.

"I cannot answer that, sir," I managed to respond, and
willed myself to sound calm.

No, I was not interested in discussing my feelings for Alejandro with my father. After his betrayal of my aunt, leaving
her to die a hideous death at the hands of Marcus Dent, I did
not consider he had any right to interfere with my life.

"Cannot, or will not?" he muttered.

"Forgive me, Father," I said abruptly, getting to my feet,
"but unless there is something you wish to discuss, I will go.
I have urgent matters I must attend to today."

My father stiffened, a flash of anger in his eyes at the way
I had just dismissed his authority.

"Insolent girl!"

I thought for a brief moment that he would strike me. But
his eyelids dropped to hide his rage, and he seemed to regain
some control. His mouth twitched, then he turned on his heel
and limped to the fireplace.

"Well, you know your own mind," he admitted grimly.
"But while you are under my roof, I would ask you to abide
by my rules. The Spaniard must leave as soon as he is able.
And until he has gone, I would rather you spend no more

time alone with him. You are still unmarried, and that boy is a Spaniard and a Catholic, long enemies of this country. It is not right."

"Not every Spaniard is our enemy, Father!" I protested. "Our Queen is married to the King of Spain, if you recall. And we are all supposed to be Catholics now."

He looked at me sideways, a strange expression in his face, then nodded stiffly. "Of course, of course... Forgive me. How could I have forgotten the change in our country's fortunes?"

The apology had been mechanical, forced from his lips. He thought I was his enemy too, I realized with a shock. My heart thudded erratically.

My father had never looked at me the same since the night I had broken out of my bedroom by dissolving the entire wall, tossing chunks of masonry about like pebbles, in order to confront Marcus Dent. I had not wanted to make my power quite so apparent to my family, but they had forced my hand by locking me up when Alejandro was in danger and needed me.

Besides, I had restored the wall on my return, and was no danger to anyone here at Lytton Park. So there was no need for my father to be quite so wary around me these days.

Yet he was afraid of me now, and the knowledge made me sad. I had only ever wanted us to be close: father and daughter, flesh and blood, bound together by love. Instead, there was this distrust and fear between us, and not a little anger.

My father stirred, crossing to his desk. He sat heavily in his seat, aimlessly rearranging the open books and documents on his desk, not looking at me.

"Nonetheless, if you wish to remain here at Lytton Park under my protection, you will tell that boy it is time he returned to the Lady Elizabeth at Hatfield." He drew an unsteady breath. "The King ordered him to guard the princess, you told me so yourself. There is no longer anything here for him, so he may as well leave. No, do not argue with me. I am master in my own house and you are still my daughter, bound in obedience to me."

"Father…"

"I want that Spaniard to leave my house!" he insisted, lifting his head to stare at me, his eyes glittering with frustration. "I have been patient enough. You will tell him today that his stay here is over. Is that clear?"

I took a deep breath and forced my itching fingers to be still, though it was difficult to control the fury coursing through my own veins. I was not "bound" to him in obedience, even if I was his daughter, and one word from me could make him forget this conversation for ever.

Yet he was my father, this was his house, and for the moment I had nowhere else to go. Or nowhere as safe from Marcus Dent. That much was true, and all the spells in the world would not change it. And he was right too: Alejandro had been charged to protect the Lady Elizabeth. Who was I to stand between him and his duty?

"It is almost Christmas Day," I muttered. "May I spend the holy day with him first?"

My father hesitated a moment, then nodded. "Very well, Alejandro may stay until Christmastide is over. But do not let me catch you alone with him again," he reminded me harshly. "And more, Meg. No more spells, you hear me? Not while you are a guest under my roof."

"Yes, sir," I agreed reluctantly.

He stood, pushing back his chair, and began to pace his study restlessly. "You think me cruel, and perhaps I am. But I swear this is for your own good, Meg. Your mother, Catherine Canley, was an extraordinarily beautiful woman. So beautiful that it was rumoured she had even caught the eye of the King. She was slender and graceful as a faery's child, with long fair hair that fell past her waist, and eyes blue as the summer sky. I will not deny it, I was captivated by her wit and beauty. But I could not overlook her sins against God, and told her so when I asked her to marry me."

I stared, speechless.

"On the day that we were wed, your mother promised me faithfully that she would stop casting spells. That she would be nothing but an obedient wife and mother to our children. But she lied. Oh, I daresay Catherine no longer slipped out at the full moon and danced naked about the circle like her wicked sister, Jane. But there were signs, and I am not a fool. Your grandmother was a witch too, you see, and neither of her daughters ever quite found the strength to give up their hellish power." My father turned, looking at me grimly. "But you will find that strength, Meg. Or leave the safety of these four walls."

It was St Stephen's Day and snow was falling all around us, fragile white blooms of ice that melted as soon as they touched my cheek.

Christmas had come and gone with horrible speed, and now I must tell Alejandro to leave Oxfordshire.

Staring into whirling whiteness, I longed to capture this perfect moment for ever and keep it from changing. But I had promised my father not to work magick at the house. Though outside in the grounds, of course, I was not exactly *under his roof.*

Still, it was dangerous to work magick without good cause.

Perhaps I should swear to give up magick, as my mother had done on her wedding day. Certainly my magick only seemed to endanger those I loved.

I drew my fur-lined mantle tighter.

Now that Christmas Day was past, the weather had turned

colder along with my mood. Indeed, I ought to have been freezing. But Alejandro had thrown his cloak down for me under the frost-spangled oak, and the fine wool was still warm from his body.

Besides, how could I be cold in Alejandro's company? We had been fighting, and the heat of his dark gaze was still scorching me.

"Meg," he growled softly, then knelt beside me on the cloak, catching at my hand.

"No," I insisted. "You know what I want, Alejandro. You cannot persuade me with kisses. I will not bend to your will."

"It would be a mistake to fight me on this, Meg."

"Then don't fight *me*."

With painstaking care, Alejandro peeled off one of my leather gloves, then interlaced long powerful fingers with my own. His eyes darkened until they were almost black, his gaze seeming to burn into my soul.

The snow fell softly about us in the silence, tiny white stars that melted as they landed on his dark hair and broad shoulders.

I stared back at him, breathless.

It was hard to believe a girl like me could ever have captured the attention of the beautiful and aristocratic Alejandro de Castillo, who might be in training to be a lowly priest but whose father was one of the most influential noblemen at the Spanish court.

I knew his bronzed face and watchful eyes, the vital strength of his body, his lean agility on foot or on horseback, as well as I knew my own person.

I had little beauty and less breeding, and I knew it. Slight and small-boned, unfashionably fair, my hair dishevelled under my hood, I was no match for those dark-eyed beauties who had tried to catch his eye at court.

Yet here he was, down on his knees before me.

"I will not bend to the will of your father and leave here while you still need me. Nor will I bend to your will either," Alejandro continued in that deliciously husky Spanish accent. "Do you hear me, Meg Lytton? I will not leave Lytton Park. I am still your betrothed, in case you had forgotten. Wherever you are, I must be also."

"But my father is right. The Lady Elizabeth needs you, and you promised King Philip that you would remain at Hatfield and protect her. Just because her ladyship has dismissed me from her service does not mean you cannot fulfil your duty."

"That was before I realized in what danger you stood, *mi querida*. King Philip is a Spaniard and a man of passion. He will understand my dilemma."

"Yet the King has left his wife and sailed for France," I pointed out, "abandoning Queen Mary with our country still in turmoil."

"His Majesty will no doubt return when his war against the French is won."

I raised my eyebrows. The last time I had seen King Philip, he had been furious with Queen Mary and determined to leave the shores of England—and his stubborn wife—far behind. That was why he had ordered Alejandro to remain with the Lady Elizabeth. Because Philip feared what the childless Mary might do to her younger sister if she grew unhappy enough. For if the elder sister could not safeguard the English throne for him by providing Philip with an heir, then perhaps the younger Elizabeth might be more able....

"All the same, you must return to Hatfield. It has been weeks now, and her ladyship will not excuse you for ever." I paused. "My father has reminded me of your duty, and I fear you may lose your position in the Lady Elizabeth's household—lose it because of me—if you do not leave in the next few days."

"In the next few days?" he repeated, his voice suddenly hoarse.

"*Dios!* Are you trying to kill me?" Alejandro drew my hand to his mouth, then bent his head to kiss my fingertips, one by one, his lips lingering on my cold skin. "How can I leave you?" he demanded, and the agony and indecision in his voice almost broke my resolve. "We have no way of knowing where Marcus Dent is, or what he may be planning. What if he returns after I have gone, hoping to take his revenge?"

"Still in the guise of a bird, no doubt." I tried to tease him, recalling how my enemy had transformed himself into a screaming hawk last time we met. "If Marcus returns, I will lose no time in running for help while he hops after me, fixing me with his beady eye."

"Meg, be serious for once and consider your own safety. Or if you will not think of yourself, then spare a thought for me. Think of how my heart will suffer if you die…*again*…at the hands of that foul creature."

He was thinking back to that terrible night at Hatfield when I had tried to exorcize the dark spirit accidentally loosed upon the world, and only succeeded in getting myself killed.

Luckily my death had been of short duration.

The talisman of his cross, set about my neck as a protective device during the ritual, had kept my soul from harm and ensured that I could return to my body once my magickal death had been reversed.

"Alejandro." I stripped off my other glove, then placed my bare hand against his cheek. "I have no intention of dying again just yet, at Marcus's hands or anyone else's."

His fingers were still entwined with mine. I could feel the

heat of his palm, and was struck by the way we were kneeling so close, facing each other, our gazes locked together.

His eyes became smoky with darkness, his need for me coiling and flaring inside each velvety black pupil. "I am glad to hear it. For I could not live in this world knowing I had failed to protect you."

A cold fear gripped my heart at this frank admission.

"What are you saying?" I demanded, and my voice rose in anger.

"Alejandro de Castillo, you are not such a coward as that. I could not love you if I thought even for one moment that you... Speak to me, Alejandro! Tell me you did not mean that?"

There was a long silence.

His dark gaze seared into me, despair on his taut features.

"Forgive me," he managed to answer at last. His eyes dropped from mine as though in shame. "I did not mean it."

"I should think not."

Suddenly Alejandro jerked my hand to his chest. My hood fell back and my eyes widened on his face, startled. He placed my hand over his heart where I felt the deep *thud-thudding* of an erratic beat beneath his shirt.

"But you *are* my heart, Meg Lytton. I wish I could freeze time so that we would never be apart. To return to Hatfield without you is unthinkable, and it will destroy me to spend even one day away from you."

"Think of your duty, then. *I* have let the Lady Elizabeth down—she cannot have a suspected witch in her household. Do not make me the cause of her losing a further protector as well."

"My duty is to you, *mi alma*," he growled. "You are my betrothed. We are to be married one day."

It felt as though there was broken glass in my throat. "You forget, I have not given you my final answer yet."

He stilled. "You mean to refuse me?"

I drew an unsteady breath. "When we wed, will you ask me to put witchcraft aside?"

"No."

"But you could not marry me otherwise." I looked at him tenderly. "Admit it, Alejandro. Your Holy Order permits marriage. But not to a suspected witch."

His jaw was clenched hard. "It could be difficult for us if you refused to give up the craft, yes."

"You already know that I would refuse to do so."

"Meg, I love you. You are the boldest, most exciting woman I have ever met. You are as brave as any man, and although you often act rashly, your instinct is always to attack. You think and act like a soldier, and you are willing to die for what you believe in. I want you for my wife, Meg Lytton, and would never ask you to give up your power. That is a decision that must come from you, not me." He paused, meeting my gaze, then continued more slowly. "But there *would* be danger for us both if you practised witchcraft after our marriage, I cannot deny that. Especially if I took you back to Spain to meet my family."

"To meet your family?" I shook my head, feeling as though I were living in a nightmare.

"Of course." Alejandro frowned. "My father can be very strict in the way he lives, it is true, and sometimes his view of the world is narrow. But no more so than any other high-ranking Spanish noble. My family are not ogres. If I took you home, they would embrace you as my chosen wife. At least, my mother would."

I felt his hesitancy. "Are you sure?"

"No," he admitted reluctantly. "But you will be my wife, and I would defend you to the death."

My heart hurt. "I know you would. And that's the problem. Because, oddly enough, I would rather not be the cause of your death." I sighed, picking my next words carefully. "There is no hurry to make this decision, Alejandro. Let us put the thought of marriage away for now, and let our lives unfold as they should. There is no shame in service to a noble cause. I will serve the Lady Elizabeth by staying away from her, and you will serve her by returning to Hatfield. And perhaps that is our destiny."

My hand was still lying on his chest. He took a shuddering breath, then pressed it deeper against his warmth, his fingers covering mine.

"Mi querida," he said hoarsely, and looked deep into my eyes.

"If I do what you ask, if I return to the princess at Hatfield, promise me you will not work magick while I am no longer here to protect you."

"I will not be alone," I said tersely. "My brother William is good with a sword. And Richard has power. He will guard my back."

His eyes narrowed. "So long as that is all he does."

"Jealous?" I forced myself to sound amused, desperate to lighten the darkening mood between us. "Of Richard?"

"That boy loves you."

Heat flared in my cheeks. "Alejandro, don't."

"You do not believe me, Meg? Or do you not wish to hear the truth?" His eyes were very dark. "I saw Richard's face the night you died at Hatfield and he carried your dead body back to the house. He looked like a man with nothing left to live for. I recognized his agony, what it meant. For it was on my face too that night, and stamped on my heart like a brand. I shall never shake it loose."

"Whatever you think you saw, you are wrong. I feel nothing for Richard."

"De verdad?" he asked grimly, and I knew he did not believe me.

"Come on, we should head back to the house before my father misses me and comes looking," I murmured.

It was the most painful thing in the world to part from him, but I had little choice. For the more I knew Alejandro, the deeper I fell in love with him, the more I realized we were not suited to each other.

I tried to wriggle my fingers out from under his. "Please, Alejandro. You know how little my father likes you. I do not wish to offend him further by being caught alone in your company."

But to my chagrin he did not move away. Instead, with incredible gentleness, like a butterfly's wings brushing my skin, he leaned forward and put his lips against mine.

My breath hissed in. Then my fingers raked through his hair, jerking him forward, clutching him to me. He made a rough sound under his breath, and suddenly he was kissing me in earnest, his arm about my waist, dragging me closer.

My heart stuttered violently. Alejandro wanted me as much as I wanted him. He was lost to reason, his eyes closed, his mouth slanting over mine, possessing me.

I was almost lost myself, yielding to the sweetness of his lips against mine. But part of me knew we had to stop. I had just hinted to Alejandro that we could never marry. All this kiss would achieve was confusion.

Confusion and an aching heart.

I had promised my father I would not work magick here at Lytton Park. But I had to distract Alejandro.

I broke off the kiss. "Look," I whispered.

His eyes opened slowly. The dark smoky pupils of his eyes had blurred with desire. "What is it, *mi alma?*"

"The snow…"

He lifted his head, following the line of my pointing finger. All around us, in a cold and silent pocket, the snow had ceased to fall—in mid-air. Beyond our protected circle, snowflakes were still fluttering and shifting on the slight breeze, falling as nature decreed. But here, the snow had stopped in mid-fall and hung suspended about us, tiny white crystals that seemed to sparkle as they spun gracefully in the air.

Staring at the motionless snowflakes mere inches from his face, he muttered, "How is it possible?"

"You said you wished you could freeze time," I reminded him softly. "I cannot quite manage that. But here in this space, the snow will not fall until I allow it."

He turned his head back to me, his eyes questing for mine. I saw astonishment there. "Meg, you never cease to amaze me," he muttered.

He put out an experimental finger: a suspended snowflake melted on his fingertip, and he smiled. "A perfect distraction."

My little ruse had not fooled him for one second. But it had worked. We were no longer kissing. The mood had shifted.

"Meg!"

Our heads both turned at the shout, which had come from the direction of the big house, its high brick chimneys hidden behind the trees.

Richard, I thought ruefully.

My concentration snapped and the snow began to fall around us again, icy and ethereal, slowly blurring my vision.

"We should head back," Alejandro said.

I did not argue, and he stood, helping me up. My body had healed since the terrifying fall from Dent's cursed tower, thanks to Richard's skill as a healer. But I was still a little stiff at times, and I had a suspicion my arm would never be strong again, despite my attempts to break my fall magickally.

Richard came into view, followed by my brother William, who looked quite wise and dependable, though he was only a few years my elder. Both young men had spades over their shoulders.

Alejandro frowned, staring.

"Your father is busy with his yearly accounts," Richard told me cheerfully, and threw his spade at Alejandro, who caught it one-handed. "Time for a little digging, don't you agree?"

"Sounds like the perfect time." I grinned at my brother, whom I was steadily growing to trust. He might have made some poor decisions in the past, but he seemed intent on making up for them now. "You in on this madness too, Will?"

William shrugged. "If the ghost of our mother said to dig under the old pigsty at Home Farm, then that's where we'll dig. What are we expecting to find there, by the way?"

"Nothing, probably," I admitted. "Except perhaps a mouldy old book."

My brother's smile was crooked. "Lovely."

4

GRIMOIRE

"So what do you think might be in there?" William asked again, his arms folded across his chest. "Something dangerous? It's too heavy just to contain a single book, however magickal."

Kneeling before the locked casket, my fingers drumming restlessly on the damp wooden lid, I shrugged.

"I doubt Mother would have sent me to dig up this box if what was inside could hurt us." I took a cloth and brushed the last stubborn smudge of dirt from the box. "But let's see, shall we?"

We were downstairs in my father's house, in the narrow, low-ceilinged room that had once been used by my aunt for weaving, but now had some purpose as a storeroom. It was far enough from my father's study and the servants' quarters to allow us some privacy, though we had to keep our voices down, for the window overlooked the old herb garden, its formal beds kept in good order while my aunt was alive, though now a mass of straggling and woody plants that nobody had cut back after the summer's growth.

I looked around at their intent faces, trying to gauge the mood of our little band. Alejandro, standing above me, his eyes wary. My brother William, loyal to me now, but who had never felt quite comfortable with the knowledge that his mother, aunt and sister were all witches. And leaning forward in his seat by the fire, fists clenched as though in anticipation of some dread revelation, John Dee's apprentice, Richard.

"Come on, Meg," Alejandro urged me softly. "Before your father comes back from his meeting with the steward."

Tentatively I tried the lid once more. It was locked, of course, the key lost long ago. But I knew a spell that would open it.

Muttering *"Aperi!"* under my breath, I heard the muffled internal click of the lock.

The rusting hinges sat slightly askew, and I had to lay the lid back carefully so it would not break.

Gazing down, I scanned the dusty contents of the box. There was a smaller box with a painted lid, a black-handled knife like my aunt's athame, some ancient candle stumps, dried herbs, and a large book of loose papers sewn together into a manuscript.... This last I removed very gingerly, fearing it might fall apart in my hands. But it seemed strongly bound, and the writing, though stained with damp in places, was still legible.

"Our mother's hand?" I whispered, and passed the damp manuscript carefully to William. "This must be her grimoire."

"What is a grimoire?" he asked.

Richard had risen and was looking at the manuscript over William's shoulder. "A grimoire is a book of spells," he muttered, "intended for magickal ephebes to study."

"Magickal whats?"

"Novices in the art of magick. Those still learning the craft." Richard frowned. "Though this manuscript bears all the marks of a Book of Shadows, as your mother suggested. This may have been a record of her spells and magickal encounters with spirits. You see there?"

Richard pointed to one of the pages. William stopped flicking through and studied it more closely.

"There is the date and time of her spell. And these small marginal drawings indicate the plants she used, and their effect." Richard nodded, glancing down at me thoughtfully. "You could learn much from this book. Perhaps more than my master could teach you, for he is not privy to women's magick."

I nodded, glad that Richard was on hand while I explored the contents of this box. For he had been trained by the conjuror John Dee and was the only other one here with any skilled knowledge of magick. Indeed, Richard was everything Alejandro was not. With his dark brooding looks, surly manner and his limp, he was every inch the Devil's child his father had cruelly called him.

I secretly thought Richard rather handsome, but I had seen the servants crossing themselves when he entered a room, and knew they would be glad to see him gone.

Alejandro was also eyeing Richard with dislike. "Are you not privy to women's magick, then? I would have thought you well-suited to womanly spells."

"It is not my domain," Richard replied coldly, looking Alejandro up and down as though contemptuous of the stylish Spanish-made clothes he was wearing. "Any more than magick is yours, priest!"

I sighed, and reached down into the box again. At least they were not *constantly* at each other's throats here, as they had been at Hatfield. Though if Alejandro stayed much longer, they would undoubtedly come to blows. I knew the two were only civil to each other when I was in the room, for they usually knew better than to prick my sharp temper by arguing in my hearing.

I drew out the small painted box next.

"So what is in here?"

I lifted the lid, and my breath stuck in my throat at the beautiful jewellery nestled within: a fine gold necklace ending in a large single pearl encased in gold, some slim gold rings, two bracelets decorated with precious stones, a brooch of seed pearls and what appeared to be a diamond; and a strange, red-gold, double-coiled ring, which I held up to the light.

"I have never seen its like before," I murmured, then slipped it onto my finger.

"Wait!" Alejandro grabbed at my hand, removing the ring. He shook his head, his eyes very dark. "Do not put it on again, *mi querida*. You have no idea what may happen."

Richard stirred. "For once I agree with your Spaniard. It could be dangerous to be too free with any of your mother's possessions, in case there are malignant effects." He held out his hand.

Reluctantly, his jaw tight, Alejandro dropped the red-gold ring into Richard's palm.

The young apprentice examined it carefully, eyes narrowed. "I will write and describe this ring to Master Dee. He may know its use."

"Don't be a fool," Alejandro growled. "You could put the entire household in danger by committing such information to a letter."

"I shall write my letter in code, as always." Richard was bristling with irritation, as so often when Alejandro was around. He handed me back the red-gold ring before turning to face Alejandro.

"Very well, let us have this out. You have been spoiling for a fight for days. What is your problem, priest?"

"You are my problem, apprentice."

"Oh, for pity's sake, be quiet, both of you, before one of the servants comes to see what the noise is." I crouched again to the box, replacing the ring where I had found it, then hunting deeper inside.

"I need help from you, not childish squabbling." I paused. "Look at this now, it must have been my mother's athame."

The sacred athame was the ceremonial knife of the witch. This one was older than Aunt Jane's, the handle cracked and worn. It must have belonged to another witch before my mother, I realized. Perhaps my grandmother? My father had indicated that she too had been a witch, just as Aunt Jane had told me.

The blade looked wicked, glinting as I turned the knife over in the wintry sunlight. I felt the weight of it in my hand, then laid it aside to be examined later.

"A knife I can understand. But what is *that?*" William asked in surprise, peering into the box.

Poking out from under a roll of coarse black linen was a small metal bowl. I picked it up, frowning. The outside was dented and blackened as though by fire, but the inside was smooth and clear except for a few scratch marks, which might have been made by a blade.

"A cauldron," Richard informed him coolly.

"So small?"

"Easier to hide or carry. Hard to explain keeping a vast pan in your possession, unless you are travelling. This bowl would do for a simple spell, and rouse little suspicion if found on your person. Many witches use whatever is to hand in their own kitchens, I believe."

Richard looked at me for confirmation, and I nodded silently, the hairs rising on the back of my neck as I cradled my mother's cauldron in my arms, smoothing my hand over its

dark, battered exterior. How strange and yet somehow com-
forting it would be to use magickal instruments that had once
belonged to her, my long-dead mother.

Would my mother be there at my side while I scratched out
the circle with her knife and incanted the sacred words over
her bubbling cauldron? There was only one way to find out.
I made a solemn vow that I would bring these forgotten objects back to their proper use at the first possible opportunity.

"The same pot a woman uses for a stew will do as well for
a cauldron," Richard continued, "and her sacred knife may
be whatever is kept for boning meat. The spells will work as
well, if not better, for the witch being so familiar with her
instruments." He hesitated. "May I look?" He was gesturing
towards my mother's casket.

"There's nothing much left," I told him, but moved aside.
"Some sachets of dried herbs, almost turned to dust. Oh, and
this must be a mandragora root!" I lifted it out, a wizened cloven root, blackened with age, mostly used for dark magick or
divination. Then I glanced back down. "What's that?"

Richard leaned over and picked it up for me. A slender piece
of wood, lovingly smoothed and shaped, but very old, oddly
discoloured in places. He ran a finger experimentally along
its length, his head cocked to one side, as though the bumps
and nicks along the wood could reveal secrets.

I put down the mandrake, and Richard passed the shaped
stick to me almost reverently. "A hazel wand. Careful, it has
power."

I felt it too, and drew in my breath, handling the wand
with the same reverence, for my fingers had also tingled as
soon as I touched it.

So my mother had used a wand. Like my aunt, I had always used a knife for sacred rituals, and my hands and voice
for spells. That was how I had been taught to work magick.

But Aunt Jane had mentioned that some witches used wands, and found them more effective than an athame or hands alone.

With the slender hazel switch in my hand, I felt suddenly connected to everything, able to see and influence the very fabric of the world. It has to be an illusion, I thought, a little dazed by the power coming off it in waves and leaping up through my fingertips into my body.

I moved the wand from right to left, and it resisted slightly, as though the air itself had weight and substance, and was pushing back on it. I looked at Richard—knew he fully understood the power of a wand such as this—and he smiled back at me, a smile of complicity.

Alejandro was very still, watching us.

There was a haunted look in his eyes. Did he suspect I had fallen in love with Richard?

That would better explain why I was sending him away, after all—for Alejandro knew that I had the power to change my father's mind in an instant. Easier to believe perhaps that my affections had been transferred to Richard than that we were not suited to wed.

I lowered the wand. "Alejandro…"

But Alejandro bowed, his face stiff. "Forgive me, I must go and speak with your father. He promised to loan me a horse for the journey back to Hatfield."

Richard looked round at him, surprised. "You are leaving Lytton Park?"

"My duty lies with *la princesa,*" Alejandro explained tersely, not meeting my eyes. "I swore to protect and watch over her, and I have neglected my oath too long. So I must return to Hatfield. Perhaps tomorrow morning."

So soon?

But of course it was for the best if he left swiftly. I could hardly complain when I had suggested such speed myself, using my father's ultimatum to support my argument.

Richard was frowning. "Surely you are aware it's not safe here, that Marcus Dent may come back in search of Meg at any moment?"

"I have waited here a full month and Dent has not shown his face. Perhaps Master Dent is too weak for another confrontation. Once I am gone though, you can redouble your spells of protection. Keep Meg indoors and under guard at all times. You and William—" and here he glanced at my brother, who was staring, as surprised as Richard by his sudden departure "—will keep her safe between you."

"And if we cannot?" William asked, clearly alarmed by the prospect.

Alejandro took a deep breath and expelled it slowly, then fixed my brother with his darkest stare. "You will keep her safe," he said, his tone final.

Richard's tone was scathing. "So you're leaving us? Leaving Meg? Just like that?"

"One of us must petition *la princesa* on Meg's behalf so she may be allowed to return to Hatfield House," Alejandro pointed out, heading for the door. "Meg will be safer there against Marcus Dent, for he would surely not dare to attack the Lady Elizabeth, not when she is so close to the throne. Unless you would like to volunteer for the task of persuading her, apprentice? Or you, William?"

The room was silent.

"I thought not," Alejandro commented, then looked back at me from the doorway.

"Forgive me for not staying," he said softly, "but a magickal ring, your mother's grimoire... I am not the right person to advise you on the use of such mystical objects. But perhaps Richard is. I hope you find the answers you seek, *mi querida*."

And the door closed behind him.

The morning was still and milky, barely dawn, snow still scattered white across the frozen ground. To the far north the skies were still dark, the clouds looming, heavy with snow. It would be a cold day, I thought, and a bad night to come. Nevertheless, the road south should be passable, though by no means an easy ride.

In an old gown, wrapped in a shawl against the cold, I stood in the doorway and watched as Alejandro saddled his horse swiftly and skilfully.

He had slung his sword belt about his waist, his fine Spanish sword hanging by his side, and although the cloak looked vaguely clerical, his suit beneath fitted tightly, a doublet and worn black hose borrowed from my brother after his own had been damaged.

I was not surprised to see him dressed so plainly, however. Alejandro was part priest, part soldier, as the Holy Order of Santiago demanded, and he looked the part today.

Alejandro straightened from his task, carefully attached his pack to the saddle, then turned to face me. I saw the dread on his face, the reluctance to leave, and felt the same pain inside me.

"I am ready," he muttered, and came to kiss me farewell.

It had been foolish of me to get up early to see him off. This was just another opportunity for us to hurt each other. I gazed up at him achingly, memorizing the stern line of his jaw, skin drawn tautly over his cheekbones as he stared back at me.

"I do not want to leave, Meg." Alejandro cupped my cheek with a gloved hand, his eyes very dark.

"I do not want you to go," I managed to respond in a whisper. "But you must. The Lady Elizabeth needs you more than I. And my father will not allow you to stay any longer." I sighed. "I believe too that we both need time apart to think."

The house behind us stood silent, the hallway empty. No one else had come downstairs. Most of my father's servants were still asleep on this bitter, frosty morning, only the cook and his kitchen assistant awake at this hour, to heat the oven for the baking of today's bread. Smoke from the kitchen chimney was wreathing a thin grey path through the frosty air, and I knew the whole household would be awake within an hour or two, with Alejandro already miles away.

"Promise me you will not try to find Marcus Dent," I said suddenly, my breath steaming in the cold.

He was still touching my cheek. "I cannot promise that, *mi alma,*" he said. "It is unfair to ask such a thing of me. I am still clinging to the hope that you will consent to be my wife one day, and that man is your enemy."

"But Marcus will kill you!"

"Will he?" His eyebrows rose and a dry smile played about his lips. "Is it so inconceivable that I might kill *him,* my love?"

I could not say yes. That would destroy him as surely as if I had plunged the sword into his body myself.

"Marcus Dent is not like other men," I tried to explain, and found myself compromising under his narrowed stare. "Marcus is dangerous. You remember what my mother said. He has powers now that he didn't have before. Promise me you won't go looking for Marcus."

"Your protection is all that matters to me."

"Brave words." Terrified that he was indeed planning to hunt down the witchfinder, I let my temper slip. "But somewhat poorly thought-out, Alejandro. After all, you can hardly protect me or the Lady Elizabeth if you are foolish enough to get yourself killed."

I caught a flash of anger in his eyes.

His lips parted, sucking in a breath to tell me exactly what he thought of my opinion. Then his eyelids lowered to hide his expression, and he reined back whatever he had been planning to say, his shrug eloquent enough to express it without words.

I had wounded him. Yet still he refused to retaliate.

"Perhaps we should leave it at that, *mi querida,*" he murmured, and there was a hint of bitterness in the way he rolled that Spanish endearment off his tongue.

I suddenly wished I could unsay what had offended him. But it was done now, part of the pattern.

"It is a long ride to Hatfield and well past dawn already," he continued. "My horse will be getting cold. I should be on my way."

"Please, don't go on an argument," I pleaded. "Let us part as friends, at least."

"Muy bien," Alejandro agreed, unsmiling. "As friends."

I stared back, thinking *kiss me, kiss me, kiss me.*

But a kiss would only make the inevitable pain worse. So I held back slightly, my expression saying *do not kiss me, please do not kiss me,* and he responded to my withdrawal with perfect stillness, as he always did.

"God be with you, Meg Lytton," he murmured, and I thought that was it.

Then his hands dropped lightly to my shoulders as though he still planned to embrace me. I froze, barely daring to breathe. He held me for a long moment, his dark eyes searching my face. I could not tell what he was thinking, but I sensed his frustration, held tightly in check, and beneath that, some powerful emotion I could not place.

Suddenly he bent his head to kiss me.

I ought to have refused his kiss. But I was weak and a fool. I raised myself on tiptoe and our mouths met. Far too eagerly.

We should never have touched, for that dangerous instant of contact unleashed feelings and desires that would have been better kept on a leash, controlled, hidden in the silences between us.

His arms came round me, pulling me compulsively against him, and I did not resist, lost in the moment.

He groaned my name, then buried his face in my throat. "This is madness."

I could not disagree with *that*.

"You are trembling. I have kept you outside too long." Slowly he released me, his eyes on mine. "Farewell, *mi amor*."

Alejandro bowed, then turned swiftly to his horse. In a moment, he was mounted and riding away, straight-backed in the saddle, just as when I had first seen him at Woodstock, riding in armour across the sunlit grass.

I watched him canter neatly down the narrow, icy track until he was out of sight, then went inside and closed the door. The hall was dark and silent.

My lips still tingled from his kiss, my heart racing. Temptation assailed me.

Would it be such a terrible thing for me to give in and marry Alejandro, to become a wife and mother instead of a witch?

Yes, my head told me furiously. Yes, it would.

5

NO GOING BACK

Two days passed while I wandered the house like a ghost or sat hunched by the smoking fire in my bedchamber, wrapped in furs, brooding over what I should do about Marcus Dent. No answers came to me in the dark, though Alejandro's face did, haunting my dreams and leaving me more dejected than ever.

When the third day dawned still cold but sunny, snow finally beginning to melt on the path into the woods, I knew what I had to do. Tired of my father's unspoken disapproval over my relationship with Alejandro, and having to face Richard's narrow stare everywhere I went, I decided to get away from the house and seek inspiration in my mother's spell book.

First, I took the red-gold ring out of my mother's casket and examined its strange double coils, slipping it momentarily onto my finger.

The air stirred oddly when I wore it, and my fingertips tingled as though the power was about to descend on me. Hurriedly I put the ring away again.

Richard had warned me not to wear the ring at least until he heard back from John Dee, and it was time I learned to be cautious about the practice of witchcraft. Even if my new-found caution came too late to save me from being dismissed from the princess's service.

Instead, I took the more innocent-looking hazel wand and slipped it into the gartered top of one of my woollen stockings. It was an uncomfortable arrangement but one that I would have to bear if I wished to avoid being seen with it. My father had no knowledge of these instruments of my mother's craft, and it seemed wiser not to flaunt them before him, given his recent display of temper.

With the grimoire concealed beneath my cloak, I muttered to William in passing that I needed a walk in the fresh air but would not go far, then hurried through the kitchen and out of the back door before my brother could protest.

I took the path into the woods, walking quickly and with purpose, and was soon lost to sight amongst the frosty trees.

With snow still on the ground, it was too damp to sit and read out of doors. But I knew a place where I could be both private and dry: Home Farm, the long-abandoned farm where I had seen the despicable Marcus Dent in a vision, and where we had dug up my mother's magickal box.

Too dangerous to leave my mother's precious belongings there unless hidden as well as she had hidden them. But back there perhaps I would find some peace. And a safe place to practise magick without breaking my promise not to cast a spell under my father's roof.

On reaching Home Farm, I hopped over the mossed pile of stones, which had once been a boundary wall, and made my way towards the old barn. I had often hidden there as a child, high up in the hayloft, thinking and dreaming on my back in the straw. Now, though, the upper loft door stood permanently open like an unlidded eye, and I could see that a bad storm had whistled through and brought the roof in at one end, for all the timbers were bowed, the whole building leaning towards the scene of devastation.

Gingerly I made my way across the uneven mud and debris, climbed the ancient ladder with half its rungs missing, and pulled myself up into the hayloft.

I turned on my heel to survey the damage, and was pleased to see that the far end of the barn roof was still intact. Even if it rained, I could stay dry here.

The wooden floor creaked ominously underfoot though, and I was forced to drop to my hands and knees, then crawl to my old place near the open doorway, where I could see clear across the icy white meadows to the river.

Breathing deep, I opened the grimoire to the first page, and my mother's name leaped out at me, written in fading ink.

Catherine Canley.

I traced her hand, admiring the curls and loops and flourishes of a bold female temperament. Bold or not, my mother had put aside her magickal gifts for ever when she married, knowing she could not be both wife and witch without the risk of bringing disgrace on her family. She must have loved my father very much to make such a sacrifice, just as I loved Alejandro.

Could I ever find the strength to make that sacrifice for love? I rather suspected my resolve would prove weaker than my mother's.

I turned the next few leaves, reading slowly through the early entries. There I found her thoughts on the craft. Her fears of discovery and death. Tales of how her own mother had taught her the best times to gather herbs and plants, then prepare them for spellwork; which moon was right for a love-spell, which for fertility rituals; the way to read augurs and omens, how the path of birds in flight could foretell the future.

I was frowning over her description of how to read the bones—for some details differed from my aunt's teachings—when a noise made me stiffen.

I listened, and heard it again. The gentlest rustle below me in the barn, a sound like dead leaves stirring in the wind.

The day was still though, not even a light breeze blowing through the hayloft door, which stood broken and open to the weather. Through that gaping hole in the wattle and daub, men in my great-grandfather's day would have thrown winter hay down for the beasts, or dragged up the freshly gathered bales at harvest time, binding them with rough twine, and whistling or singing as they worked.

Today Home Farm was a wasteland, completely deserted except for me—and whoever was standing exactly below me in the barn.

Gently I closed my mother's grimoire, picked up the hazel wand lying beside me, and waited.

Eventually I heard the noise I had been expecting. A tiny click, then a rustle, then another click. Someone was climbing the broken ladder into the hayloft, moving as slowly and silently as they could. Though only a ghost could have avoided making a noise on that ancient contraption, which shifted and creaked under the weight of a very mortal being.

I prepared myself, my heart racing, my mouth suddenly dry as I considered the various outcomes of being discovered with a book as dangerous as this.

A face appeared, frowning up at me from the narrow hole in the floor.

"I don't believe it!" I lowered the hazel wand with a mixture of irritation and relief as I recognized my stealthy visitor. "Did you follow me all the way here?"

Richard glanced at the wand, then hauled himself into the loft. He seemed unconcerned by the swaying and groaning floorboards, limping towards me without any change of expression, his hand held out as though for a gift.

"A simple tracking-spell. It works best with deer," he said drily. "But you would not have been hard to find even without it, the clear trail you left behind."

"Go back to the house, Richard. I came up here to be alone."

He raised his brows, for my tone had been sharp. "Missing your one true love?" he sneered.

I glared at his outstretched hand. He had not bothered with gloves, despite the cold weather. "Why are you here? What do you want?"

"I want you to give me that wand before you do yourself a mischief with it." Richard halted in front of me, then crouched down, reaching for it. Before he could take it though, I muttered a word and the wand disappeared. His frown deepened. "Don't behave like a child, Meg. Give me the wand."

"It's mine."

"I do not doubt it. But you must let me take it. It's too dangerous, it's not for a novice. You can have it back when you're an adept."

"I am hardly a novice, Richard. You have seen what I can do with my voice and hands alone. My skill is equal to the task. Besides, the wand is mine and I will not let you take it."

"Have you ever worked magick with a wand before? Do you even know the properties of wood from the hazel tree?"

"I know it is the wood of white magick, that it protects the witch and helps her see far," I told him, struggling to answer his questions while keeping my spell steady to prevent the wand from reappearing. "I know it brings healing, and… and great wisdom."

"And that a circle drawn by the hazel wood is one of the strongest barriers against evil," he added, then nodded grudgingly, dropping his hand to his side. "Very well. If you will not relinquish the wand, so be it. But try to be sparing when working spells with it, Meg. You may find its effects more powerful than you intend."

"Thank you. I shall bear that in mind."

"You should not have disappeared today without telling anyone where you were going."

"I wanted to be alone."

"Marcus Dent is still out here somewhere. And he wants you dead."

"Sometimes I think everyone wants me dead."

"I don't." His mouth twisted. "And nor does Alejandro. Though your doting Spaniard will want me dead if anything should happen to you again in his absence."

"Better make sure it doesn't, then."

His frown disappeared at that and he grinned, seating himself before me. "That is my plan." He looked at the grimoire. "So, what have you discovered?"

"Not much," I admitted, and passed him the book.

He flicked through the pages as I had done, almost idly, then paused, raising his eyebrows.

"What?"

He shook his head. "Nothing." He turned a few more pages, shrugging. "There was a spell to see from a distance, that is all."

I stared, not understanding, then held out my hand for the grimoire. "Let me read it."

"No."

"The book belongs to me, not you. May I have it back, please?"

"No point," Richard said shortly, turning the pages with a

distracted frown as though looking for something. "It won't work. My master tried to develop a similar spell some years ago and it was a disaster. I doubt a country witch would have fared better than the Queen's conjuror."

"A country witch?" I gasped. "Richard!"

"How else would you describe her? Oh, yes, I remember now, your mother served Queen Anne when she was younger. A court witch, then. But all the same, only a *woman*." He glanced at me sideways, surveying my face. The straight line of his mouth twitched. "You go very red when you're angry, did you know that?"

I wrestled with the desire to turn Dee's arrogant apprentice into a toad, or some other slimy or scaly creature, and watch him hop away, croaking. He would not be able to mock me then, nor withhold my mother's grimoire from me.

"Give me the book," I said, emphasizing each word so he could not fail to miss how annoyed I was.

Richard shrugged, then deposited the manuscript heavily in my lap. He stood and muttered, "Take it," then limped to the broken loft door as though intending to jump down into the farmyard.

But of course he did not jump.

Leaning against the gap in the wall, Richard looked out in silence, staring across icy tumbling meadows to where the river twisted and broadened in the valley bottom. It was a beautiful view, and one that I had always loved, but it was clear his mind was elsewhere.

I was puzzled by his abrupt withdrawal, and more than a little concerned that I had offended him. I had few friends and none but Richard who understood magick as I did. Chastizing myself for a too hasty tongue, I considered how I could mend this. It would be stupid to lose his friendship because of my headstrong temper.

"Forgive me," I said in the end, unable to bear his silence. "It was my fault. I'm too ready to speak when I should listen."

He made no reply, still staring down towards the river. But I saw his hand clench into a fist.

"Perhaps we could go through the spell together," I suggested lightly, hoping he would take the bait. "It might work better with two."

His head turned blindly, his face tight, the hurt shining in his eyes. "You do value my judgement, then?" he asked. "I thought you did not."

"Only because I am a stubborn idiot." With my best smile, I patted the floor next to me. "Come back, I pray you, and help me decipher my mother's hand. Many of these spells are in Latin and I cannot always make them out."

Richard was flushed, his gaze not quite meeting mine. I must have offended him indeed, I thought, and was at once contrite.

"I have a sharp tongue and often forget to be grateful. It is a fault that has been much remarked by my father, my brother...." I had sent Alejandro away and might never see him again—I did not wish to lose Richard too. "I value your judgement very much, Richard. Please come and sit down with me."

At last he moved, pushing away from the wall and limping back to my side. His eyes met mine briefly as he took the manuscript back and set it down in front of us on the dusty floor.

"Very well, but we shall share the reading," he muttered, still defensive, then gave me a dry smile. "If that suits you, madam witch?"

"What can you see?"

My eyes were closed, my hands resting lightly on my thighs as I knelt in the chilly hayloft. I had let my mind empty of distractions, or as many as I could block out. Now I drew a slow breath and tried to obey the terms of the spell.

But it was not a promising start.

"Nothing," I admitted.

"I told you the spell would not work." Standing above me, Richard waited another moment, then made an impatient noise. "Come on, we might as well go back to the house. It must be nearly suppertime."

"Not yet," I insisted. "My mother would hardly have gone to the trouble of inscribing such a lengthy and detailed spell in her book if it did not work. Five more minutes, then we shall go back for supper. You have my word on it."

When the place was still again, I tried harder, letting my mind sink into the silence, thinking as powerfully as I could of my father's house. I conjured up in my mind the creaking stairway from the hall to the bedchambers, the narrow landing with the crack in the floor where you could see straight down into the heat and bustle of the kitchen, the smell of fresh-baked bread and meat turning on the spit rising to the rafters....

"*Aspicio*," I whispered. Suddenly I was flying.

I gasped as my body left the ground. There was a frightening weightlessness, and a tight feeling in my chest, a fear that I might fall. Colours spun about me in a blurred rush, green fields and the cold grey of the wintry sky. My hair was loose, blowing back over my shoulders as wind dragged past me, my body flying faster and faster.

Yet I knew that I had not moved, that I was still kneeling in the abandoned hayloft with Richard watching me.

Abruptly the world tilted.

My eyes opened, and that was when I realized they had been screwed tightly shut, for the flying sensation had left me a little sick. I gazed about myself, breathing shallow, my eyes slowly adjusting to darkness. I was standing on the upper landing in my father's house, looking down the stairs into the hall. Or rather my mind was there, my body still a good two miles away in the hayloft.

The detail shook me. I could see knots and cracks in the wall beams, a beetle crawling in the dust at the top of the stairs, and down in the hall I watched as one of the servingwomen came hurrying out of the scullery, three or four brown eggs cradled in her apron.

There was a sound behind me. I turned in my dream, and saw my brother's door open.

Without moving, I found that I was inside his bedchamber, as though my thought alone had taken me there.

William was lying on his bed, his arm over his eyes, a small book open on his chest. As I watched, he sighed deeply as though distressed by some memory or imagining.

"Alice," he whispered. "Alice…"

After a moment, his arm fell away from his eyes and I realized that he had been crying.

William rolled onto his side and continued to read from his book. In my head, I heard him reciting a poem softly to himself. A love poem. The words fell away into shadow, but my brother's red-rimmed eyes were clear enough.

"Meg."

I started violently, thinking William knew I was there in his chamber and was saying my name. My eyes blurred, there was a hideous rushing in my ears, then I was back in the hayloft, staring at nothing like a mad thing, my whole body aching, with Richard on his knees before me, his face pale and drawn.

"Come back to me, Meg," Richard said urgently, and snapped his fingers in front of my face.

A shudder ran through me, everything turned misty, and I felt horribly sick.

Richard nodded unsympathetically. "Good, you're awake."

"What...what did...?" I tried to stand up but Richard pushed me back.

I did not argue, for I was dizzy, my head spinning unpleasantly.

"Stay where you are. God's blood, Meg, you turned cold and seemed to lose your senses there. I could not rouse you for several minutes. I told you not to be too free with these spells from your mother's book, that they were dangerous." He sounded furious. "When will you listen to me?"

"Never," I muttered.

Richard crouched down, looking at me, his head on one side. "I'm not made of stone, Meg. I have no taste to see you die again under my care. I have not forgotten that night at Hatfield. Having to carry your dead body back to the house nearly finished me. Not a night I wish to live through again."

"But it worked," I said eagerly, and struggled to my knees, blenching when my stomach rebelled at the too abrupt change in position. I put a hand to my mouth and waited, eyes closed. "Oh, God." I slowly dropped my hand as the sickness abated. "Richard, I have to tell you," I whispered. "I was there."

"Where?"

"I thought of my father's house. Built it in my mind's eye as the book says to do, then said the spell. And straightaway I was flying. At least, it felt like I was flying, and I could see the ground flashing past me. Then I was there, *in the house.*"

He was staring. "Go on."

"I saw my brother—" I began, then stopped myself. I had been going to say "crying" but it seemed unjust to betray William's privacy, for if he had known anyone was watching, he would never have wept. And over Alice too, the Lady Elizabeth's maid. I had not realized his feelings for the girl ran so deep, though I remembered now they had grown close during the autumn we passed at Hatfield.

"Reading a book," I finished lamely.

Richard's eyebrows shot up. "Reading a book? How very exciting."

He clearly did not believe me.

"Listen, I was there," I insisted, "in my father's house. I saw my brother reading a book, and stood as near to him as you are to me, and he never saw me. It was no dream, nor was it a memory. It was a true seeing."

For a long moment Richard looked at me without speaking, seeming to consider that possibility. Then he took up the grimoire and studied it, running his finger across my mother's spell.

"If what you say is true, this spell could..." Richard hesitated. "It would be a powerful work of magick indeed."

I held out my hand. "Help me up, please."

He did not argue this time, but stood and took my hand. His grip was strong, reassuring. "Lean on me."

"I thank you." My legs were still trembling from the power of the spell, and the heavy folds of my gown were always a hindrance, so I did not consider it a weakness to ask for his help. "Now you can kneel where I was, and try my mother's spell for yourself."

"What?"

I almost smiled at his stunned expression. "Why so surprised? You will not need to 'believe' if you can see for yourself that the spell works."

Richard shook his head. He handed me back the manuscript, this time taking more care not to damage the fragile binding. "Forgive me, but I cannot. I do not have your skill as a witch."

"I have seen you use magick."

"Nothing akin to this."

"Oh, come!"

He folded his arms, looking at me grimly. "I am serious, Meg. Catherine Canley's book is not for me. It is women's magick. To be permitted to observe but not to speak. To see great works, but not influence them yourself. My art lies in quite another direction." He paused. "Besides, her spells may only work for you because you are her daughter."

That had not occurred to me. But it was possible.

"Women's magick," I muttered, and tucked the book under my arm, for I felt too tired to continue that day. It seemed that "far seeing" was a physically exhausting spell, even though no actual movement was required on the part of the one travelling. "And what is a man's magick, pray?"

Richard grinned, knowing how much such jibes infuriated me.

"Everything that is not for a woman to perform. Which is most things."

I resisted the urge to hit him with my mother's book, for I knew he only spoke thus to tease me. "Come on, I'm eager to get back to the house and see William. If he tells me he was in his chamber all morning, reading a book, we will know it was a true vision."

"Which it was." Richard believed me *now*. "Wait, you'll need this." He threw my cloak about my shoulders and took a long moment to fasten it against the cold.

I studied him, amused by the look of concentration on his face.

He must have cut his hair in recent days, for the dark unkempt curls that used to brush his shoulders had been shorn, his hair razored short up his neck. The forelock that always hung over his forehead like a pony's was still in place though, giving him a vaguely dishevelled look, as though he had only just risen from his bed.

Richard was an attractive young man, I realized. Then I

could not believe I had just thought such a thing. But it was hard not to at least acknowledge it when he was standing so close.

"Though if your brother was out on his horse this morning," Richard added cheerfully, unaware of my thoughts, "or helping your father catalogue his book collection, then it was a deception of the mind and we must beware your mother's spell book. Agreed?"

Climbing the stairs of my father's house, I hesitated, then turned towards my brother's chamber. The door stood open.

I pushed it slightly, just as I had done in my dream, and peered inside. My brother's bed was empty and in disarray, his bolsters askew, the blankets tossed higgledy-piggledy onto the floor.

"Looking for me?"

I jumped, turning to find William directly behind me on the narrow landing. He looked at my face, grinning. "Did I startle you? You look as though you've seen a ghost."

A ghost, I thought faintly. I had seen one or two in my time, thinking back to the dark spirit I had inadvertently summoned at court, to poor Anne Boleyn's silvery outline floating above the Lady Elizabeth's bed. And to my own mother...

I would almost have welcomed a ghost at that moment if it meant my mother's spell book could be trusted. It would kill me to think that her spells and secret musings on magick—written in her own hand and set down purposely for me to study—should be considered suspect.

"What have you been doing this morning?" I asked.

"Nothing much. I was just reading, that's all." William pushed past me into his chamber, his look defensive.

I followed him, noting the shutters thrown open to admit the chilly daylight, and the general untidiness of his room, soiled clothes strewn on the floor, last night's candle a puddled stump on the table beside his bed. "Reading what?"

My brother was frowning, a slight colour in his face. "And how is it your business what I was reading?"

"Will, please tell me."

"Very well," he said gruffly. "I was reading poetry. There, now you know the truth. Will you tell me what all this is about?"

So it had been a true seeing.

I shook my head. I was not ready to tell Will about the far-seeing-spell, nor admit that I had spied upon him in the privacy of his own chamber.

"I have never known you read poetry before." I smiled, teasing him. "You must be in love."

"*In love?*" Now my brother was scarlet, stumbling over his words.

"I have no idea what you're talking about. If you were a man, Meg, and not my sister, I'd…I'd…" Then William saw my knowing smile, and his confusion grew even worse. "Oh, forget it!"

A NATURAL DEATH

The weeks advanced with infuriating quietness towards spring at Lytton Park. The snow stopped falling and a wintry sunshine melted the last of its icy whiteness from the verges. New flower stalks broke the hard earth, the trees in the park came into bud at last, and my father's vast sow gave birth to a litter of eight wriggling piglets. A robin redbreast came to sing and beg for crumbs on my windowsill every morning, its nest hidden amidst the tangle of foliage below. The world felt very fresh and new, though the air was still chilly in the early hours when I would wake from some confused dream and stare up at the stars.

Meanwhile, I walked or rode out with William and Richard during fine weather, helped to run the household for my father, and spent my evenings by the fire in my chamber, reading my mother's grimoire and occasionally heading outdoors to attempt a few of her minor charms when neither Richard nor my father were on hand to catch me.

Then one afternoon in late February, supervising the beating of some filthy old tapestries hung over a wall in the spring sunshine, I heard a shout and turned to see the outline of a horseman riding steadily down the track from the main road, the sun at his back.

I blinked and coughed in the wealth of spinning dust from the tapestries, unable to see clearly. Above me, William was hanging out of one of the casement windows, no doubt to get a better view. He shouted again and began waving his hand violently. I could not hear him, so turned, asking the servant to stop beating the tapestry for a moment.

I shielded my eyes against the sun, frowning up at William. "Who is it? Can you see?"

"It is Alejandro de Castillo," he called back excitedly. "Your Spaniard has come back!"

I went hot and cold at the same time, and my belly clenched like a fist within me.

"Oh," I said faintly, and looked down at myself. My apron was soiled with dust, my hair too no doubt, for my cap was askew, and I was wearing my worst workaday gown, with rips at the hem and a torn sleeve.

Richard came limping round from the stables, his gaze also fixed on the approaching horseman.

"Oh, the Spaniard again." He turned to study me, noting my flushed cheeks. "Come back to claim your hand in marriage, has he? Better make yourself look presentable then, or he might ride on."

I met his eyes, and a shiver ran down my back at the bitter intensity of that look. "Don't," I muttered, then dragged off my apron and thrust it into the servant's hand. I tidied my dusty cap and hair, but had no time to do much else but pinch my cheeks and hope I did not look like a complete scarecrow.

Alejandro spurred on his mount, seeing me ahead, and swung out of the saddle while the horse was still moving.

I stood watching as he strode towards me. I was suddenly unable to move, light-headed, my breathing shallow. I had forgotten how his presence alone was enough to make my heart beat faster. What did that mean, if not that I was in love with him?

He looked tired, yet his gaze was as dark and intense as ever, meeting mine with a shock that left me speechless.

"Meg," he said deeply, and dropped to both knees before me, raising my hand to his lips as though I were a princess. "Meg, *mi alma,* how I have missed you." He rested his forehead against the back of my hand, muttered something in Spanish that sounded like a brief prayer, then stood and bowed more formally. "I bear an urgent letter from *la princesa* and am instructed to return to Hatfield with you at once."

Richard, standing just behind me, expressed my own feelings of shock when he swore lengthily under his breath. "What did you say, priest?"

Shooting him a look of acute dislike, Alejandro did not repeat his message but turned instead towards my father, who had appeared in the doorway with William, both of them looking perplexed.

"Sir," Alejandro greeted my father, bowing rather stiffly, feathered cap in hand.

"Señor de Castillo?" My father was his usual unfriendly self, frowning at our visitor from within the shade of the doorway. Even the ancient gargoyle peering over the stone lintel above his head looked more welcoming with its crude squat face and protruding tongue. "What brings you back to Lytton Park?"

"Forgive my intrusion, sir. I have returned on the orders of the Lady Elizabeth." He unfastened his leather pouch, drew out a crumpled-looking scroll of paper, and handed it to me. "Read it."

He stepped back into sunlight, seemed to stumble over a deep rut in the path, and almost fell.

"Alejandro," I cried, and reached for him, but he held me off with a stern hand.

"It's nothing," he said shortly, and straightened again, though with an effort. His jaw was clenched, the skin of his face stretched taut, a hollow look in his eyes.

"Are you unwell?"

"Please." Alejandro drew a sharp breath, nodding to the letter in my hand. "Meg, read what *la princesa* has written. The sooner you read it, the sooner we can start back to Hatfield."

"Will you not at least come inside and take a cup of wine? You look weary from the long ride...."

"Read it!" he insisted, and I did not dare argue any longer, for though his face was grey, his eyes burnt into me so fiercely I could only wonder what might be in the letter.

I broke the princess's seal, unrolled the paper, and read her brief message:

M, you will return to me at once in the company of Señor de Castillo and the boy Richard, if he is still with you. Do not refuse to come or it will prove my undoing. I am in the gravest state imaginable and only you can help me. E.

I stared at Alejandro, my head reeling. "Her ladyship bids me come at once. That if I do not..." After the curt and abrupt manner of my dismissal from Hatfield, I was shocked by this strange summons and could not quite believe it. "But what is the matter? Is the princess sick?"

"I cannot tell you."

Richard stepped between us, his lip twisted in a snarl. "Cannot, or will not?"

Rounding on him, Alejandro took a swift pace toward

Richard, half drawing his sword from its sheath. "Speak to me again, conjuror's boy, and it will be the last word you ever say."

"Alejandro, no! Richard is our ally."

At my protest, Alejandro hesitated, his face still hard, then seemed to collect himself. He slammed the sword back into its scabbard, drew an arm across his forehead as though to wipe away sweat, then stumbled again as he stepped backwards, only righting himself with difficulty.

"Forgive me, sir," he muttered, turning to address my father, "I did not come here to start a brawl. I shall walk my horse round to the stables and await your daughter there. Though if you could lend me a fresh horse for the return journey, I would be grateful. This poor beast is done and must rest."

"It is you who must rest," I told him sharply. "When did you leave Hatfield?"

"I am not weary, I—" But his face became suddenly pale and he crumbled, leaving the rest unsaid. I caught him as he fell, and with Richard's help lowered him to the ground. He lay like one dead, his eyelids closed, lips slightly parted, his body still as stone.

"Alejandro," I said urgently into his ear, kneeling at his side. "What is it? Are you hurt?"

"Your priest is in a swoon and cannot hear you," Richard said, frowning down at Alejandro. Abruptly he tugged the folds of the cloak aside, revealing a dark stain on the left side of Alejandro's black doublet. With swift practised fingers, he unfastened the doublet and lifted that too. Beneath it, Alejandro's shirt was sticky with blood.

"And this is why."

"Alejandro!" I exclaimed in horror, and clapped a shaking hand to my mouth.

For a moment I was filled with unthinking panic, watching

as Richard began to uncover Alejandro's wound. Then I saw one of the servant girls peering out past my father to see the handsome Spaniard returned, and my good sense returned.

"Quick now, Susan," I called out to the girl, and was astonished that my voice did not quake the way my insides were doing. "Hurry away and fetch warm water and clean strips of cloth. Tear up one of the old linen sheets if you must. And have a bed prepared for Señor de Castillo."

Her eyes widening, the serving girl stared first at me, then at Alejandro, before scurrying away on her errand.

With exquisite care, Richard lifted the shirt away from the bloodied skin, and we both stared down at the terrible gash in his side.

Richard considered it coolly. "A sword thrust, I'd say. Or a long knife blade. Another few inches higher and it would have pierced a lung. I saw that happen once in a street fight. A bad death, to drown in your own blood." His mouth tightened. "Your priest is lucky to be alive."

Alejandro did not stir, still lying unconscious on the cold earth. I wondered how he had been able to sit a horse with such a wound, let alone ride such a long distance. His wound did not look freshly got, even to my inexperienced eyes. So he had been attacked soon after leaving Hatfield.

But who could have stabbed him, and why?

There was so much blood....

"We must get him inside," I said curtly.

"William, help me carry him," Richard said, glancing up at my brother.

Together they eased him up off the ground and bore him past my father into the shadowy house.

"Careful, go slowly now." Richard turned his head, waiting for me. "Up the stairs?"

I thought quickly. "Yes, take him upstairs. He can lie in my bedchamber."

My father, watching this, made some noise of protest as Alejandro was carried upstairs but I ignored him.

"You and William are already sharing, so there's no space in your chamber. I would never expect my father to share with a wounded man, and Alejandro cannot sleep on the floor like one of the servants." I ran ahead of them up the stairs and threw open the door to my chamber. "This is the best place for him. Lay him on my bed and I will tend his wound."

William shook his head. "Meg, it's not right to take him into your bedchamber."

I rounded on my brother. "Peace, I pray you," I hissed as Alejandro stirred at the sound of voices. "Do as I bid you, and stop arguing."

Once they had laid Alejandro on my bed, I made him as comfortable as I could, removing his boots with William's help, then placed a bolster beneath his neck to cradle his head. I stood over him while Richard took a knife and slit his shirt open, exposing the gaping wound in his side, and tried not to swoon myself at the sight.

"God's blood. I do not wonder at his fainting now. He must have been in agony," I whispered.

Richard nodded, thrusting his knife back into his belt. "Unless he is made of stone, yes. It is a serious wound." His eyes narrowed.

"And it looks like we are not the first here. Someone has attempted to cauterize this with some kind of hot metal. Very clumsily too."

A tentative knocking at the chamber door made me turn, startled.

"Mistress Lytton?" Susan stood in the doorway with a copper bowl of steaming water in her hands, coarse linen strips draped over her arm.

"Thank you." I dredged up a smile for her. "Put them on the table, then go down to the stables and make sure the señor's horse is well cared for."

When we were alone again, I turned to William and Richard.

"Forgive me, but I need to do this alone."

Richard nodded, seeming to understand, and went straight to the door. William, however, hesitated, glancing dubiously at the unconscious man on the bed.

"But if he should awake while you are tending his wound…"

"I will call you if I need you to restrain him," I told my brother firmly, and pushed him out of the room after Richard. "Why do you not go and pack your bags, unless you would rather stay here with our father? The princess has summoned me back to Hatfield House as quickly as may be, so I will be leaving as soon as Alejandro recovers enough to ride and I suspect you may wish to accompany us." I could not help a little smile as I thought how eager William would surely be to see his Alice once more.

"If he recovers," Richard murmured, but slipped hurriedly away, no doubt reading the threat in my eyes.

I closed the door and leaned my forehead against the wood, half afraid to find myself alone with Alejandro, wounded and unconscious.

Then I remembered how he had prayed over my dead body at Hatfield, not knowing my death was a magickal one and therefore reversible. Alejandro had been brave beyond imagining that night, putting aside his pain to light the candles and perform the last rites for the dead. And though his wound looked grave, he was not yet dead. There were still things to be done for him, and quickly. Magick to be worked that might save his life. I was scared, yes, but his courage must inspire mine.

I turned to find him looking at me. He must have woken from his swoon when they laid him on the bed.

"Alejandro," I choked out.

He managed a faint smile, struggling to sit up.

"No, don't move." Hurrying, I knelt beside him, rubbing my cheek against his hand. His skin was so cold it terrified me. "You are badly hurt."

"It looks worse than it feels," he whispered.

"Oh, Alejandro, you fool." I stared at him accusingly. "Why did you not admit at once that you were wounded?"

"A mere scratch..."

"A scratch that could kill you. What happened? No, do not tell me yet." I stood to fetch the steaming copper bowl, tossing a handful of linen strips onto the bed beside him. "Let me tend the wound first. You will need your strength for that."

I wetted a cloth and pressed it gently against his wound, heard Alejandro suck in his breath, and looked up to see his jaw clenched, his eyes dark with pain.

"Forgive me," I muttered. "I know it will be painful, but the wound must be cleaned." Nonetheless I worked more carefully, dabbing at the ragged edges of his wound. "Who did this to you, Alejandro?"

"Two men. Hooded. I did not recognize them. They must have followed me from Hatfield."

His breath hissed again as I reapplied the cloth, then he continued his tale more slowly.

"We fought on horseback, then on foot. It was an ugly fight.

"They had daggers and cudgels, I had only my sword to keep them at arm's length. I sorely wounded the villain who gave me this—" he indicated the wound, his mouth twisting with satisfaction "—then the other man dragged him up onto his saddle and both rode away, leaving me for dead." He saw my look and managed a laugh. "Not so surprising. I was face-down in the dirt, there was blood everywhere.... They must have thought my wound mortal."

"I cannot believe you continued into Oxfordshire, wounded so badly."

"An old shepherd came across me a short while later. Like the Good Samaritan that he was, the old man helped me to his hut, fed me ale, and pressed hot iron against the wound." He managed a grin at her expression. "I know, it hurt worse than taking another blade in my side. But it stopped the bleeding long enough to let me ride on."

"Well, you are bleeding again now. And if I do not heal you, you may die from it."

"Heal me?" His dark eyes narrowed on mine. "With magick, you mean?"

"Of course. There is a spell for staunching blood." I wrung out the bloodied cloth, trying not to look at the water turning slowly scarlet in the bowl. His wound had reopened as they carried him upstairs, and was now bleeding profusely. "My aunt taught me. I have never used it for a wound as deep as this, but if I change the wording a little—"

"No magick."

"Alejandro, it must be done."

He shook his head, a stubborn look on his face. "This is not your choice, but mine. I got this wound through my own carelessness.

"If it is the Lord's will that I should be healed, then so be it. But I need no help from the dark arts."

"Healing charms are not the dark arts," I pointed out as patiently as I could, for he was serious.

"To be healed by a charm is not natural."

"And bleeding to death is?"

"Perhaps." There was a grim humour in his voice. "If God wishes for my death, then so be it."

"Then I am to do nothing?" I demanded, helpless and frustrated.

"You rode here on my account, Alejandro. Now you tell me I must sit idly by and watch you bleed out your heart's blood when I could save you with a word."

"You are afraid, Meg, and I do not hold that a fault," he said, watching me. "I was afraid too, that time at Hatfield when I thought you were dead. I would have done anything to see you restored to life. And perhaps God heard my prayer that night rather than it being my talisman that saved you. Have you considered that?"

"No," I replied flatly.

He sighed. "You must see that I cannot allow you to change the will of God with magick. You might well succeed, I do not say you would fail. But no good would come of my survival, not at such a perilous cost to both of us."

"Then what can I do?"

"Promise me you will not interfere," Alejandro said, leaning back against his pillow as though exhausted, a frown in his eyes.

"That you will work no magick to heal me."

"Alejandro, I cannot promise that."

"Then you had better leave," he muttered, and watched me go reluctantly to the door. I could see pain in his eyes, and knew it was not merely physical. "I wish you had more faith in me, Meg."

Hurt and confused by this pointless refusal to be healed, I left the bedchamber without further argument. "I wish you had more faith in *me*," I said silently to the closed door, then ran down the stairs.

7

WORK NO MAGICK

To my relief there was no one in the shadowy hall below, its corners chill with gathering dusk. My hands trembling, I did not stop to think but fumbled for a new candle and kindled it from the low-burning fire in my father's empty study. Then I knelt by the hearth, called on the four directions, and began the spell without even bothering to cast a circle. I needed certain herbs, but the spell would work as well with the few pinches of herb-dust I kept in my belt pouch.

Seeing Alejandro so badly hurt had made me realize how much I loved him. I had still been right to send him away, for we could never be happy together while he hoped I would give up magick after our marriage. But the thought of his death, the imminent possibility of that horror, had left me destroyed.

I could not stand by without acting and allow him to die. His decision was akin to self-slaughter.

Had sending him away given Alejandro this death wish?

Sprinkling the dust over the candle flame, I closed my

eyes and whispered the first words: "Bind the bones, slow the blood, knit the skin, heal Alejandro."

I thought of how the enemy's steel must have plunged inside him, splitting his skin, cutting him deep, then envisaged the blade pulling out again, the bloodied edges of his skin knitting together in its wake, healed and whole again. I spoke the charm thrice through, only this time my voice faltered as I came to the place where his name should fall in the spell.

Promise me you will not interfere. That you will work no magick to heal me.

I buried my face in my hands.

Suddenly I heard a familiar sound outside the door. Pinching out the candle flame between finger and thumb, I stood and brushed the hearth dust from my gown. Then I went to the door and opened it.

"Richard?"

Dee's apprentice was standing at the foot of the stairs. He turned and stiffened, no doubt reading the horror and fear in my face. He came towards me at once, taking my hands, rubbing my cold skin.

"What is it?" His eyes met mine. "Has he worsened?"

"Alejandro will not let me heal him," I whispered. "He says I must not use magick, but let God heal him."

His mouth tightened. "Your Spaniard may have glanced at magick for your sake, but he still intends to be a priest. What else did you expect?"

"Richard, I am afraid he will die."

"Then work the spell."

I shook my head reluctantly. "I cannot. It would destroy him. Destroy us."

"So let the novice priest take his chances with God. He has made his choice." Richard shrugged, turning away. His lip had curled. "What more is there for anyone to do?"

I caught at his sleeve. "Wait, please. Alejandro may put his faith in God, but I would rather put my faith in you."

He looked startled. "Me?"

"You can heal him, Richard. I know you can. Not with magick, but with your skill as a healer. You know better than me which plants to use, how to staunch the blood and keep the wound clean to prevent infection."

"I am no physick. I have no training in that art."

"Do not lie to me. You told me yourself that Master Dee taught you as a boy, showed you everything he knows of healing and physick as well as magick and the art of summoning spirits." My grip tightened on his coarse sleeve, and I was encouraged that he had not yet shaken me off.

"Please, I beg of you to help him."

"And if he does not want my help, but only God's?"

"I think Alejandro will allow it if no magick is involved. He *must* allow it." My voice broke, seeing Richard still so cold and obdurate. "It is his only hope of survival."

"And if your priest lives," he said with quiet savagery, "you will marry him?"

"N–no." I twisted my hands together, suddenly nervous. "We may be in love, but we are not right for each other. Not for ever and ever."

"Does Alejandro know that?"

I swallowed. "He suspects it. It is why he does not push me for an answer...." It was not the whole truth, but it was true enough for now.

Richard looked down at me, studying my face through his lashes. I could not read his expression. His hand lifted to brush my cheek, then he gave a crooked smile as though mocking himself. "So there's hope for me yet?"

"Don't," I muttered, and his hand fell away.

"Very well," Richard agreed after a moment's consideration.

"For your sake, I will try to save your stubborn priest, assuming he will allow my very earthly intervention." His voice rose as I dragged him exultantly to the stairs. "But I cannot promise to succeed!"

I waited in the chair beside the bed while Richard worked by candlelight, his hands slow and patient, first cleansing the wound with a foul-smelling herbal preparation of his own making, then stitching it closed with a sewing needle and a length of catgut.

The catgut had been William's idea: upon hearing that we intended to stitch the wound, he had come to my bedchamber bearing an ancient lute, its wooden belly cracked but the catgut strings still intact. Richard painstakingly unthreaded and cleaned the strings, then used the catgut as thread to stitch the sides of Alejandro's wound together.

Trying not to betray my anxiety, I watched Richard set a neat row of stitches into Alejandro's tortured side, each movement slow and methodical.

"That smells grim."

Richard shrugged. "I made it with my own urine. Mixed with an infusion of last year's betony. The two together make an excellent cure-all."

Faugh! I wrinkled my nose.

Richard glanced at me. "What? You think I carry pots of ointments about with me like some travelling surgeon? It may stink, but it was the best I could do in a hurry."

I said nothing, merely raised my brows. Though if it worked, I would never grimace at the stench of the privy again.

Alejandro himself slept like the dead throughout the surgery, drugged by a cup of strong wine mixed with a little black fluid, which Richard had warned me not to taste, for he said it could be "highly poisonous" if too much was consumed. Indeed, when Alejandro finally awoke he was sweating and shaking, then violently sick, his pallor deathlike. But the catgut stitches held firm, and after an hour he lapsed back into uneasy sleep, still sweating but less pale.

"Will he live?"

Richard had crouched beside the hearth, washing the blood from his hands with a pitcher of warmed salt water. "Perhaps. And perhaps not." His face drawn with fatigue, he yawned, then reached for a rag to dry his hands. "These things can be difficult to predict. His wound was cleaner and less jagged than I expected. But he lost a great deal of blood on the ride here, and that weakness may weigh against him when the fever sets in."

"Is he feverish yet?"

"A little." He shrugged, straightening up with a grunt. "If your priest makes it through the next few days, his chances are good."

I was dissatisfied, but it was the best answer I could hope for and I knew it. Between Richard's skill as a healer and Alejandro's unshakeable faith in God, he might yet survive.

"So we wait."

"We wait," he agreed.

Richard limped to the window and looked up. The full moon had risen above the house, clear and ghostly white in the black heavens. Its silver beams fell across the floor in strips, not quite reaching the bed where Alejandro lay sleeping.

"And the princess will have to wait too," he added drily, "for Alejandro to return to Hatfield in your company. Even if he recovers, it could take a while before he's able to sit a horse again without bursting those stitches."

It was the first time I could remember Richard using his name, not contemptuously referring to Alejandro as "your priest" or "the Spaniard."

"Thank you, Richard."

"There is no need for thanks." He yawned and stretched, a flicker of pain on his face. "God's blood, I need to rest."

"Go to bed then, you have done enough here." I smiled. "I will sit with him, and call you if there is any change."

On his way to the chamber door, Richard stopped before me, dragged me forward without warning, and pressed a kiss on my lips. Not a gentle kiss, nor a brotherly one either, but a man's kiss, hard and demanding. I felt my heart begin to race, my cheeks flushing, and stared up at him in confused shock when he pulled away.

"You owed me that kiss, Meg," he whispered, meeting my gaze.

"Call it my fee for helping your priest. Besides, you can hardly begrudge me one kiss if he lives. For he will take all the rest."

After Richard had left the room, I glanced at Alejandro and was relieved to see him still deep in slumber. If he had been awake to witness that kiss, and how I had blushed under it…

He would certainly have burst his stitches then, I thought ruefully, and got up to throw another log on the fire, glad of an excuse for the heat burning in my cheeks.

The next few days passed in a blur of anxiety and sleepless nights at his bedside. Alejandro's fever grew after that first evening, leaving me numb with fear that he would die, then broke so abruptly that Richard queried whether it had been his careful stitching or indeed God's will that his servant still lived.

The day after his fever broke, Alejandro woke and spoke lucidly with both of us, though he was still very weak. The following day, he was able to sit up in bed and eat a light meal, and indeed seemed eager to be mended enough to ride back to Hatfield.

It did feel like a miracle. But Alejandro was young and

strong, and Richard had great skill as a healer. That was what I told myself anyway.

"I know what your Spaniard will believe," Richard commented drily, watching from the hall as I carried a tray of bread and broth upstairs. "That God saved him."

I shrugged. "What difference would it make?"

Alejandro was a fervent believer whose chief desire in life was—or had been, until he met me—to serve God. It was not beyond all possibility that God had intervened to save him. Though in my heart I felt certain it had been Richard's neat stitches that saved his life. After all, over the past year Alejandro had allied himself with a witch—that was unlikely to have won him any favours with the Almighty.

"None whatsoever. Just so long as you do not also believe it," he said pointedly.

"I am not such a fool," I told him, then pushed my way into the bedchamber, where I had left Alejandro sleeping, hoping he had not woken during my absence and overheard our conversation.

I nearly dropped the tray in shock when I found Alejandro out of bed, already dressed in the coarse brown shirt and hose William had lent him.

"What do you think you're doing?"

He looked up at me keenly, a slight colour in his cheeks, buckling his sword belt about his waist. "Ah...I had hoped to be downstairs before you returned. Look at this!" Perhaps thinking to distract me, he indicated his leather sword belt. "This is too loose. I will need to make a new hole with my dagger. Though no doubt a few good meals will render that unnecessary. Where is my dagger, by the way?"

"You're not going anywhere. Get back into bed."

"No need, I am much recovered this morning." He bent

for his doublet and grimaced. His hand flew to his wounded side, hidden by his shirt.

"Alejandro!"

I pointed towards the bed, but Alejandro refused to move, his hand still clamped over his wound, his lips curled back from his teeth in a kind of pained growl.

"Leave me to finish dressing," he muttered, not looking at me.

"Forgive me, I have no wish to be ungrateful. I know what diligent care you have taken of me since I returned to Lytton Park. But I am not an invalid and do not need to spend any more days in bed."

Richard limped into the room. His lightning glance flashed across my face, then assessed Alejandro.

"I expect he'll live," he told me drily when I had explained what had happened. "You had better wait downstairs though while I check his wound. Go on, your father is below and wishes to speak with you."

I left the room, but reluctantly.

I hated the pained look in Alejandro's eyes, and the fact that it had deepened when he glanced from me to Richard. His jealousy remained unspoken, but that did not mean I was unaware of it.

Downstairs, my father called me into his study, his face stern. I could already guess what he wanted to say and stood in an agony of impatience, wishing I knew if Alejandro's wound had split.

"I imagine the Spaniard will be ready to return to Hatfield soon," my father began coldly, standing by the fire with his hands clasped behind his back, "and you no doubt intend to accompany him back there. With or without my permission as your father."

I shrugged, not bothering to respond. I was no longer a

child, being almost seventeen years of age, but my father believed he still had the right to pass judgement on my decisions.
It had been one thing to respect his feelings as master of this
house by asking Alejandro to return to Hatfield. But now apparently I needed my father's permission to leave Lytton Park
in his company. The injustice made my lips tighten.

There was a chilly silence between us. The fire crackled
and I stared at it, not prepared to meet his gaze.

"If you leave Lytton Park, Marcus Dent will find you,"
my father said pointedly, "and destroy you. When he came
to visit me before you returned home, Dent made it clear he
would remember our friendship and not attack you while you
remained under my roof. So you see, you cannot go back to
Hatfield if you wish to live."

"Marcus lied to you," I said impatiently. "He cannot attack
me here because the place is beset with protective spells. Not
because of his old friendship with you."

My temper, always quick to rise, flared; I could not help
myself. "Anyway, what do you care if Marcus does attack me?
You have never shown me love or understanding. You have
only ever disapproved of me and tried to control me."

"How dare you speak to me like that!" he blustered, glaring
at me. "I am your father. You owe me respect, girl."

I held my breath, counting to ten as I tried to calm down.
This argument was foolish and pointless. My father could not
hold me here, and we both knew it. It was better to speak
calmly and leave his house with some dignity.

"I shall return to Hatfield with Alejandro as soon as he is
able to travel, and probably take William with me too. The
Lady Elizabeth has asked for me in person and I am still loyal
to her ladyship, even if she saw fit to dismiss me in the autumn." I glanced from the smoking fireplace to the ugly faded
tapestry on the wall. "Surely you see Lytton Park is no longer

for me? I was made for more than hiding quietly beneath my father's roof like a mouse under the floorboards."

I went to the door, but my father had not finished. He followed me in haste, his chest rattling with deep, harsh breaths.

"You will regret leaving here," he warned me. "This is the only safe place in the country for you."

I turned on him in the doorway. "Being here did not help Aunt Jane when Dent burst in and dragged her away to her death. Dent might leave me alone for a few years, but eventually he would grow impatient and come for me." I glared back at him until his gaze dropped. "And what would happen if you were to die, Father? Would Master Dent still honour his promise to leave me alone?"

"You seem very keen for my death," he muttered savagely.

"I am merely aware of my vulnerability if I make the tactical error of standing still—and letting him catch me."

"Meg, stay with me." His voice faltered. I realized with a shock that his mouth was trembling. "Please."

"Forgive me, but it is my duty to serve the Lady Elizabeth at Hatfield. Besides, there is nothing left for me here," I told him flatly, unwilling to hurt him but equally unwilling to stay.

"Then tell your brother to stay with me. I am no longer young, I need one of you here."

"That must be William's choice, not mine."

He hit out angrily. "William will not stay at my bidding. I have already asked. He wants to return to Hatfield too— he mentioned some young woman in the princess's service."

I nodded. "Alice."

"Is she of good family?"

"I believe so, yes. Close to the court, like the Canleys were. And they are Protestants."

"Well…" My father grimaced. "That's good news, at least.

I could not have stood to see both my children wed to Catholics."

I looked away. He still thought I might marry Alejandro. Was he right…? My father seemed very old suddenly, his hair silvering, his face drawn in tight lines. I hurried to embrace him, and felt his body tremble slightly against mine.

I kissed him on the cheek. "Never fear. Marcus will not harm you once I have gone. And I will return by and by."

"I am not afraid of Marcus Dent," my father said sharply. But he had a strange expression on his face when I curtseyed and left him.

Richard was descending the stairs when I entered the hall, with Alejandro a few steps behind him. I was relieved to see Alejandro up and about, but equally concerned that he would set his recovery back by rushing to be well and whole before he was ready.

"Well?"

"I told you, he'll live," Richard said laconically. "But he's not yet ready to sit a horse."

Alejandro's mouth was a straight line as he reached the last step, his brows knit together with concentration.

"I disagree," he insisted, addressing Richard without even looking at me. "I am in a little discomfort, that is all. The wound is healing well, by the grace of God."

"And thanks to my intervention," Richard added, but held up a hand when Alejandro's eyes narrowed angrily. "Peace, priest. I am not interested in arguing with you over God and his mercy. And I agree that you need not delay your return to Hatfield any longer. But it would be madness for you to sit a saddle in your condition."

I frowned, not understanding. "Then how…?"

"He can travel in a litter."

Alejandro stiffened, then looked from Richard to me, clearly aghast at this suggestion. "Like a woman?"

"No," Richard commented lightly. "Like a wounded man lying in the back of a cart. And Meg will be safe—both William and I will be on hand if there is any trouble. Will can drive the cart and I shall ride alongside."

Alejandro straightened, meeting Richard's gaze squarely. "The journey to Hatfield will take twice as long with a cart, and we have delayed long enough as it is. I'll take my chances on horseback, I thank you. And I too can fight if necessary."

"Then your stitches will burst, the wound will fester, and you will die a painful and horrific death."

My stomach turned. "Alejandro, please." I went to him, my gaze searching his face. "Do not be stubborn. My father will lend us his cart. You can sit up, you need not lie down. No man will think any the less of you for it, not after the wound you have sustained."

He looked at me silently for a moment through his lashes. "Will you travel with me, *mi alma?*"

"In the cart?"

Alejandro nodded, still watching me.

I felt heat in my cheeks. "Yes, of course. If you wish it."

"I do," he murmured, then took my hand and lifted it to his lips. There was the suggestion of a smile in his dark eyes, though I could not be sure I had not imagined it. "If you are there with me, it will not seem such a hardship."

Richard made a choking noise under his breath. "Have you no shame?" he muttered, averting his eyes from such unwanted intimacy, then turned on his heel and headed for the back door. "I think William's in the stables. I need to find him and arrange which horses we can take."

I ignored him, smiling back at Alejandro. I did not want to deceive the Spaniard into thinking we would definitely

marry, for I felt sure that possibility was becoming more remote every day. But I loved Alejandro, and would do whatever he asked to ensure that he looked after himself properly.

"Pack up what you need, Meg, and say your goodbyes,"
Richard called back curtly over his shoulder. "We leave for
Hatfield first thing tomorrow."

The weather stayed cold but dry for the next two days as
we made our slow way cross-country from Oxfordshire to
where the Lady Elizabeth made her lodging at Hatfield House,
a remote country mansion where we had lived very happily the year before. The road was uneven, little more than a
dirt track in places, but while Alejandro winced at the worst
bumps and jolts, he said nothing, his jaw set hard, never once
calling a halt.

I sat beside him on the cart, cross-legged, and played at
cards with him, then dice, then listened while he read aloud
to me from a long poem by Ovid that he had borrowed from
my father's library of books, translating smoothly from the
Latin as he read.

We slept at a rough tavern on the first night, too tired
to do more than close our eyes, but on the second day had
not been riding many hours before we came in sight of the
narrow, smoking chimneys at Hatfield House. With the sun
hidden behind clouds, the great house looked shadowy and
a little sinister. The windows on the west side were all shuttered against the daylight, like a row of blinkered eyes. The
entrance yawned dark at the centre, shrouded in ivy.

I shivered, studying it as we approached. I had never seen
the place look so grim and unwelcoming.

"Look, I can see the house plainly now!" William exclaimed, driving the cart. He turned and grinned back at
me. "We are nearly there, little sister. Still thirsty?" We had
finished the last of our meagre supplies the night before and

had not thought to ask the tavern keeper for more on our departure that morning.

"My throat is a little dry," I admitted, then looked across at Alejandro, who had fallen asleep in the chill sunshine, wrapped in travelling furs.

His face looked as beautiful as an angel's now that the lines of pain had been straightened out, his body relaxed as he slept, one arm slung over my mother's chest of magickal instruments—which I had insisted on bringing away with me—and his short dark hair ruffled by the breeze.

I had been examining my mother's ring on this last leg of the journey, for I was still curious to know its purpose. So far we had no word from Master Dee about it, and the only way I could think of discovering its use would be to wear it.

Now the ring glinted in the sunlight, inviting me.

I slipped it onto my finger and held it up, admiring the way it caught the light. At once I felt more awake, stronger somehow, as though I had just drunk one of Richard's healing draughts. And my finger began to tingle, growing almost hot.

I frowned, turning the ring on my finger. The heat was not uncomfortable nor unpleasant. Indeed, it was rather like the tingling itch I felt in the fingertips when the power descended upon me. But this heat seemed to be trickling back along my hand and wrist, up my arm and into my shoulder bones, spreading warmly towards my heart....

Richard kicked his horse into a trot, riding past with a quick glance down at Alejandro, and I hurriedly slipped my glove back on, concealing the ring.

"Best wake your sleeping prince," he told me, unsmiling. "See, they have heard the horses."

Sure enough, the entrance door had been thrown open, and I recognized Alice at once, standing out on the path with her hands on her hips. The maid's face creased into a broad smile at the sight of William, then she waved at us, calling something back into the house.

A moment later, a taller figure joined Alice on the path. Only it was not the Lady Elizabeth as I had expected. It was the dark, sombre figure of Kat Ashley, staring at us from beneath her old-fashioned French hood.

"Don't fret," Alejandro murmured beside me. When I turned, surprised to see him awake, he managed a reassuring smile. "You will not be turned away this time. It was Mistress Ashley herself who bade me ride for you."

"Mistress Ashley was behind this summons?" I was amazed, for she was the one who had ordered my dismissal upon her arrival at Hatfield.

"But it was she who called me a witch and sent me home to my father's house."

He yawned, stretching as he stirred from his bed of furs. I tried not to stare at the perfection of his body, not even the humble clothes my brother had lent him able to disguise his muscular strength.

"That was before the Lady Elizabeth had special need of you. Things have changed now."

I frowned, wondering what he meant.

Alejandro threw back the furs as we approached the house. When William had drawn the cart to a halt, he stood, holding onto the swaying side of the cart, and I recognized a certain bold recklessness in his expression. He did not wish the princess, nor any of her ladies, to think him weak. However much it cost him to pretend he was not injured.

He jumped down without waiting for William's offered hand, then turned to help me.

"Meg," he murmured, and caught me by the waist, lifting me easily down onto the path. He frowned, his hands slipping to my hips and lingering there a moment, disapproval in his face. "You have lost weight."

"I'm just growing taller," I joked.

"You should not let yourself become too thin," he insisted, then smiled into my eyes, the warmth of his smile filling my heart. "Thank you for keeping me company on the journey. And do not allow Mistress Ashley to intimidate you. You have the power here, not her."

My eyes widened at this dangerous suggestion. But I could not ask him to elaborate; Mistress Ashley was already upon us.

She took my arm in a clawlike grip, shooting a grim look at Alejandro as she pulled me towards the house. "Why has it taken you so many days to answer her ladyship's summons? Was the urgency of the request not made clear enough to you? We had almost given up all hope of you arriving at all!"

"Forgive me," I answered her, more sharply than was entirely polite, "but Alejandro was injured on his return to Lytton Park, and we could not—"

"Injured?" She had stopped dead on the path, staring back at Alejandro. Her hand dropped from my sleeve. "What nonsense is this girl speaking?"

"A mere scrape," Alejandro told her smoothly. "Nothing more. You must forgive my slow progress, Mistress Ashley."

"Señor de Castillo might have died if we had not stayed a few days to tend him properly," I corrected him, ignoring the warning look in his eyes. "You should be grateful we are here at all."

"Indeed?" she countered, her tone haughty.

I could not help glaring at Mistress Ashley, even though it was rude. The first and only time we had met, the princess's former governess had wasted no time in turning Elizabeth against me and bidding me leave Hatfield for ever. Now she was treating me like the lowliest of serving girls.

"When I left, Mistress Ashley," I said coldly, "you accused me of witchcraft and told me I could never return while you were in residence. What can possibly be amiss that I am summoned back with such urgency?"

Her mouth tightened with fury. "I have not changed my opinion of you one iota, witch girl. Do not be deceived by this summons. But my mistress is in dire need of your skills. She is unwell and has been worsening every day since I sent Señor de Castillo to fetch you." As we turned towards the entrance, Mistress Ashley glanced up at the gloomy house. Something akin to fear flickered in her face. "No more talk now, you must be taken to my mistress with all speed."

I followed her inside, managing a brief smile for Alice as I passed. Her bright eyes were so eagerly studying my brother that I was left in no doubt of her affection for him. That was one good thing to come out of this strange summons, at any rate.

Inside the walls of Hatfield House, I drew my cloak more tightly about my shoulders. The great house felt colder and damper than when I left Hatfield in the late autumn, and although a fire was smouldering resentfully in the huge grate in the hall, filling the air with smoke, it was making little impact on the chilly air.

Indeed the only hot thing was my finger, still encased in my sheepskin glove, which seemed to be pumping warmth around my body. Perhaps the ring's purpose was to keep you warm in a snowstorm, I thought, and had to conceal my grin.

"Her ladyship is still abed?" I asked in a whisper. The shadowy interior felt oddly hushed, more like a crypt than a house, and I did not like to speak too loudly.

"The Lady Elizabeth has not left her chamber in days."

"But what ails her? Is she sick?"

Mistress Ashley looked at me sourly, her skirts gathered in

one hand, breathing hard as she climbed the stairs. "Señor de Castillo did not tell you?" She made a rough noise of contempt. "Her ladyship is not sick, you foolish girl. She is *bewitched*."

An old fear gripped my heart and I stared at the woman, barely able to speak, the hated name burning in my mind.

"By...by Marcus Dent?"

She frowned then, looking back at me. "Who?"

I stared, then realized my mistake. She knew nothing of my enemy, and this was unlikely to be his handiwork anyway. Marcus Dent could not have penetrated the magickal defences about Hatfield House and its grounds. Or could he?

"Nobody," I said swiftly. "It does not matter."

Kat Ashley raised her thin brows but said nothing. I could not see her face clearly, for she had not brought a candle. But I sensed that she loathed me and wished me anywhere but there. Simply because I was a witch, I presumed.

Reaching the top of the stairs, she swept along the landing ahead of me in her black weeds, never missing her footing despite the darkness. I followed her wearily, studying the back of her head with acute dislike. Mistress Ashley was a shadow among shadows, a black crow in the house of the dead. She had banished me from here once, and she could do it again with a click of her fingers. Just as soon as I had served her mistress. If we ever got to her room.

My skin crept with sudden dread. Yes, why was it taking so long to reach the princess's bedchamber? I recalled it being only a few steps along the landing. But perhaps my memory had deceived me.

Glancing past Mistress Ashley, I saw a host of doors ahead, more than I remembered. Hundreds, possibly. I blinked, bewildered and no longer trusting my eyes.

It was no dream though. I pinched myself and the corridor still stretched on for ever, the far end shrouded in sinister oblivion, each door yawning open on either side like a row of black toothless mouths.

We could be walking for days, I thought in horror, and never reach Elizabeth's room.

Then I became aware that we were not alone. The hair rose on the back of my neck. Someone was following me. I could hear the thin scraping of a shod foot along the floorboards, and the brush of thick cloth from a long robe....

I whirled in terror, my heart thundering wildly.

But there was nobody there. All I could see was the reddish glow of firelight on the wall above the stairs. Then I heard William's deep familiar voice greeting the hall retainer below, and the sound of laughter from the servingwomen.

I am the one bewitched, I thought, and shook my head in dismay. First, the tinglings I had felt on the cart when I first set my mother's ring upon my finger, and its strange warmth, both of which seemed to have vanished now. Now I was beginning to hear things that were not there. Perhaps I needed more sleep.

"Did you hear what I said, girl?"

I turned, hot-cheeked. "Forgive me…what were you saying, mistress?"

To my relief, the long black corridor ahead of us was gone. The landing was just as I remembered it, unlit but otherwise perfectly ordinary.

Mistress Ashley had paused before the Lady Elizabeth's door, her hand raised to knock. Her voice dropped to a whisper. "I said, the Lady Elizabeth is bewitched by love."

I had paused to remove my glove, slip off my mother's ring, and conceal it in my belt pouch. But at this I looked up at her, astonished.

"By love?"

"Yes."

Her voice hissed through the darkness, leaving me cold. A restless shadow-spirit had stalked this house when I was here before, terrifying us in the night and haunting our daydreams. It might have gone now, blown back to its kingdom in the realm of death but something dangerous still stirred here in the dust. I could feel it in the uneasy drumming of my blood.

"The Lady Elizabeth has fallen in love and is bewitched by her passion. So bewitched, she has barely eaten nor slept nor spoken to a soul this past month, and lies near to death." Kat Ashley met my gaze fiercely. "And you will break the spell that binds her."

Part TWO

HATFIELD HOUSE

MUCH SUSPECTED

I had seen the Lady Elizabeth in many different moods since first entering her service over a year ago: I had seen her proud, joyful, furious, commanding, even frightened. Yet never before had I seen the Queen's sister *broken*.

Not lying in bed as I had expected but seated in the window-seat in her nightgown and lacy mantle, the Lady Elizabeth seemed to be waiting for someone whom she knew would never come, staring out into the wintry sunlight without hope.

Her small dark eyes were red-rimmed and swollen as though she had been crying, her face paler than ever. Her knees drawn up to her chin, she hugged them tight, rocking slightly back and forth on the window-seat, her air that of a distressed child.

It was strange and disquieting to see the princess, five years my senior, reduced to this childlike state.

Blanche Parry sat in a high-backed chair beside the fire, her face pinched, not sewing or occupying herself with some mundane task as she habitually did, but watching her ladyship with a scared expression. As I entered she looked up in brusque recognition. There was relief in her face. We had never been friends. But I knew the princess's lady-in-waiting held me in some awe since the night I had "died" and come back to life. Her eyes had never quite met mine after that. But I could tell from her face that she hoped I had come to cure Elizabeth.

"My lady," Kat Ashley murmured, dropping to her knees before her mistress, "Meg Lytton is here." When she received no response, she plucked nervously at the princess's sleeve. "My lady…can you hear me? The young Spaniard has come back at last. And he has brought the witch girl with him, as you requested."

The Lady Elizabeth stirred then, frowning, and looked down into Kat Ashley's face as though she had only just noticed she was there.

"Meg Lytton?"

"I am here to serve you, my lady." I dropped a low curtsey, shocked to see my former mistress so disconsolate. "In whatever way I can."

What could have happened during my absence to reduce the Lady Elizabeth—whom I remembered as so regal, so composed—to such depths? At once I shared Mistress Ashley's suspicion that she was bewitched, for surely no ordinary man could have brought the proud daughter of Anne Boleyn to this.

My instinct told me this was not the witchfinder's work though. Dark magick felt entirely different. Yet who else but an enchanter could be responsible for her tears?

"I was told you were sick, my lady," I ventured when the princess did not reply, "and had kept to your chamber these two weeks at least. I am no skilled healer, but if the cause of your sickness is magickal…"

Elizabeth said hoarsely, "'Tis not magickal."

I was surprised by such a flat denial. And suddenly uncertain of my territory. If my talent as a witch was not required, why had the princess summoned me?

"Then how may I be of assistance to your ladyship?"

"How indeed?"

The princess closed her eyes, leaning her head against the window frame. Her reddish hair glinted in the sunlight, unbound and hanging to her waist. For a while there was silence in the room. Then her eyes flew open and she beckoned me nearer, as though she had just reached a difficult decision.

"They say every poor village witch knows a spell or a love potion," she whispered, watching me intently, "to charm even the most impossible lover. Can you do this for me, Meg? Can you brew a love potion that will bring me the only man in the world I want?"

A love potion?

I avoided Kat Ashley's sideways glance. So she was right. The princess was indeed bewitched. But by love, not Marcus Dent.

"What..." I licked my lips, almost too afraid to ask the question. "What man is this, my lady? What is his name?"

Blanche Parry made a noise of protest, but I kept my gaze on Elizabeth and waited.

"His name is Robert Dudley," the princess said softly. "His father was the late Duke of Northumberland."

"His father was the D-Duke of Northumberland?"

I stared, horrified by her admission. Before Queen Mary came to the throne, after their young brother King Edward had died, the Duke of Northumberland had gathered together his own supporters in an attempt to put his daughter-in-law Lady Jane Grey on the throne before Mary Tudor could be crowned.

Needless to say, the duke's rising had been put down with

little difficulty, and those involved had paid with their lives. Or most of the ringleaders, at least.

"But was the Duke of Northumberland not executed for treason?"

The Lady Elizabeth nodded, and hugged herself tighter. "His sons were imprisoned too," she admitted sadly, "and stripped of their titles and estates. His son Guildford was executed along with him, and his son's wife, poor Jane Grey, a sweet child who was once a friend of mine and whom they had hoped to set upon the throne in my sister's place. I too was suspected for a time, and thought to lose my own head." Her voice snagged on pain, then recovered slowly as she continued. "The Queen agreed to release Robert from the Tower and allow him into her service. His family lands and title are still forfeit though, so for now he must be plain Master Dudley and earn his keep like any other man at my sister's court."

"I see," I murmured, trying to hide my reaction.

But it could hardly be worse. The Lady Elizabeth had fallen in love with a suspected traitor like herself. How had this disaster occurred? Out here at Hatfield she was isolated from everyone at court, or so I had thought.

As though sensing my confusion, the princess managed a wan smile. "I met Robbie when we were imprisoned in the Tower at the same time," she explained quietly. "We are the same age, so were naturally drawn together at that dark time. Robbie is witty, clever, so amusing…and yes, though Kat hates to hear me say it, he is good to look upon. The most charming and handsome courtier I have ever known, and the truest."

"Yet you have never spoken of Master Dudley in my hearing before today. Are you sure this is not some idle fancy that will soon pass?"

This remark was rather too blunt for Kat Ashley's liking. She stiffened and hissed at me, "Silence, witch girl!"

Blanche Parry was on her feet too. "You had best mind your manners, Meg," she told me fiercely, hands on hips, her mouth pursed with disapproval. "Remember, Lady Elizabeth may be your future Queen. Do not forget your place."

"Forgive me," I said, looking at the princess.

But Elizabeth waved her ladies to sit, a grim smile on her face.

"No, the girl is right to question the strength of my attachment to Master Dudley. The truth is, I thought Robbie lost to me, that he would eventually meet his end on the scaffold like his ambitious father and brother. So I said nothing and told myself to forget him.

"For over a year I struggled to put Robert from my mind, to keep my heart hardened against love. A suspected traitor makes a dangerous friend, especially when I was so newly returned to my sister's favour myself. But then the unexpected happened. Robbie came to visit me himself, soon after you had returned home to Oxfordshire. He stayed secretly in the old shepherd's hut so the servants should not know of his visit. I visited him there after dark each evening, and we... we talked for hours."

I was astonished and a little shocked by this admission.

My stillness must have communicated itself to the princess. A small red spot burnt in each of her cheeks and Elizabeth could no longer meet my gaze.

"I did not intend to encourage him, but I could not help it. Robbie has a fiery nature like my own, and can be very persuasive when he wants to be. He made it clear that his affection for me had grown rather than waned since our last meeting. And I am afraid I did not hide my interest from him either."

"But now he has left Hatfield?"

She nodded. "Robert has returned to court in the Queen's service. Mary means to send him abroad soon, I would guess.

Robert is an excellent soldier as well as a skilled courtier, and already has some reputation as a leader of men. No doubt my sister feels he may be useful to her at the head of her troops. And she is right to do so."

There must be something she was not telling me, for this matter seemed simple enough to me.

"But there is nothing to fear here, my lady, if both of you are in love and willing to marry. You merely have to wait until your sister..."

I hesitated, seeing the quick twitch of her brows. She had never liked any of us to mention the succession aloud, even here in the relative safety of Hatfield House, her childhood home, as a matter of precaution against spies and eavesdroppers.

"Until you inherit the throne," I continued more cautiously, for it was dangerous to speak of the failing health of her much older sister, Queen Mary, "and then marry Master Dudley when you are free to do so."

The princess's eyes turned to me, burning with a strange dark flame. "It is a lovely future you spin for me there, Meg. And I wish with all my soul that such simple happiness could be mine. For I admit, Robert Dudley fascinates me more than any other man in the world. I was drawn to him from the first moment we met, and kept him in my heart during my tedious months at Woodstock. But now, having spent many hours in his company, I cannot seem to stop thinking about him, talking about him...even dreaming about him." Her gaze searched mine intently. "Is that love, Meg?"

My lips curved into a slow smile. For what she had described was a perfect mirror image of how I felt about Alejandro.

"It certainly sounds like love."

She closed her eyes. "I feared as much."

"But if Master Dudley loves you, and you love him too and wish to marry him, this is merely a matter of patience." I frowned, bemused now by her forlorn expression. "Forgive my impertinence, my lady, but your problem will be solved by time. I do not understand why you had me summoned here."

"Meg, we cannot be wed," Elizabeth whispered, her face suddenly ashen again.

"But you said—"

"Robert Dudley is already married."

"Already married?"

"That's what her ladyship said."

Alejandro looked thunderstruck. Seated under the window in his candlelit chamber, his legs covered by a horsehair blanket, a book open on his lap, he raised his gaze to mine.

Ignoring that look, for I knew what it signified, I paced from the bed to the door, then back again. This would not be an easy tangle to unravel. Even with magick.

My brother was playing cards with Alice on the bed. He turned his head to ask, "To another woman?"

"That is the ordinary way of things, yes."

William gave a bark of laughter. "I am not a fool, little sister. I only meant, it was not an admission that she is already secretly wed to Master Dudley?"

I shook my head impatiently. "Dudley's wife is called Amy Robsart. They were married young. Childhood sweethearts, her ladyship said. Only Master Dudley now swears that he no longer cares for his wife, and is in love with Lady Elizabeth instead. And she with him. But the case is hopeless, since she cannot fall in love with a married man. Not if she hopes to be Queen one day."

"So why summon you?" William frowned over his cards, then played his hand. "You are not his Holiness the Pope, you cannot grant this man a divorce so the two can be legally wed."

Alejandro intervened just as I opened my mouth, no doubt sensing my irritation. "The Lady Elizabeth is sick, my friend," he explained.

"If you could have seen her these past few weeks, never sleeping, refusing food, lying near to death at times, you would not mock her need for help."

"But a love potion?"

Alejandro paused, frowning. "No love potion can untie the marriage knot. No, if *la princesa* has summoned Meg, she must have some special reason for having done so."

I could no longer hold back what I knew. "Elizabeth wishes to see Robert again, even though he has returned to court. She has to know if he feels the same, once and for all. She must go to her sister's court."

"Impossible!" Alice exclaimed, staring up at me over her cards, wide-eyed and a little flushed. William had been making her giggle ever since he pulled her onto Alejandro's bed, which explained her heightened colour. Now though she seemed worried, the game abruptly forgotten. "Queen Mary would never allow such a thing. And the Lady Elizabeth would get in dreadful trouble for it."

"Her Majesty will not even know of her visit." I smiled at Alice, trying to reassure her. "Trust me."

I had not had much of a chance to speak with Alice since my arrival, which is why Alejandro had asked her and William to come to his chamber, where we could more safely meet without being overheard by the servants.

I had been worried that Alice might have grown cold during my absence. God knew I was not always an easy person to like. Yet our friendship seemed as strong as ever. And as uncomplicated, for Alice had a bold nature but a pleasingly simple one.

Where she loved, Alice clung tight and would not let go. I was glad she had welcomed my brother to our small circle, for the bouncy, curly-haired maid would be a good influence on him. Of course, I knew his affections were engaged there but could not be sure how Alice felt about him. She often smiled at him, but that meant nothing. My brother needed such allies, I thought suddenly. It was not so long ago, after all, that William had betrayed both me and the Lady Elizabeth, and almost his country too.

Alejandro was frowning. "But this sounds like madness. How can the Lady Elizabeth visit her sister's court without anyone's knowledge?"

I looked at him and raised my eyebrows.

"I see." He closed the book on his lap and laid it aside, his voice dry. "With magick."

William grinned across at Alice. "Wait for it."

"And why not?" I demanded of Alejandro, at once on the defensive. "I brought my mother's chest of instruments with me from Lytton Park, and her spell book. With such help, I will be stronger than ever before."

"And Richard sees no harm in her magickal instruments?" Alejandro persisted.

"Why must you always look to Richard for reassurance?" I was suddenly annoyed, my jangling nerves not helped by my brother's prickling asides to Alice. This was none of their business. But I directed my irritation at Alejandro, who I strongly suspected of thinking me addicted to the dark arts. "Is my own judgement in matters of magick not to be trusted?"

Alejandro hesitated, his dark eyes searching my face. "It is not a lack of trust, *mi querida*. These magickal objects belonged to your mother. It is only natural that you should view them more generously than Richard, and not see the very real danger in using them."

Almost as though he had heard his name mentioned, there was a quiet knock at the door.

"Come in," I called.

Richard put his head round the door. His lips twitched into a smile as he took in the sight of my brother and Alice playing cards on the bed, Alejandro resting in the chair, a coarse blanket over his knees, and me standing by the window. It must have seemed a very domestic scene.

"So here you all are," Richard said, his gaze meeting mine first, as it always did when he entered a room. He came inside without waiting to be invited. "I have been looking for you everywhere. Mind if I join you?"

"Do we have a choice?" Alejandro drawled, but did not protest when the conjuror's apprentice made himself comfortable, leaning against the closed door.

"I have just written to John Dee," Richard said, ignoring Alejandro's taunt, "to let him know where I am." He looked directly at me. "Since Dee did not reply to my last letter at Lytton Park, I have asked again about that ring of your mother's. Just in case my last letter went astray."

Alice looked alarmed. "Astray?"

"Their letters are written in a special code known only to a few people," I informed her, seeing the concern on her face. "The code was devised by Master Dee and is quite fiendish without a key. Even if one of their letters was intercepted, it would be next to impossible for anyone to get at the truth."

"*Next* to impossible," Alejandro echoed softly, a warning note in his voice. "Not absolutely impossible."

Alice suddenly jumped up, a guilty look on her face. "Oh, forgive me, I nearly forgot—" She hurried out of the chamber, returning a short while later with a mud-stained leather pouch. She opened the pouch and handed a letter to Alejandro with a shy smile and a curtsey. "This arrived a few days ago by courier. As you see, it is addressed to you, Señor de Castillo."

"Alejandro," he corrected her, smiling.

She hesitated, then tried his name. "*Ale-Ale... Handro.*"

"*Muy bien,* Alice."

Alejandro glanced down at the letter, marked with his nàme in a neat but florid hand, and the approving smile died on his lips. I had the impression he had recognized the handwriting and was disturbed. He made no comment though, merely dropping the letter unopened beside his chair and covering it with the blanket that had been warming his knees.

"I have had enough of this tiresome infirmity. Surely soon I will be recovered enough to rise and make my apologies in person to *la princesa?*" Alejandro stood without any help, supporting his weight on the table, though I saw him glance at Richard for confirmation. "*Si?*"

Richard shrugged. "You heal fast, I'll give you that."

"Now perhaps you will respect the power of prayer, heathen," Alejandro told him loftily, brows raised, goading the apprentice. He looked in my direction, holding out a hand, and I saw his dark eyes soften. "Come, with your help I will walk in the garden, regain my strength to visit the Lady Elizabeth."

"You do not wish to read your letter first?"

He did not even glance at it, holding my gaze unswervingly, almost as though he knew I was testing him but had no plans to satisfy my curiosity yet.

"Later, perhaps," he said lightly. "I would rather have your company for now, *mi querida.* Unless you wish to deny it to me?"

9

A QUESTION OF BLOOD

The Lady Elizabeth's condition worsened the next day. When I tried to attend to her, Mistress Ashley sent me away, declaring sharply that her ladyship could not even rise from her bed, let alone discuss matters that would only distress her. I waited in my chamber for a few days, reading through my mother's grimoire, hunting for some useful solution to Elizabeth's problem. Richard came to study the book with me, pointing to an occasional spell over my shoulder, and Alejandro always seemed to drift past the doorway just as we were laughing over some obscure Latin phrase or scribble in the margin.

At last a summons came.

I found Elizabeth propped up on pillows in a darkened chamber that smelt of incense and burnt herbs. "I am at my wits' end, Meg. This cannot continue. You must do whatever you can to cure me of this sickness."

"You mean love?"

Elizabeth nodded, her face pale and haggard. "I have

changed my mind. I no longer desire to travel to my sister's court to see Robbie. I cannot bear my own weakness where he is concerned. There must be a spell against impossible desire, Meg. I need you to perform it tonight. I cannot live like this, not even for another day. I am locked up in Hell."

She clutched feebly at my hand as I stood by her bedside. I thought she had never looked closer to death.

"Please," she begged, as though afraid I would refuse, "help me escape the chains of this love, and when I come to the throne, I swear you will be rewarded. I do not care what horrors your spell demands. I will drink blood and dance naked under the moon, whatever you tell me."

"There is a spell," I admitted, remembering something we had found in my mother's grimoire. "But it requires the use of a cauldron, and cannot be cast here in the house for fear of discovery."

"Where then?"

"The old shepherd's hut? The place is very private, and it is open to the working of dark magick, which is no doubt why Master Dee always stays there when he visits." I looked at her dubiously. "But will you be strong enough to walk there, my lady?"

Her mouth tightened. "I must be, it seems. What do you need for this spell?"

I named some of the ingredients, and her face lightened. "Oh, those are easily procured. Bess in the kitchen will help you with the herbs. And there are toads enough in the garden. Look under any stone. But the wild plants…"

"I can gather those myself, my lady," I reassured her. "But if you wish the spell to be performed tonight, I must hurry. It may prove difficult to hunt down some of the woodland plants once dusk falls."

"Go, then," she agreed, and sat up in bed, a slight flush in her cheeks. "I will prepare myself."

The princess was looking relieved as I hurried out, and small wonder, this love had her so bewitched. Whatever Elizabeth felt for Robert Dudley, she had been taken over by it, her whole being possessed.

I met Alejandro on the stairs. He was walking with a stick to avoid being forced to remain in bed. But I could see that he was still in pain.

"Going out?" He had noted my cloak and walking boots. "Not alone, I hope. It will be dark in an hour or two."

"Come with me, then." I handed him my basket for a moment while I fastened my cap, then took it back. "I should not be too long. I am only gathering ingredients for..."

Alejandro raised his eyebrows when I hesitated. "For a delicious supper?"

"That's right," I said drily, then glanced at his stick, adding cautiously as I knew his pride, "Will you be able to walk as far as the woods? We only wandered in the garden yesterday and yet it seemed to pain you...."

"I will manage," he insisted, and held out his arm to me. Alejandro was so stubborn and proud, he never liked to admit when he was hurting. It was a trait that irritated me. All the same, I disliked admitting when I was in trouble. Two sides of the same coin, perhaps.

We made our way down the stairs and into the formal walled garden, where I saw Bess collecting herbs for that evening's meal and stopped to ask her to set a few aside for me. My story that I was making up a herb sachet for the Lady Elizabeth did not sound very convincing to my ears, but the servingwoman did not seem to notice, nodding cheerfully as she continued to snip at the tender young rosemary shoots.

There were signs of spring everywhere at Hatfield. I bent

to turn over a few stones, and eventually found a recently dead toad. Spells that called for parts of birds and animals always made me squeamish, for I disliked taking a life to make magick. So to find one already deceased was a blessing.

I slid the dead toad into my basket and covered it carefully with a cloth.

"What?" I demanded, seeing Alejandro's expression.

"Oh, nothing," he said drily. "Only remind me to skip supper if you're cooking."

The red-brick walls of the formal garden were softened by a tangle of ancient climbing roses, their pruned-back top stalks just starting to grow back again. Periwinkles had seeded themselves in the sandy soil between herb beds, and a few mint shoots trickled thinly over the lip of a tall clay pot against the wall. In the vegetable patch, a stone rhubarb bell lay on its side, waiting for the first immature stalks of rhubarb to appear.

"I wish we knew who had attacked you when you left Hatfield, and why," I commented, nudging a pretty little periwinkle with my boot.

"No doubt it will become clear in the end," Alejandro said unfathomably.

We came to the gate that led away into meadows bordered by a wild tangle of woods. He pointed ahead, leaning on the gate. "The woods. It will be dark soon. You sure you want to go on?"

Still trying to protect me from the darkness, I thought, even though I was long past being protected.

I glanced back over my shoulder at the long house of soft red brick, its twisted chimney stacks smoking peacefully, and wondered where Richard was today. I had not yet spoken to him about the odd experience I had on arriving at Hatfield— seeing and hearing things that were not there—and though I wanted to discuss it with someone, I knew Alejandro would only worry if he knew.

It hurt to say, "I can carry on alone if you prefer to go back."

"Not a chance," he said shortly, and I tried not to be glad of his company. He tucked his stick under one arm and held the gate open for me. "Come on."

The air was cooler and darker in the woods, damp with a suggestion of impending rain, and the warning calls of birds sounded among the branches.

"The villains who attacked you, do you think they could be Marcus Dent's men?" I persisted.

"I told you, both men were hooded. I did not see their faces."

He sounded exasperated. "Meg, please. We have more important things to discuss than robbers on the Queen's highway. Stop a moment, let's talk."

I halted under a broad-trunked, low-branching sycamore and bent to gather some honeysuckle stalks, their new budding leaves fresh and soft.

Looking up, my heart ached at the expression on his face. The fact that Alejandro could not see how dangerous I was for him made no difference to me. The game had gone on long enough, but it must stop here, in this shady woodland on the edge of Hatfield House. It had been lovely to pretend over the past year that we could be together, that life would work out for us. But I could not allow Alejandro de Castillo to suffer for the choices I had made.

I was already convinced that Alejandro had been attacked because of his association with me, even if I was uncertain who had been behind it. But those men would try again one day if he stayed at my side, of that I was sure.

"In a short while," he said quietly, watching as I dropped

the wild flower stalks into my basket, "it will be a year and a day since I asked you to marry me."

"I have not forgotten."

"You made it clear that you are unlikely to say yes, and of course I would never try to force you." His voice hardened; he might not want to "force" me, but neither would he give up without a fight.

"I still hope to make you change your mind though."

"Impossible."

He looked at me broodingly for a long moment. "Is that so? I've seen the way the wind has been blowing since I left Lytton Park. You would prefer an English Protestant husband, is that it?"

"No!"

Alejandro continued doggedly, "Richard understands your art too. He has his own power. There would be no *conflict* there."

"Yes," I muttered, "but no love either."

"I know you do not wish to live in Spain, and why. But what if we were to marry and stay here in England?" he asked as if he had not heard my response, his head bent in thought. "I could give up the priesthood."

Anger leaped in my heart. "Don't you dare! I know how much it means to you. Besides, it would not solve anything. You are a Spanish nobleman, Alejandro. Even if you gave up the priesthood, when your father dies, you will inherit his title and his duties. You will be required to attend the Spanish royal court, and oversee your lands and tenants." He did not reply. I persisted with my argument. "Is that not true?"

He lifted his head and his gaze met mine, a stormy black velvet shot through with frustration. *"Si."*

"In other words, if you are crazy enough to marry me, a commoner and a suspected witch, you will bring double disgrace on your family whether we stay here or live in Spain. And then the Inquisition will come beating down your door."

"Those dogs would not dare touch the wife of a nobleman—" he began hotly, but I interrupted him.

"The Spanish Inquisition would dare anything. Have you forgotten how they dragged me away and tortured me when we were at court? I was under the protection of the Lady Elizabeth, but they thought nothing of *that*."

Alejandro shot a lightning glance at my hand. Señor de Pero, the Chief Inquisitor, had torn one of my fingernails off while torturing me for information, and the finger had never quite healed.

He took me by the shoulders, staring into my face. His voice was clipped, self-condemnatory. "Yes, and that was my fault. I did not believe de Pero would torture you, but I was wrong. Badly wrong. I should have worked harder to get you out of there."

"You couldn't have saved me, you will never be able to save me. I'm…I'm not someone who *can* be saved." My heart thumped at the sudden flash of fury and helplessness in his eyes. But I needed him to accept the truth. "I'm a witch, Alejandro. I'm meant to be alone."

He held me at arm's length, his expression bleak as he looked me up and down. "So let me see if I have understood you, *mi alma*," he said stiffly, a muscle jerking in his cheek. "You will not listen to my suggestions. You wish us to go our separate ways once you have helped *la princesa*, and never see each other again?"

Somehow I managed a nod. "That would be for the best."

"So this is the end?"

"This is the end," I repeated heavily.

I could hardly breathe, the pain in my heart was so intense. Having my fingernail ripped off by the Spanish Inquisition had been more bearable than telling him we were finished. If my spell stripped away Elizabeth's desire for Robert Dudley, perhaps I should use it on myself and Alejandro. Set back our hearts to the moment we met and alter fate so that we remained strangers. Cold, indifferent strangers.

Then at least I would not have to suffer the agony I could see reflected in his eyes too.

The hour was late, the night outside dark. The old shepherd's hut danced with shadows, lit only by a candle lantern and the low fire I had kindled. The smoke wreathed its way out of the broken rafters while I stared through it at the Lady Elizabeth, kneeling opposite me within the circle I had marked out in the dirt with the rough end of my hazel wand.

Outside the circle Blanche Parry stood to one side, studiously not looking at what we were doing but reading Elizabeth's book of the psalms instead. The lady-in-waiting had stoutly refused to leave her mistress alone with a witch in this "nasty, dirty hovel" but was also clearly horrified at the thought of witnessing magick. So the psalms it was.

Somewhere outside the shepherd's hut I knew Alejandro was also on his feet, waiting for the spell to be finished so he could escort us back to the house. He had not spoken to me on the way down to the hut tonight, supporting the Lady Elizabeth instead, though he himself was hardly more steady on his feet.

Alejandro had not forgiven me for rejecting him. Perhaps he never would. Well, I would probably never forgive myself either. But it had still been the right thing to do.

I set the cauldron on the flames, waited patiently for the oil to smoke, then threw in the toad entrails, a slimy pinkish-brown tangle.

The smell of roasting innards filled the hut at once, and the Lady Elizabeth blenched.

She did not cover her nose though, much to her credit, but at my whispered instruction threw in her own ingredients: a shred of paper with *Robert Dudley* written across it, a dried petal of eglantine he had pressed inside a letter for her, and a scattering of rosemary.

"Have you ever wished to be free of love, Meg?" she asked curiously, watching as I stirred the ingredients gently together.

I kept my eyes on the cauldron. "Yes."

"With Alejandro?" Her smile was thin when I looked up in surprise. "I know you are still secretly betrothed. I have seen how you look at each other. But you must know such a match to be impossible. Indeed, I should have said something before, but my mind was elsewhere...."

I looked at her, steeling myself, for I knew before she spoke what was coming next.

"I know it will be hard, but I need you to stay away from Señor de Castillo while you are here. You must never be alone with him in your chamber, as you often were when you served me before. I was taught that a princess must always be in charge of her ladies-in-waiting, especially the younger ones, and has a duty to ensure they remain...untouched." To her credit, she looked very uncomfortable as she said this. "You understand what I mean?"

I nodded stiffly.

"Good, I'm glad." Elizabeth bit her lip, gnawing on it as she stared at the cauldron between us. For the first time I saw her as a girl rather than a princess, only a few years older than me, and very much in love with a man she could never have. "Now to rid myself of unwanted love, and we can both be chaste together."

I had earlier had a very similar conversation with Alejandro, of course, and could have smiled about that if my heart had not been bleeding inside.

"If you are ready," I said huskily, adding a crushed handful of the wild flowers I had gathered in the woods, "recite the words we practised. But *backwards,* remember, and three times exactly. Then we must keep vigil until everything inside the cauldron has begun to blacken. That's vital, my lady, or the spell will not work."

Elizabeth nodded, a look of utter concentration on her narrow-chinned face.

"Dudley Robert," she intoned with great seriousness, staring at the sticky mess inside the smoking cauldron, "thee for... love my away take. Dudley Robert...thee for love my away... take." She paused, suddenly shivering, then finished in a rush. "Dudley Robert thee for love my away take."

God's blood, I thought grimly, those toad entrails stink. I tried not to show my revulsion before the princess though. If she could stand it, so could I.

Nonetheless, gathering the ingredients for the spell, consulting my mother's grimoire, even scouring out her old travelling cauldron—these simple acts had brought me closer to my mother. Now it felt as though Catherine Canley were there by my side, advising me how to work the spell. And I felt sure she would have performed such spells for her own mistress, Elizabeth's mother, Queen Anne herself.

The disgusting mixture in the cauldron was brown now, turning to black at the edges. I looked at the Lady Elizabeth, but she was staring at the various objects I had laid out on the dirt floor beside the fire, her face distracted.

Suddenly uneasy, I glanced at the cauldron, then the door, closed against the cold night air. What was troubling me? The hairs prickled on the back of my neck as I became aware of a presence with us in the hut. My mother's spirit? Or something more sinister?

The place was so still. Perhaps I was imagining things. It was very late, and I was tired after a restless night.

The pot hissed and I peered inside, squinting through the heat haze, the thickening smoke as the ingredients blackened. When I leaned back again, I felt dizzy. Then stupid somehow, as though I had been drugged.

Had I unwisely inhaled some of the smoke? But there was no warning in the book about doing that....

I turned to consult the grimoire for the next step, and found Elizabeth turning the pages, her look fascinated.

"My lady," I began tentatively, then saw what she was wearing on her slender middle finger.

My mother's ring!

"No!" I exclaimed in horror and lunged across the cauldron for her hand, not caring how insolently I was behaving towards a princess.

I never reached her.

In that instant, Blanche Parry stumbled forward with a yell as though to prevent me from molesting the princess.

I leaped up, startled by this violent response, but one glance at Blanche's face told me she was not even looking at us. She was staring at the cauldron, its contents now a foul stinking mush.

With a surprisingly powerful kick, Blanche launched my mother's battered cauldron off its iron stand, then stamped on the fire, all but destroying it. Blackened toad entrails, ash and burning brands—some still white-hot—went flying towards the princess, who jumped to her feet to avoid being burnt by the shower of hot debris.

The fire hissed out.

The hut was dim, the only light coming from the princess's lantern, the flickering gloom thick with smoke.

Blanche stood in the centre of the circle, head bent, her large body shaking as though with an ague.

"Blanche!" the princess gasped, her face paler than ever. "What on earth were you thinking? You've ruined everything. The spell will not work now. And you've burnt my hand! Look!" And she thrust out her slightly reddened hand, still jewelled with my mother's ring, for the woman to see.

"Blanche?" I murmured, rather more cautiously, and laid a hand on the woman's heaving shoulder.

The lady-in-waiting swung abruptly to face me, crouching low as though about to spring at me. Her mouth opened. But no words came out. Only a terrible snarling like a rabid dog, her lips damp with spittle.

Elizabeth was staring now, her eyes almost black. "God's blood, what is that infernal noise she's making? Have you lost your wits, Blanche?"

But Blanche did not reply. Her cap had tumbled off, her hair hanging loose. Her features were twisted in an ugly grimace, almost unrecognizable. Some evil creature of pure evil had taken possession of her body and was staring out of her normally placid face with a malevolence that struck terror into me.

The door to the hut crashed open and Alejandro stood there, breathing hard, his gaze locked on me. Then his eyes widened at the sight of Blanche in the circle, crouched with bared teeth like a wild animal.

"Madre di Dios!" He crossed himself rapidly, then lifted his silver crucifix to his lips, staring at Blanche. "I heard shouts. What in God's name has happened here?"

"We don't know," I muttered, looking away from him, though I was secretly relieved to see him.

It was a lie, of course. I had a strong suspicion that Marcus

Dent might be behind this. But Alejandro did not need to know that. It would only make it harder for him to let me go.

Blanche had turned to inspect him, still growling low in her throat. Now she suddenly sprang at him with a wordless cry, rigid fingers outstretched like claws.

Alejandro seized her by the wrists, struggling for a moment while the lady-in-waiting screamed and raked at his face, then crashed heavily to the dirt floor with her. The violent shock of their landing seemed to shake the demon out of Blanche, and she cried out in genuine terror, "Lord save me!"

Alejandro released her and stumbled to his feet, a smear of mud on his cheek. "Mistress Parry?"

"Forgive me, forgive me," she babbled, then hid her face in her hands.

He swung to face us. "I don't understand what's been going on here——" he began in a hostile tone, but then broke off, staring at Elizabeth. She had been studying the back of her hand with a perplexed frown, and he must have seen the glint of my mother's ring on her finger. "My lady? Why are you wearing that ring?"

The princess looked up with narrowed eyes, clearly shocked to be addressed so peremptorily.

"Sir?"

I stepped forward, holding out my hand. "My lady, you must remove that ring. It is a magickal object."

"What, this? But it's so beautiful. I saw it lying on the floor, and I just had to put it on…." With obvious reluctance, the princess slid the ring from her finger and placed it on my palm. She bit her lip. "Was it the ring? Did I cause this?"

"I don't know," I admitted, closing my palm on the reddish-gold ring. It felt cool and smooth, and I was suddenly tempted to slip it onto my own finger, remembering how strong and confident it had made me feel. "Though I doubt it. This felt more like dark magick."

"It's curious though," Elizabeth murmured, frowning down at her hand again. "I could have sworn— The skin was burnt, I'm sure. But there's not a mark there now."

"How lucky for you," I said with mild irony, then caught Alejandro looking at me darkly and regretted it.

But the princess was not listening. She had hurried across to comfort Blanche, embracing her with the warm affection she seemed to reserve only for her ladies-in-waiting, and murmuring reassurances in her ear.

"We had better get back to the house," I said to nobody in particular.

I bent to rescue my mother's grimoire, brushing off the ash before closing it. Aware of Alejandro's gaze burning a hole in the back of my head, I tucked the ring safely back into my pouch, where it should have remained. The strange thing was, I did not even remember removing it.

10

INVICTUS

"Say that again. You did what?"

I gaped at Richard, disturbed and horrified by what he had just told me.

It was three nights since the fiasco in the old shepherd's hut when my spell had been ruined and Blanche possessed by some demon, possibly Marcus Dent. Poor Blanche had spent the next day in bed, claiming "wobbly legs," but seemed otherwise unharmed by her possession. All the same, Blanche was clearly avoiding me—as though she blamed me for what had happened; and perhaps she was right to do so—as was marked by her absence this evening.

Richard and I had been summoned alone to the princess's bedchamber and were seated on the floor, a single tallow candle lighting our faces.

There was one chair, set aside for the princess, but Elizabeth stood by the window instead. She was never able to settle for long, staring out at the dark now as though waiting for a signal. A small fire burnt steadily in the hearth, the damp logs crackling as they were consumed.

It was a windy evening, and the leaded glass in the window was a poor fit; as a consequence the candle flame dipped while we spoke, sending shadows rippling across the walls and our faces.

"I said, I removed the spells of protection about Hatfield House once you had returned home last autumn," Richard repeated, shrugging.

"But why do such a dangerous thing?"

"What's the matter?" He sounded defensive. "They were set around the house to guard against Marcus Dent, and it seemed unlikely he would bother coming here when you were in Oxfordshire. Besides, I found them problematic. They prevented the working of certain spells in and around the house. It took a while to dismantle them," he added grudgingly. "Your spellwork is strong for a woman. But eventually I found a way to take them down."

"How?" I demanded, feeling ruffled. If Richard could remove my ring of protective spells, perhaps Marcus Dent could too. And once someone had broken through, stamped their presence on the house, it would be hard to keep them out again.... I shivered. "*How?*" I asked again. I needed to know what mistake I had made.

"You left some of your things here." Again Richard grinned, aware of my outrage and enjoying it. "Small items. A few hairpins, a pair of old shoes...I used them to work the counter-spell for me."

"And now that I have returned?"

"We should erect the protective barrier again." Richard met my eyes. "Tomorrow after breakfast?"

I nodded. I disliked the idea that anyone, even Richard, had found a way round my spells of protection. But I couldn't close my instinctive thought that it would be too late anyway to erect the barrier—a man as powerful as Marcus Dent would surely cloak his own spells, make it nigh impossible to keep him from us once he had breached the boundaries. It was a weakness in my armour that I had not foreseen. "I must be more careful what I discard in future."

"Burn everything," Richard agreed cheerfully. "Or bury it. That is my master's way. John Dee leaves nothing for his enemies to use against him."

"How is Master Dee?" Elizabeth turned from her silent scrutiny of the dark grounds. "I often think of the astrologer. His advice to me at our past meetings seems more true than ever these days. Have you heard from him since the last letter you showed me?"

"No, my lady."

"I shall write to him myself." Elizabeth bit her lip. "Oh, but I can't. He is still in Bishop Bonner's employ. It would not be safe."

Bishop Bonner. A devout cleric who famously spent much of his time questioning Protestant heretics and sending to the stake those who would not abandon their faith. The Lady Elizabeth was right to fear him.

Richard hesitated. "If you can tell me what message you wish to relay, I can write in code to my master."

"Thank you, I shall." With a gesture she dismissed Kat Ashley from the room, then turned to me sharply as soon as the three of us were alone. "I have been thinking, Meg. The failure of the spell to turn my love away from Robbie must surely mean that it is a pure love, a love that cannot be blocked by magick. So, Meg, have you considered how to bring me to visit Master Dudley without discovery? Or at least fetch me news of him and his wife, Amy? I must know if he is truly happy with her.

"For if he is happily married," she continued, "if Robert has lied to me for the sake of advancement when I am Queen, then I will abandon this madness without the need for any further spells, no matter how pure and honest my love. I am no thief, to steal away a man whose proper place is in another woman's arms."

I had been thinking of the far-seeing-spell in my mother's grimoire for the past few days, and decided to mention it now, though I felt sure Richard would not approve.

"How about if I were able to visit Master Dudley on your behalf, and bring back news of him?"

Her head swung sharply, her small dark eyes narrowed on my face.

"When?"

"This very night. Here and now, if you can put your trust in me."

I saw disbelief in her face. She looked hard at Richard. "This can be done?"

"I believe so, my lady."

"How?"

Richard spread his hands in a gesture of helplessness. "I have no answer for you, my lady. The thing is possible over short distances. Though Master Dudley is at court, is he not?" He looked at me warningly. "That may be too far for Meg's power to reach."

"I do not know where Robert is," the princess admitted. "He may be at court. Or he may be at home with his wife."

"It will be difficult if I do not know for sure where he is." Then I remembered how Richard had lowered my barrier of protective spells. Perhaps there was a lesson to be learned there. "Do you have anything of Master Dudley's? A letter, perhaps? Or a keepsake?"

She stared, and I saw a haughty flash of anger in her eyes.

The Lady Elizabeth disliked her private affairs being too openly discussed.

"Why?"

"It may help my spell."

"I see." The princess looked pained, then seemed to come to a decision. "Look away and close your eyes. Both of you."

Surprised, I closed my eyes and bent my head. A moment later, I heard a rustle, then a quick step, and something cold was placed in my hand.

"There," Elizabeth said huskily. "Robert Dudley gave me his likeness as a keepsake. It was painted by one of his sisters some three or four years ago. He would have been about twenty then. And here is a letter he wrote to me." Elizabeth handed it to me reluctantly, rolled up and tied with a red ribbon, though from its creased state the paper looked to have been studied many times. She added hurriedly, "Only you must promise not to read it!"

"You have my word on it, my lady."

I looked down at the miniature portrait of Robert Dudley, done rather neatly considering its size, then set into a circular frame. Dark eyes, dark hair, a sallow complexion. Robert Dudley might almost have been Spanish, but for the stoutly English way he bore himself, one fist at his hip, the other resting on the head of an adoring hound.

Master Robert Dudley looked very young, but bold with it. There was a steady look to his eyes, a daring fearlessness that was most attractive and I saw at once why Elizabeth had fallen in love with such a man, a fellow prisoner in the Tower, a noble stripped of his lands and title, and almost deprived of his life....

It must have been hard for Elizabeth not to think of her own suffering when she witnessed his.

"Well, what do you think of Master Dudley?" Elizabeth

asked at last, a note of impatience in her voice, and I realized she had been watching me eagerly as I studied the miniature.

"He is very handsome, my lady."

"Yes, he is." The princess drew a long breath. Her chest rose under the narrow bodice, her lips curving into a rare smile. "And I wish he were here with me now, however wrong that might be. Then at least I would know he is safe, that his enemies at court have not gained any advantage over him. Both his enemies and mine, for they are the same."

"I shall do my best to bring you news of him, my lady. I do not know how successful the spell will be, when the distance to be travelled is so far…. Well, let me try."

I set down the miniature and letter, and placed a hand on each, closing my eyes as I let their essence rise up through my fingers.

As soon as I took up the hazel wand, its power filled me. My fingers tingled with that old familiar sensation, painful and exciting, of having been stung with nettles. I thought of Robert Dudley, saw the handsome young courtier in my mind's eye, and silently asked the hazel wand to find Dudley for me, to "take me to him."

Eyes still closed, I murmured the command word, "*Aspicio*," lifted the wand, and almost immediately felt a tugging at my back and shoulders.

Startled, I turned my head blindly, questing for the others, thinking Richard or the princess must have touched me.

But all was still. There was no longer anyone beside me.

My body rose, floating a moment, then turning on the air, oddly weightless. I kept my eyes shut, afraid to look down and break the spell. Wind lifted my hair and my cheeks grew chill. Suddenly I realized that I was no longer in the Lady Elizabeth's candlelit chamber but flying through the night, voyaging the long darkness that lay between Hatfield House and the south.

I opened my eyes. The rushing darkness made me dizzy, and when I glanced down, the height was simply terrifying. Fields and vast black trees, shimmering rivers and hills, even the looming bulk of houses flitted beneath me at lightning speed, faster and faster as I flew south, my mother's spell rapidly and irresistibly closing in on the location of Master Robert Dudley.

What if I should fall and kill myself?

I almost laughed. This was no journey of the body. I could not tumble out of the sky like Icarus in the Greek myth, the boy's wax-bound wings melting when he flew too near the sun. This was a spell, a magickal voyage of the mind. All that could happen was that I might be woken before I had completed the spell....

I was not reassured by that thought. Last time I had felt queasy and off-balance after Richard panicked and broke the spell after a few minutes. This time I might be gone for hours. What would happen if one of them brought me back too early?

Suddenly my journey was over. Blackness descended and the night wind stilled. The air around me blurred, then I landed on my feet, standing in a torch-lit passageway.

This was the residence of some person of importance, I realized, glancing about at the expensive wood panelling and lavishly embroidered tapestries on the walls depicting Biblical scenes: Adam and Eve, the woman's face cast down in disgrace as they were evicted from Paradise; Lot's wife being turned into a pillar of salt; the beautiful Salome admiring the severed head of John the Baptist.

Stairs led up into darkness; all was silent up there. But to my left a door stood partly open, and I could hear voices within.

I frowned, finding one of the men's voices oddly familiar. Surely I knew that man?

At that moment, two servants emerged from the room, carrying empty platters in each hand, leaving the door closed.

They were heading straight for me.

I stiffened, my heart thumping as I stared from one unsmiling face to the other, and I mentally scrabbled for some reason for why I should be standing there, eavesdropping....

But there no was no need for explanations. The men walked through my body as though it were not there, and continued down the passageway, giving no indication that they had seen me.

Like a ghost, I thought unsteadily.

I studied my bare hands. To me, I looked—and felt—solid enough. But to them I must be invisible, just as before when I had spied unseen on my brother.

Putting my hand to the door, I tried to push it open, but it would not budge. I had no substance there. Yet suddenly I was inside the room. I glanced back. The door was still closed. So I could pass through solid objects at will, I thought wonderingly, not just have them pass through me!

There were four well-dressed people seated about the table, which had been set for a lavish meal, silver platters and wine goblets gleaming.

"Come, sir, you and your wife must take more of this excellent Spanish wine," insisted the portly, red-cheeked gentleman at the head of the table. He snapped his fingers and a servant hurried forward with a brimming flagon. "I cannot stand to see my guests' cups and plates empty. Especially not when you have come so far to eat at a humble churchman's table."

I judged the man to be somewhat older than Kat Ashley, who was now past her fiftieth year, and very well-fed by the look of his paunch. He turned jovially to the woman on his left, who looked terrified at this attention. "Not hungry, mistress? The last course was a little rich, I agree. And all those raised pies and pastries give one terrible indigestion when consumed this late in the evening. Though the larks' wings and venison in the gravy were rather tasty...." He rubbed his large hands together, smiling broadly. "But there is a syllabub coming, and I promise you it will be a triumph."

I moved forward, taking in the place to which I had been brought. The dining chamber was well-lit with candles, a large fire burning in the hearth and fresh rushes on the floor, the windows shuttered. I did not know the "humble churchman" at the head of the table, dressed in the finest clerical robes and with a black velvet cap on his head, but the young man to his left was unmistakably Master Robert Dudley.

I studied the young man's profile with interest as he stretched out his goblet to the servant. Yes, the portrait had been a good likeness.

Opposite him sat a woman whom I assumed must be his wife. Amy was fair and not unhandsome, but seemed very meek, for she barely raised her head when the churchman addressed her.

The fourth person was sitting with his back to me. But as I slipped round the table and saw who it was, I realized why one of the voices had seemed so familiar.

It was John Dee, the Queen's astrologer, and a secret long-time supporter of her sister Elizabeth.

"I shall take more wine too, if I may," Master Dee was saying meekly, raising his own goblet to have it refilled. "It is not bad, as Spanish wines go. But I do prefer a red Burgundy. So much smoother on the palate."

The churchman looked at him sharply. "It is unlikely we will enjoy much Burgundy at our tables this year, Master Dee. Not while His Majesty is waging war against the French. Unless your *charts*—" and here he paused, an edge of contempt in his voice "—have revealed to you the outcome of this conflict? If so, you should share such information with the Queen at once."

"No, indeed, my lord," Dee replied uneasily, and I guessed that the man at the head of the table must be his master, the dreaded Bishop Bonner.

I studied the bishop closely, feeling sick. One of the most feared men in England, he had recently committed the elderly Thomas Cranmer, once the Archbishop of Canterbury, to the bonfire in nearby Oxford. Having watched my own aunt die in the same way, I knew such cruelty could never be justified. Yet here he was, mopping up his gravy with a hunk of manchet bread, more intent on his dinner than on burning as many of his fellow men as he could.

"This man," Robert Dudley announced with a determined laugh, "would have us think him an expert in wines. But indeed when I was a boy, and he was my tutor, I swear he barely touched a drop. Still a young man himself, he would drink nothing but the weakest ale or mead."

My mouth fell agape.

John Dee had been tutor to the young Robert Dudley?

I stared, bemused, at the astrologer; his eyes were shadowed with recent pain, yet his face still looked as handsome and unearthly as when we had first met, his hair long enough to fall down his back like a woman's.

I knew John Dee to be as learned as any university tutor, and wise too in the occult arts, a conjuror of dangerous spirits, a great magician, and a bold astrologer who had come near to losing his life over the royal charts he had dared to draw up. I simply could not imagine such a man as a humble tutor, even to rich and noble youths such as the Dudleys must have been before their family's disgrace.

What on earth had Dee taught Robert as a boy?

Instantly I imagined a dark room of zodiac charts, star

maps, large bottles of pickled newts, with forbidden books and heretical texts strewn open amid a mass of black candles…. I shook the foolish vision away. He would have taught the Dudley boys Latin and Greek, some French and Italian too, mathematics and history, shown them a map of the globe, discussed politics, philosophy and the economics of nations. The same things Elizabeth had been taught as a girl, and which she often discussed with Alejandro.

"And he was right to do so." Amy Dudley managed a smile for the bishop, but I thought she looked strained and unhappy. "Better a sober tutor than a drunken one. Is that not so?"

"Indeed, indeed," the bishop muttered, and pushed the sopping bread into his mouth.

Dee managed a thin smile. "I often drank as a student at Oxford. I have not always been so…restrained."

"Oxford." Bishop Bonner looked directly at him, his heavy brows frowning. "Don't mention the accursed place. I have seen enough of Oxford these past few months to last me a lifetime. Back and forth from London on Cranmer's case. First old Archbishop Cranmer refuses to acknowledge the Queen's authority over the church, then he rejects the Mass itself. Next thing, when he sees his old friends roasting in the street for their stubbornness, he tries to recant and turn Catholic again." He shook his head, glancing at Mistress Dudley when she made a rough noise under her breath. "Forgive me. You have heard all this nonsense, no doubt?"

Her cheeks suddenly white as snow, Amy Dudley gave the bishop the tiniest nod. "Something…" she whispered.

"Well, Her Majesty could see the truth of the matter and she would have none of it. I mean, the law states that if a man recants, he should not burn. We all know that. But a lie uttered in fear is never a true recanting. Besides, old Cranmer had it coming, and I for one do not mourn his death." Bonner drank deep from his goblet, then belched loudly. "Nor the manner of it. He will face hotter flames in Hell, will he not?"

The room fell silent, but the bishop did not seem to notice, clicking his jewelled fingers for the servant to fill his cup again.

Robert Dudley turned to his former tutor, clearing his throat.

"I am glad to have a chance to talk with you again, sir. It was kind of Bishop Bonner to extend an invitation for us to dine here tonight."

"His lordship is a very generous man," John Dee agreed, smiling awkwardly at the bishop.

"Tell me, what news of the Queen? You must have been at court more frequently than I these past few months, for I fear Her Majesty has not forgotten my family's wrongful support of the rebellion."

The court astrologer steepled his fingers together under his chin, regarding his former pupil. "Her Majesty has been unwell in recent months. She suffered much under the influence of Saturn last year. But Venus is on the rise. Her health will soon be restored."

Dudley's smile looked forced. "That is excellent news and I rejoice in it." He raised his goblet. "Long live Her Majesty, Queen Mary!"

His wife drank too, nervously. "Long live Her Majesty!"

Someone knocked at the door, then entered swiftly. A man came to the table and presented a note to the bishop on a silver platter. Bonner wiped his mouth and fingers on his napkin, then unrolled the message, frowning as he read it.

"Nothing wrong, I trust?" Dee asked solicitously.

The bishop grunted, pushing back his chair. "A letter that requires my personal seal. Another of these cowardly heretics who believes he can avoid the fire by swearing he has changed his mind at the eleventh hour. But he will burn tomorrow if his recantation is a false one." His smile made me feel sick. "And I can always tell the false ones. They are the men and women who make the most noise when they first see their burning place." He threw down his napkin and strode to the door. "Enjoy your syllabub when it arrives. I must compose a reply to the prison warden. I shall soon return."

The heavyset bishop walked straight through me, and I shuddered, even after such a ghostly contact. Then I noticed how the others waited with downcast faces until the bishop had gone, their silence conspicuous.

John Dee clicked his fingers to the one servant still remaining.

"Go see if his lordship still has a cask of that good Kentish ale in his cellars, would you? I have a thirst tonight this Spanish wine will not quench."

Once they were alone, Dee leaned swiftly across the table. "We may talk freely for a few moments, until Bonner returns. Only keep your voice down, Robbie. You never know who may be secretly listening."

Indeed not, I thought drily.

"A strange reunion, this," Robert Dudley said wryly. "At dinner with a man who would condemn us all to the bonfire if he could read our hearts. But seriously now, what news of the Queen's health? Is she indeed recovered?"

"I fear so, yes. The Queen is often confined to bed these days, but we cannot hope for her death just yet." Master Dee shrugged.

"Still, Mary has long suspected the Lady Elizabeth of having put a curse on her. Her return to health should quash that rumour, at least."

Robert grinned. "If any woman could curse her own sister and make it stick, it would be Elizabeth."

"Then perhaps you are not so well-acquainted with the Lady Elizabeth as you suggested in your last letter. I have always found her a most regal and even-tempered lady."

"Or perhaps I am better acquainted with her than you." Robert glanced at his wife, then sat back in his chair, looking at Dee through narrowed eyes. "But enough of that. In truth, what do your charts say of the succession? Will the Spanish King succeed in getting himself an heir?"

"The charts suggest there will be no further pregnancies. Unless Queen Mary should die, and Elizabeth take her place as his wife."

Robert's teeth were bared. "That will never happen. I would kill the Spanish King before he could force her into marriage."

"A trifle drastic," Dee commented without heat, and sipped at his wine.

"Tell me, Master Dee, how are you finding the daily arrests and burnings?" Robert asked tightly. "I must admit to some surprise on hearing of your new post with Bonner. You make an unlikely sniffer-out of heretics."

"I agree. Yet what else could I do? Ignore the bishop's offer of employment and face death myself?" He shrugged, dabbing his mouth with his napkin. "In a cruel climate, one must bend or be broken.

"But you must have learned that lesson yourself, Robert," Dee continued more softly, "for you spent long enough in the Tower after your family's rebellion. Your father executed, your poor brother Guildford too. Yet here you sit, with your head still on your shoulders."

Robert said nothing, watching him intently.

"I am not happy with the work Bishop Bonner gives me. But at least this way I may survive to serve the Lady Elizabeth when her time comes to ascend the throne." Master Dee crossed himself delicately.

"Until then, may Heaven forgive my sins, past, present, and future."

"Amen." Robert glanced briefly at the door, then lowered his voice. "Have you heard from the princess? You keep a boy in her household, I believe. Your apprentice?"

"Yes, Richard is loyal to me and sends me word of the Lady Elizabeth from time to time. And of her maid, Meg Lytton, who has some minor power in the dark arts."

I glared at him, unseen. *Some minor power?*

But in my irritation I had missed something. Some brief look and whisper had passed between the other two at the table. Suddenly Robert Dudley was on his feet, following his wife to the door. She turned at once, speaking sharply under her breath. Robert tried to steer her back to her seat, and her eyes flashed fire at him.

"Sit down, Amy," Robert said angrily. "Don't make a fool out of me at Bonner's table."

"You are in love with her!" she exclaimed.

"Not here, in God's name. Not here."

Glancing back at his former tutor, Robert Dudley bustled his wife out of the room, and I heard the couple arguing in the passageway beyond, still keeping their voices down even in anger as though such caution had become a habit.

So all was not well between Robert Dudley and his wife, Amy. This was news the princess would embrace. But what had caused their quarrel?

You are in love with her!

Had Amy guessed the reason for his interest in Elizabeth?

"Meg? Is that you, Meg?"

I turned, startled at the sound of my name.

John Dee was standing too. I looked back at the fair-haired

conjuror, baffled. He had turned some old parchment out of his pocket, a torn scrap on which I could see his own black spidery handwriting, and was unfolding it as though to show Robert when he returned.

But to my amazement Dee's eyes were on my face.

"Meg Lytton?" he whispered, then his strange gaze shifted and he looked past me, then around the room. "I sense a strange presence here. If there is a spirit with me, knock on the table to let me know you understand."

I raised my eyebrows. Knock on the table? I attempted to do as he asked, but my hand passed straight through, making no sound.

"So much for that," I muttered, and was taken aback when he turned at once in my direction again, his handsome face questing.

Could he *hear* me?

"Meg," he whispered, fumbling with the paper in his hand. "If it is indeed you that I sense in this room, I received Richard's letter—thank him for me—and have news in return for you." He tapped on it, waving the scrap in the air as though inviting me to take it.

"*Invictus.* You see?"

Invictus?

I leaned over and looked at what he was waving. There was a drawing on the scrap of paper. A sketch of a ring, and beneath it the Latin word *Invictus,* underlined several times as if that were the ring's name. He was tapping this word, and staring about the room.

"*Invictus,*" he repeated. His whisper became hoarse. "Only you must beware, it can be dangerous. If you begin to feel—"

But I missed the rest.

Something hit me hard on the side of the head, violently enough to make the world turn black.

POSSESSION

My eyes opened slowly. The world was blurred now, instead of black. That was an improvement at least. I was lying on the floor, back in the Lady Elizabeth's bedchamber at Hatfield House. Everything appeared to be sideways, but when I attempted to right myself, my head throbbed like the Devil himself had struck it with his trident.

I winced at the thunderclap of pain across my temples. My tongue felt like a dry piece of cloth rolled up inside my mouth, and when I tried to speak, the words came out wrong. "What...what juth happened?"

"Don't try to get up. Or speak."

Richard was kneeling before me, his face very pale. Gently he brushed the hair back from my forehead, dragged up my eyelids one by one, then examined my face with an intensity that frightened me.

"Thank God," he muttered. "You are properly awake at last. I thought we would never get you back."

"So you hit me to make sure of it?" I demanded indignantly.

The Lady Elizabeth appeared behind him. She handed me a white handkerchief drenched in rosewater. "Richard did not strike you. We could not rouse you from your trance, though it has been nearly an hour since you last spoke. Your eyes were closed, and you were so still...then quite suddenly you fell over and woke up. That is all we know."

I looked at the floorboards accusingly. "So I did this to myself? I lost my balance and hit my head on the floor?"

"You did." Richard leaned back with a strange expression. "But at least the shock brought you back. I had begun to worry we might lose you again. How do you feel? You look feverish."

The rosewater smelt wonderfully refreshing. "I'll live," I managed to say, and lifted the damp handkerchief to my face, cooling my skin.

To my surprise, I found Richard was right. I was burning hot. There was a fine sheen of sweat on my forehead and neck, as though I had been sitting too close to a fire, and my cheeks were glowing. Yet one glance told me the fire in Elizabeth's chamber had long since gone out.

The tallow candle had also burnt low in my absence, the chamber quiet and gloomy. I looked at it assessingly. Had I truly been "gone" nearly an hour? My head was spinning, my heart thudding, and I felt sick. So this was what happened to the body after journeying too far in the mind.

Elizabeth was impatient to hear my news. "Did you manage to see Robert? To speak with him, perhaps?"

"I did not speak with Master Dudley," I muttered, and saw her face fall. "But I saw him, yes. And I also saw..." I hesitated, glancing up at Richard. It felt strange to be here at Hatfield again, when seconds ago I had been standing in an unknown house many miles away. "Your master, John Dee. He says thank you for the letter, by the way."

"Does he now?" he said drily.

I almost smiled, but my head was hurting too much. "He was dining with Bishop Bonner tonight. The other guests were Master Robert Dudley and his wife."

Richard's eyes widened, but he said nothing.

"With his wife? And Bishop Bonner, you say?" The princess crouched beside me in a rustle of heavy skirts, her face intent. "Are you sure it was he?"

"Yes, the bishop was their host. It was a very fine house. Like a palace. I saw John Dee, Master and Mistress Dudley, and Bonner himself at the dinner table. They were discussing the Queen's health."

She drew a sharp breath. "So my sister is unwell."

"Not any more, Dee said. She was sick, but has recovered. Then they talked of…of Master Cranmer's burning." I glanced at Richard. My throat was parched. "Is there any wine? My mouth is like dust."

"Yes, poor Thomas Cranmer." The princess crossed herself, her voice cracking with pain. "I knew him all my life, he was a great churchman. Such a terrible death, burning. But my sister hated him, of course, so his arrest became inevitable once she took the throne." She saw my puzzled expression. "Thomas Cranmer was one of those who negotiated my father's divorce from her mother."

Behind her, Richard was pouring me a cup of wine. I remembered the servant pouring wine for the bishop's guests. My teeming brain seemed to jerk, and for an instant it felt as though I were back in that other space, watching them. Then I looked at the cup in my hand and could not recall how it got there.

Richard, kneeling beside me, frowned. "Meg, your eyes went all blurred again. Are you still here with us?"

I nodded, though the world was tilting slightly. I had lost

time for a moment there. Gone somewhere else in my mind
and not been able to control it.

"*Invictus,*" I muttered, remembering Master Dee's warning.

"Pardon?"

It can be dangerous.

I shook my head, struggling to put my thoughts together.
What had I been saying?

"Master Dudley did speak of you, my lady," I said huskily,
and the princess sat down to listen, her face eager.

Briefly I covered what the two men had discussed once
Bishop Bonner had left the room. Then I attempted to describe, carefully prompted by Elizabeth, Robert Dudley's
clothes, how he had been wearing his hair, his voice, what
he said, his expression at every point in the conversation, and
in particular his questions about the princess.

Finally I outlined Robert's sudden argument with his wife.
"She seemed very angry, as though she already knew about
your...your friendship with her husband."

"But he denied it?"

"I do not know. They spoke too quietly."

She nodded, looking pained, then abruptly hid her face in
her hands. "Oh, this business is so awful. Master Dudley is a
married man! I love him with all my heart, God knows that
I do. But it is a most unnatural love, an impossible love, and
I wish that I could rid myself of it."

I knew only too well how she felt.

Elizabeth looked at me through the cage of her fingers, her
eyes red-rimmed. "Oh, leave me. Go, both of you. It's late
and I need to be alone."

As we left, Elizabeth was picking up the miniature portrait from the floor where I had left it, her face pale and determined. I wondered if she would burn it, and the letter too,

ridding herself of all possessions that reminded her of Robert Dudley.

But of course she would not.

In her position, would I burn a portrait of Alejandro just because he could never be mine?

Richard squeezed my arm when we reached the small chamber I shared with Alice, stopping me when I would have gone inside.

"*Invictus,*" he said, repeating the word I had muttered in the princess's chamber. "What did you mean by that?"

"John Dee said it. There was a picture of my mother's ring on a spare parchment, and he had written *Invictus* beneath it. He also said 'it can be dangerous,' but I heard no more." I felt my sore head gingerly; there was a lump developing under my hair. "It's Latin, of course. You know the word?"

He nodded. "*Unconquered.*"

"He said it to *me,* Richard. Master Dudley was not in the room at the time."

Richard stared at me, incredulous. "Master Dee saw you, you mean? He knew you were there and spoke to you?"

"It sounds crazy, I know. But it's true."

"Or perhaps that bump on the head has affected your brain."

"So little faith in my magick. When your master's next letter arrives, you will owe me an apology." But I touched his cheek lightly. I did not want him to think me ungrateful for his help. "You are a good friend, Richard. Thank you for being there tonight. I needed you."

His gaze became intense. "Anytime, Meg. You only have to ask." He paused. "We will wait till tomorrow to set the new protective spells. You will need your wits about you for the work."

I looked along the dark corridor to Alejandro's room. The

door was closed but I had the feeling he was still awake, listening to our whispered conversation.

"We'll talk more in the morning. Right now I seem to be growing an egg on the side of my head. Goodnight, Richard."

The weather had changed, I realized, as I slipped quietly into the bedchamber I shared with Alice. It was a blustery night outside, the wind moaning around the house like a soul in torment. I kindled a light, moving softly about the room.

Gazing out through the gap in the shutters, I reached behind to loosen the lacings of my bodice. The moon was high. Clouds scudded across its white face, some smudged a dirty black, almost menacing.

Unconquered.

I frowned, the word worrying at me.

I slipped out of my bodice, then removed my foreskirt, hanging it carefully over the back of the chair. There might be another meaning to *Invictus,* of course. Perhaps Alejandro would know; his Latin was superb.

Still in my undershift, I knelt by my mother's chest to put away the hazel wand, then felt for the ring in my pouch. That should go back into the chest too. I should not be carrying it about with me like this—it could too easily be lost…and Master Dee clearly thought it held some special significance. "*Invictus.*" For some reason I thought of my champion, Alejandro de Castillo, his sword drawn against the powers of evil.

Before I could pull the ring out, a rustle behind me brought me round sharply. Alice was sitting up in bed, staring at me.

"Did I wake you?" I whispered, smiling. "Forgive me, Alice. It's been a long evening. I will only be a moment."

My heart was thumping like a scared rabbit's. God's blood! I was so nervous these days, I was seeing attackers in every shadow. Wearily I dropped the ring back into my mother's casket, closed the lid, then began to cast a slow protective circle about it. Tomorrow Richard and I would set a new circle around the house and grounds and despite my misgivings I would still feel safer....

Suddenly I felt a heavy hand on my shoulder, and turned, staring into Alice's white face.

"You cannot hide from me," she told me coldly, her empty eyes boring into mine.

Only it was not Alice's voice.

My body shook violently as I realized the trap I had walked into. I pushed the demon-creature away, stumbling backwards in my haste and knocking over the candle.

The flame guttered on the rushes and was extinguished. Now we were standing in the pitch-black together, listening to the moan of the wind, this nameless fiend and I.

In the silence, my breathing sounded loud and harsh to my ears.

I clamped a hand over my mouth, struggling to breathe quietly, to listen for *her* breathing.

I thought of escape, perhaps shouting for Richard or Alejandro. But I dismissed the idea. Alejandro was already wounded, and I did not want anyone else to be hurt on my account. Besides, she might be standing between me and the door. And instinct told me not to let her touch me again.

My eyes adjusting to the dark, I caught a faint glimmer: Alice's white nightgown moving as she turned her head, trying to locate me.

Now was my chance.

But even as I raised my hand to strike her down, I realized it could not be done. Not without hurting Alice. My friend was not my enemy. She was possessed. Just as Blanche had been in the old shepherd's hut. And now I knew why. Because Richard had lowered the barrier of protective spells about this house, now it lay wide open to whatever evil spirit or fiend from Hell cared to enter it. And chief amongst my suspects must be Marcus Dent, a man who would stop at nothing to destroy me—before I could destroy him. Richard's actions would have been as a gift to him. An invitation.

Abruptly I changed my mind. And the spell with it.

"Banish!" I shouted in Latin instead, clapping my hands as loudly as I could.

Alice dropped like a stone to the floor, a white flash in the darkness.

I thought the thud must have been heard throughout the house, and waited in expectation of running feet along the corridor. But none came.

I was on my own, it seemed.

Falling to my knees beside Alice, I fumbled in the dark for the pulse at her throat. Her heart beat steadily, as though she had been asleep the whole time. She was not dead, then. For a moment, I had feared...

I jumped up and groped my way to the window. With trembling hands, I threw back the shutters and let the moonlight flood in across her face.

Alice looked like a fallen dove, lying white as a ghost beside my mother's chest.

"Alice?" I murmured, but knew from her steady breathing that she would not waken. Not until the effects of the possession had worn off.

She needed to sleep. And so did I.

Crouching, I got my hands under my friend's arms, then dragged her over to the bed. But she weighed more than I had realized, and I was soon out of breath, grinning as I imagined what Richard would say if he could witness all this undignified puffing and panting.

Getting Alice under the covers was the hardest part, and

afterwards I slumped against her unconscious body for several minutes, exhausted beyond thought.

The last thing I remember thinking before I fell asleep was, how much had the demon seen before I broke its possession of Alice's body?

My mother's chest of magickal objects must still have been open as the creature came up behind me, the lid thrown back, everything on display.

You cannot hide from me.

Or had it said, *You cannot hide it from me?*

The next morning, Elizabeth appeared to have returned to her usual calm self. Looking at her in the Great Hall I could not see the red-eyed, lovesick girl from last night who had demanded every detail of her beloved's looks and expressions, then wept bitterly and turned us out of her room because she knew Robert could never be hers.

Today, Elizabeth was practising to be a Queen. Her voice was cool and clear as she gave us our duties for the day: I was to tidy the sewing box and disentangle a mess of embroidery threads and silks with Alice's help.

I did not mind this. Richard and I could do our spellwork later—if it were even worth doing, now I knew that Marcus Dent had made his presence felt. I shivered as I thought of the man; this time of domestic tasks would be good for me, I realized. I could not spend all my days fearing the witchfinder's arrival and hopefully my banishing-spell last night would give us at least today in which to plan, to set our defences again. And I was at least now forewarned.

Alice had smiled at me on waking, cheerful as ever, her hair tousled, and I had known at once that she had no memory of what had happened last night.

I considered mentioning it, to see if Alice could remember

anything, then changed my mind. It would serve no purpose and only distress her. No girl, after all, wanted to be told they had been possessed by a demon during the night, then man-handled back into bed afterwards.

Alejandro had offered to write out some Spanish poetry from memory for the princess to study, and Blanche and Kat were to take up their sewing on the wooden settle, the prin-cess declared. Only my brother William was given no task, but set himself to work by fetching in fresh logs for the fire.

I wanted to sit near Alejandro and ask him discreetly about last night's possession, but he had chosen the small desk under the windows for better light. So instead Alice and I arranged ourselves on the narrow bench we used at supper times, pass-ing the sewing box between us along the table.

Richard came in from outside during these arrangements, and halted on the threshold, looking embarrassed. I studied him with a secret smile, wondering what on earth he had been doing. His clothes were filthy, his long fingers soiled with dirt, and he had lost his cap. Had he been casting spells *without me?*

"Forgive my appearance, my lady," he said, bowing stiffly to Elizabeth. "The wind blew a tree down in the night across the track to the gate. I was just helping John to move it."

The Lady Elizabeth eyed him from her position by the hearth, an unfathomable look on her face. Some days she seemed to be warming to John Dee's apprentice, then other days she dismissed him as a servant beneath her notice.

"You had best go and clean yourself up, Master Richard." She looked him up and down as though she were a great Queen in the finest cloth-of-gold, not a disgraced exile forced to wear a thrice-mended gown and slippers that no longer quite fit. "For you are not fit to keep us company in that at-tire."

There was a hard look in Richard's face as he bowed again,

and took himself up the stairs, not even glancing at the rest of us. "My lady."

Satisfied that we were all gainfully employed, Elizabeth sat down in the high-backed chair nearest the hearth and began to read a letter she had received.

Kat looked up curiously from her sewing. "Is that a letter from the Queen, my lady?"

"Yes, my royal sister has seen fit to write to us at last," Elizabeth agreed, and there was an odd note in her voice. "Would you like to hear what she has to say, Kat?"

"Yes indeed, my lady."

"'My dearest sister,'" Elizabeth read out to her lady-in-waiting, betraying with only the slightest twitch of her lips how ironic she found this initial address, "'I trust you are well, and that the winter you have passed at Hatfield House was not so cold as the one we suffered at Greenwich. Here the Thames came close to freezing over, and several foolhardy youths were drowned when they attempted to walk from one bank to the other.'"

I turned my head to listen, intrigued.

The letter went on in a remarkably friendly fashion, while Queen Mary excused herself for not having written in so long, then politely requested her sister's attendance at court for some state occasion later in the year.

I frowned, wondering what could have brought about this change of heart. Last time I had seen the two sisters together, Queen Mary had been half-mad with fury, for her Spanish husband liked Elizabeth rather too well.

But perhaps John Dee was right, and Saturn's baleful influence had not only made her sick this year, but had also driven the Queen to seek some kind of reconciliation with her younger sister. It was not for nothing that Saturn was called the Great Corrector.

"Attend to your work, girl!" Kat Ashley snapped, seeing me listening. "The Queen's letter is not for such as you to hear."

A flash of temper nearly made me snap back at Elizabeth's lady-in-waiting. But I bit my tongue and suppressed the urge.

My eyes met Alejandro's across the narrow hall. A tingle ran through me at the intimacy of his dark look, then I lowered my gaze to the green silk thread I was untangling. But my hands were trembling slightly. Perhaps it would be a good idea to work an anti-love-spell on myself after all.

Elizabeth continued reading aloud from her letter, though the rest of the letter was an unexciting description of recent events at court, with little to interest me further.

"Here," I whispered, handing the box of silks back to Alice, then bent my head to wrestle with a particularly troublesome knot in one of the thin red threads.

After a while, Elizabeth stopped reading and fell silent. No doubt she too was pondering her sister's suspicious change of heart. I struggled with the knotted thread, my foot tapping impatiently. The Great Hall had grown dark and chilly in the last few minutes, I realized, catching myself shivering.

I frowned, glancing up. Had the fire gone out? My brother had brought in an armful of logs only a few minutes before, setting several pieces of freshly chopped wood on the glowing heat before slumping on the bench opposite, his elbows resting on the table. Yet now William seemed to be staring blankly at the dark wood of the table, caught in a reverie.

Daydreaming about Alice, probably. I almost snorted at the thought. William had never been able to hide his feelings when we were growing up, and it was plain to me that he found Alice a comely girl.

I only hoped his interest was not unwelcome to Alice, for she could break William's heart if she dismissed his attentions out of hand.

I looked at her, smiling wryly, and saw that Alice too was staring into the sewing box with a blank expression, her mind also presumably on other things.

Entertained by this mutual daydreaming and wishing to share the joke, I glanced over my shoulder at Alejandro, who was still engaged in copying out Spanish verses under the window.

Except that Alejandro too was perfectly still. His feathered quill was motionless, poised above the inkpot without descending. His dark head was slightly bent, long lashes hiding the expression in his eyes, but I could see him staring down intently at the parchment as though he could not quite believe what he had written.

Had everyone gone crazy today?

Then I looked across at the Lady Elizabeth, seated by the fire, and a wave of cold fear slammed into my heart. The princess was holding the Queen's letter as she had been before, but Elizabeth too had stopped moving, her lips parted, frozen in mid-sentence.

On the wooden settle opposite her sat Kat and Blanche, their needles suspended, a look of mild surprise on Blanche's face, Kat watching me through narrowed eyes, neither woman even so much as blinking.

Clumsily I stood up, the embroidery threads falling unheeded to the floor.

"Alejandro?"

But he neither spoke nor moved in response. He might as well have been made of stone, I thought, as I stared at him in horror. His name echoed about the high rafters as though the house were empty. The fire had gone out too, I realized, glancing at the hearth. The logs lay half-burned, smouldering in the ashes.

I shivered, rubbing at my arms. The hall was suddenly bit-terly cold.

Cold as a tomb.

I took a few steps towards the other women. "Blanche? Mistress Ashley?" I whispered, then looked at Elizabeth. "My lady?"

Their stillness was unnerving.

Breathless in a room of living statues, I looked about at the company, searching for some sign that they were jesting, play-ing a trick on me. But nobody moved. Even the clattering of pans and the cheerful sound of Lucy whistling in the kitchen had stopped. I had no doubt that if I were to walk down the narrow passageway to the kitchen, I would find the servants equally motionless, as though some spell had turned them all to stone as they went about their chores.

My skin crept with horror.

Only one person could be powerful enough to have caught everyone here out of time, and left me to face him alone. Someone who had shrugged off a banishing-spell as lightly as though it were a simple charm.

Then I heard it. The sharp firm clop of shod hooves on the mud track that led to us from the Hatfield road. Slowing now, coming steadily closer to the house. The jingle of a harness. The creak of leather.

I ran to the half-open door and eased round it, peering out into the sharp spring sunshine. My heart was thumping so loudly it hurt.

I had expected to see a horse and rider when I looked out-side. What I saw instead was smoke. A high cloud of smoke rolling along the track towards the front of the house.

I sucked in my breath, waiting for whatever-it-was to arrive at the door: thick black smoke travelling in a misshapen ball.

The smoke-ball was unlike anything I had ever seen before, but quite clearly supernatural in origin. It looked and smelt evil, hanging acrid in my throat. It billowed out like a gown in the wind and rippled long fingers of smoke towards the house, then slowly began to disperse, draining away as though into a hole in the ground.

Soon all that was left was a black stallion.

On the horse's back sat a rider dressed in the rich doublet and hose of a gentleman, cloak thrown back over one shoulder, a jaunty feathered cap on his head.

It was Marcus Dent.

12

BLOOD MAGICK

Marcus swung down out of the saddle and looked directly at me in the doorway.

"Meg," he said lightly, and swept the cap from his head with an exaggerated bow.

It was the Marcus Dent from my visions. Only this time there was no cloudy illusion to hide his face from me. That was when I realized what was different about him. He was almost handsome now—his face was no longer scarred, and his dead eye was whole and blue again, watching me sharply, no longer destroyed.

His hair was sleek and fair too, shining in the sunlight. "Good day to you. I trust you are in good health? What of your mistress, the Lady Elizabeth? I had heard she was unwell. But perhaps now Meg Lytton is returned to her side, the lady has miraculously recovered?"

I stared and could not speak, my insides clenching.

"What is the matter? Am I not courteous enough to match your God-fearing Spanish priest?" Marcus queried, raising his brows at my expression. His smile was wry. "Oh, my appearance. But there is no reason to be surprised. You are not the only one with a little power, my dear Meg." With a pass of his hand, he returned his face to the scarred ruin I remembered from our last meeting. The white eye stared at nothing, his lips bared to reveal broken and blackened teeth, new reddened scars like burns across his throat.

I gasped at the hideous transformation, unable to snatch the sound back, and his laughter chilled me.

"Agreed." Marcus waved his hand and his face was whole again, ten years younger, startlingly handsome. "I think this face suits me better too."

I turned to shut myself into the house, to protect those still within, and at once he was there, pushing me inexorably aside as though I weighed less than a feather.

I fumbled for a word of power and Marcus Dent smiled, placing one long finger on my lips. "Yes?"

I opened my mouth but found myself unable to speak, my voice stolen by his spell.

"The silence of a woman is a rare gift indeed." He looked past me and saw the Lady Elizabeth, frozen on her high-backed seat. "Ah yes, your mistress looks much improved. Reading a letter, I see." He crossed and plucked the letter from the princess's hand, beginning to read aloud in a mocking voice, "'Dearest sister, I trust you are well'…et cetera, et cetera. From the Queen herself, no less. What exalted company you keep here, Meg." He dropped the letter on Elizabeth's chest. "But where is your Spaniard?"

The sun, slanting in through the high windows, illuminated Alejandro's dark head, still bent over his verses. He was wearing no sword, out of deference to the princess's wishes. Though even if he had been, he could not have drawn it. For Alejandro sat deaf and dumb, unable to move and not even knowing that he needed to, so utterly blind to the danger that approached him. Vulnerable to the worst, most creeping evil...

I tried to lunge after Marcus, and found I could not move either, my feet stuck in treacle, my arms still raised towards him in a gesture of attack. My vision turned red, my fury built until I thought it would lift the top of my head off.

How was this trick done? How had the witchfinder caught us all like this, flies in his honey trap, helpless to resist? Richard, I thought gratingly. This was Richard's fault for lifting the protective spells that had kept Marcus Dent out of Hatfield. And the fool had thought himself clever for breaking my magickal barrier down, just so he could cast certain spells within it and allow visitors to come and go unchallenged!

"I can see why you would want to marry him. He is a handsome fellow," Marcus remarked, halting before Alejandro. He glanced back at me and smiled, chilling my blood, then bent and put his face close to Alejandro's. "I wonder if the Spaniard tastes as good as he looks. Shall we find out?"

I watched in speechless horror as he drew the dagger from his belt, then sliced a thin line from Alejandro's jawline to his forehead, skipping over his eye with a flick of the blade. Blood oozed out at once and began to trickle down his neck. The cut was not deep, but would be enough to scar him for life.

Marcus examined the seeping red cut with interest, leaning close into Alejandro's face. "Shame to ruin so handsome a young man. But my face has been ruined, so why not his? Perhaps you will see no difference between us once his face too is scarred and ugly." To my disgust, Marcus stuck out his tongue and slowly licked along the cut, cleaning the blood from Alejandro's face. "Hmm," he mused, straightening. He swallowed, licking my beloved's blood off his lips with apparent enjoyment, then looked back at me. "Not bad for a foreigner."

My skin crawled even as I struggled to release myself from the hold he had over me. His confidence frightened me. What kind of creature had Marcus Dent become since his trip into the void, and was there any way to defeat such powerful magick?

Of course, I should have realized the blood-licking was part of a spell. Marcus took three steps back from the window, stepping very deliberately out of the dusty beams of sunlight, then called out, "Alejandro de Castillo, I have drunk your blood and have power over your body." He clapped his hands three times. "I am your new master. Arise and do my bidding."

Alejandro's limbs jerked. The quill feather dropped from his hand. Suddenly he lurched to his feet, almost knocking the desk over, and stood before Marcus, his head bent, swaying as though half-asleep. The inkpot rolled off the table behind him, the dark stain of its contents pooling next to his feet. He paid no heed to it, his mind and soul sleeping, his body an empty shell, obedient to his master's command.

"Dance for me!"

Alejandro danced a few clumsy steps, his movements rough and grotesque.

It was not Alejandro in there, I reminded myself grimly. Merely his captive body. But it hurt nonetheless to see Marcus make him look ridiculous.

"Kiss Meg Lytton."

I wanted to scream as Alejandro approached me, his eyes empty of expression, his cheek and collar horribly bloodied, and set his lips against mine.

His lips were cold. Like kissing a corpse.

"Now take this dagger." Marcus held out the weapon to Alejandro.

"Go to the Lady Elizabeth, and stab her through the heart with it."

Alejandro took the dagger without hesitation and walked slowly towards the Lady Elizabeth, blood still trickling down his cheek.

I stared, caught fast in Marcus's spell. I could only watch in horror as my beloved approached the heir to the English throne with a dagger in his hand.

Stooping over the princess, Alejandro knocked the letter aside so that it fell to the floor in a slow rustling arc, then held the dagger aloft, clearly aiming for her heart.

"Stop!"

Alejandro froze, the dagger poised above the princess's chest. The room was silent.

"When your Spaniard has killed the Lady Elizabeth, I will order him to kill himself," Marcus remarked coolly, turning back to me.

"When her servants awake, they will see a dead Catholic priest with a bloodied dagger in his hand, and assume he drugged them, then murdered the Lady Elizabeth on the instructions of the Queen."

He was mad, I realized.

"Like most men, I could never bow the knee to an unmarried woman," he continued smoothly. "It is against the natural order of things for a woman to rule a man. I have an excellent informant though, who has seen the future and tells me of a great virgin Queen, a woman who will change the world and rule without a man to keep her passions in check."

He smirked. "I imagine you can guess her name, Meg. It is difficult enough to stomach her sister on the throne, but at least Queen Mary has seen sense and submitted to her husband's will. But a Queen who rules alone?" He shuddered. "Too horrible to countenance. So since I have the power to do it, I intend to put an end to her unnatural reign before it has even begun.

"The extent of my power is truly breathtaking. But like you, I cannot use it openly, lest I be hanged for the very crime I have so often punished with the gallows. One day, perhaps, I will be honoured for my conjurations and granted a place at court, as Merlin was in old King Arthur's day. But for now, I must bide my time. Watch and plan, as it were."

Turning to me, Marcus Dent dragged the feathered cap from his head again, then shoved a hand through his fair hair, smoothing it down. I looked on at this preening, dismayed and a little bemused. Was the villain making himself presentable to me?

"I have not made myself entirely plain, my dearest Meg." His voice softened, was almost wistful. "Your friends will die here today. Unless you choose to help me."

The sun was full in my eyes, gold and blinding, but I could neither close my eyes nor move to avoid it. Tears came instead, blurring my vision until all I could see of the witchfinder was thick dusty shafts of light cutting across the Great Hall.

If I could help Alejandro...

Marcus came out of the dazzling, swimming light. We were so close, I could hear the rasp of his breath like that of a dying animal. Yet his face was handsome even in shadow, light dazzling behind his fair head like a halo.

His blue eyes, oddly tender, came to rest on my face.

"I was angry with you last year, Meg. So very angry. For a long time I could think of nothing but your death, and the death of everyone you hold dear." He reached out and stroked a slow finger down my cheek. I could not move, not even to shudder. "But eventually I came to realize the truth."

The truth?

"You are the only one who can appreciate the extent of my power. The only one with whom I can share my ambition."

His chest was almost touching mine now. He looked down

at me for a long moment, examining my simple country gown, the tight bodice, my skirts full and heavy, then he looked slowly back up to my face. He was smiling, his eyes heavy-lidded, a slight flush in his cheeks.

"You know me better than anyone else in this world, Meg. I was wrong when I tried to kill you last year, for there is a better way to deal with you. You are dangerous. But now I am dangerous too." His gaze dropped to my mouth. "So we can fight this out until one destroys the other. Or join forces, and let the world fear us instead."

My stomach turned over as I realized what the witchfinder was considering. It was too horrible. My heart began to thud violently. I felt sick, staring back at him in a fever of disgust and loathing.

"I have dreamed of this moment, of our togetherness," he whispered. "Have you?"

Inside the blank facade, my head was working furiously, my thoughts frenzied. If he were so very dangerous, why had the witchfinder not simply killed us as soon as he walked in? We were helpless, caught up in his spell, utterly vulnerable before his power.

So why are we still alive?

Marcus put his hands on my shoulders, his eyes gleaming with triumph and excitement, then leaned forward and placed his mouth against mine.

The horror of the moment was scorched for ever into my mind as Marcus kissed me, holding me still with his spell while his mouth moved on mine, trying to awaken desire.

After what felt like a skin-crawling eternity, Marcus pulled back and looked down into my face.

"Between us we could create something miraculous. A child, perhaps." For a second his voice turned tender, persuasive. "You and I together, Meg. Nobody would have the power to stop us." Eagerly he searched my face in the silence.

I stared back with hatred in my eyes, willing him to be swallowed up by an earthquake even if I had to die with him. A cloud seemed to pass over his face, and for an instant I saw the other Marcus, the one with the terrible scars and the ruined eye. Then the handsome face took over again, forcing the other man, the broken Marcus, back inside where he belonged.

"So be it." His mouth twisted. "I should kill you and all your friends where they stand. But I am a pragmatic man. I shall let them live, and you too, if you will do something for me."

His intense blue gaze pierced me. "Can I trust you, Meg? If I release you from my spell, will you swear not to attack me? Though if you do—" and he pointed at Alejandro "—he will be the first to suffer. You understand?"

A second later, as though he had sensed my agreement, his spell released me. Slowly I lowered my aching arms to my side, waiting to hear what he intended for me.

"In your chamber upstairs, there is a wooden chest. And in that chest are some objects that interest me greatly."

I turned my head, staring at him with creeping horror. "So it *was* you in my chamber last night," I whispered. "You possessed Alice?"

Marcus smiled cruelly. "Go and fetch your mother's things down to me. If you behave, I will spare your Spaniard." Seeing my indecision, he hissed at me. "Hurry, witch, or all your friends will die."

I did not trust him to keep his word. But my instinct was to get away from him, so I could think clearly without the fogging influence of his spells.

I picked up my skirts and ran upstairs. Along the corridor I passed Richard, caught motionless like the others on his way down to us, still fastening a clean doublet, his leg stretched out mid-stride, a look of consternation on his face.

Had Richard seen Marcus Dent from his chamber window and tried to reach me in time to warn me?

The door to my chamber stood open. Bessie was inside, one of the hall servants, frozen while sweeping the floor.

I knelt before my mother's chest and threw back the lid with shaking hands. My heart was racing. There was the straight hazel wand, the battered cauldron, the ropes and cards, her old grimoire, the double-coiled ring shining up at me...

Instinctively I slipped the ring onto my finger, and felt stronger, more powerful, my head clearing at last.

Why had Marcus not made Alejandro stab the princess, rather than just threaten to do so? And why send me upstairs to fetch these things instead of coming up for them himself?

Why not just slaughter us all, and carry my mother's chest away with him on his rotten enchanted horse?

Because he can't.

My hands stilled on the rim of the wooden chest. The whole thing had been a charade. Marcus Dent did not have the power to kill any of us.

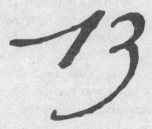

Lux

There was a noise behind me in the doorway. This time I did not pause to think. I reached inside the chest for the hazel wand and I whirled, standing up.

Marcus Dent was right behind me.

"Wait!" His blue eyes were blazing. "Strike, and I will kill them all."

"Do it, then," I taunted him. "Murder the princess. Destroy her servants. Burn Hatfield House to the ground."

"You think I cannot?"

"I think you *dare not.* You said it yourself, we need to be careful who knows of our power." I raised my eyebrows, my tone incredulous. "What, you would come here openly and kill the Queen's sister? No place would be safe for you to hide after that."

Marcus Dent screamed at me. His whole body seemed to lurch towards me, growing vast in the same instant, his bulk filling the doorway, then the whole chamber, swelling impossibly fast. He was a mass of acrid black smoke again, no longer human, billowing about the room, and in the midst of it I could see his ruined white eye glaring, watching me.

"Out!" I cried, choking, covering my mouth with my sleeve. I pointed the hazel wand towards the place where Marcus had been. The power snaked down through my arm, my wrist, my hand, flying out of my fingertips like lightning. "*Out!*"

The chamber was empty.

Next moment I was running, stumbling past Richard and touching him on the shoulder with the wand but not waiting to see if my counter-spell would wake him. There was no time. I almost flew down the stairs, finding a confused Elizabeth awake and on her feet, her ladies coughing in the smoky air.

Alice was sitting at the foot of the stairs, staring up as I descended, clearly unsure what had happened. She got to her feet as I passed, looking pale and shaken. "Meg? What happened?"

I put a hand on her arm, saying, "Forgive me, Alice. There's no time for explanations." Then I turned to our mistress. "Quick, where's Alejandro?"

Elizabeth's face flushed angrily, for I had spoken without my usual deference, addressing her as though we were equals.

Then she saw the look on my face. "I saw him go outside. But there was so much smoke in this hall, it was hard to see clearly. Is something on fire? I must have been asleep because I can't remember how—" Elizabeth called after me as I ran for the door, her voice sharp, "Meg, what is it?"

I burst outside and stopped dead.

Marcus Dent stood a few feet away beside his black horse, his back to me. Suspended in mid-air between us hung Alejandro de Castillo, his eyes still closed, his face blank.

It was such a shock to see my beloved reduced to that state, so vulnerable, so unaware of the danger he was in, I could have thrown back my head and howled in fury and despair. Instead I raised my hand, and pointed the hazel wand at Marcus.

"Remove your spell and let him go," I told him unsteadily. "Now!"

"Or what?"

"Or I will blow you back into the void, Master Dent. You remember the void? It did *that* to you." And on the word that, I flourished the hazel wand in the same gesture I had seen him use before, and his handsome mask was stripped away, revealing the grim shell of his ruined face beneath. "I wonder what it will do a second time, Marcus?"

The whole world shifted, blurring violently, and I staggered, my hand wavering, as though the earth had moved under my feet.

The sky darkened. No, it blackened. I could see nothing. Not even the wand in front of my face. The big house was gone. Alejandro was gone. There was no remnant of spring sunshine left, not a glimmer, not a single shaft.

I was inside a black cloud of Marcus Dent's making, so thick and obscure that no light could penetrate it.

And he was close by. I could hear him laughing.

A violent wind buffeted me in the blackness. I fell to my knees, my cap wrenched off, hair lifting in the wind, whipping about my face.

"Your mother's wand," his voice roared at me. "I know it is in your possession. Give it to me. Give it to me now!"

I shook my head and staggered to my feet, bent over almost in half to avoid being blown away.

Lightning seared my eyeballs.

"The wand!" he insisted. "My men failed to kill your Spaniard when he rode out of Hatfield. But I will not fail, trust me."

Rain lashed at me, beating at my face, my hair, drenching my gown through. It clung to me, a wet rag.

Marcus was behind me now, his voice a steel pin holding the darkness together. "I want that wand and I will have it. Or the Spaniard's death will be on your head." His laughter was everywhere at once. "What is it to be? Your mother's wand or Alejandro's life?"

Lightning flashed again, only a few feet away, knocking me off my feet. I pushed myself up to my knees, grass under my wet palm. Everywhere was dark.

Dent's words rang in my ears. *My men failed to kill your Spaniard when he rode out of Hatfield....*

So Alejandro had been attacked by Dent's gang on his way to Oxfordshire. Perhaps Marcus hoped that I would be weaker without Alejandro by my side. I strongly suspected that he was right. Even now, Alejandro was out of reach, in the hands of that monster, and all I could feel was my own weakness.

I could have slapped myself with sheer frustration. *Think, think, think!*

I forced myself to kneel up, peering about in the velvety blackness of the storm. Was that a gleam of sunlight I could see?

"Meg, are you there?"

With immense relief I recognized Richard's voice. "Yes, yes!" I cried hoarsely. "I'm over here, Richard. In this darkness."

"If you have it, use the wand!"

Of course, I thought. What a fool I am.

"*Lux!*" I shouted hoarsely, still on my knees, raising the hazel wand above my head, and at once the rain-smoke darkness was gone.

Dazed and blinded by the sudden glare of sunlight, but still buffeted by the driving howl of the wind, I covered my eyes with my arm. Sand from the paths was being whipped up into the air, a sea of flying grit in my face.

"Richard?" I shouted into the raging, dust-filled light, my eyes narrowed to mere slits, knowing Dee's apprentice could not be far away. Perhaps with his magickal skills we could defeat Marcus together. "Where is Alejandro? I lost him. Can you see him?"

"Get up," Richard urged me, fear in his voice. "Quick, Meg! The horse…"

But it was too late.

As I lowered my arm, I heard a thundering on the grass, then looked up at a pair of shining black hooves, reared up above me, the horse neighing wildly.

Dent's stallion!

A hand grabbed me by the arm, dragging me sideways so that I fell heavily, the breath knocked out of me. Hooves struck the ground where I had been lying, and I stared up into Richard's pale face, breathless.

"You're welcome," he muttered, meeting my eyes. He raised his hand in a swift aversion-spell, and the black stallion turned as though terrified, veering sharply away across the lawns and heading for the trees.

Richard squeezed my shoulder, suddenly grim. "Hurry, get up. Dent's coming again."

My fist clenched around the slender hazel wand, and power thrummed in me, my scalp and fingertips tingling. Where was it coming from? I felt overwhelmed by this sudden surge of power, too strong for my body, everything inside me trembling and on fire.

I turned to face Marcus Dent as he came striding across the grass. I felt as though a thousand bees were trapped inside my head, crawling about in a bee-gold huddle, buzzing at the underside of my skull, desperate to get out.

"Foolish of you, Meg. When will you learn?" Marcus lunged for the wand and hit my protective barrier, his hand bouncing back on a wave of pure fury. "Women's magick! Child's magick! It cannot last. I am the stronger here and you are only alive by my grace. Now give me that wand or see your beloved Spaniard die."

Again the world shifted. Suddenly Marcus Dent was standing before me on the grass, Richard flung backwards by some hellish wind, Alejandro held before Dent like a hostage. Alejandro's body still hung limp; his eyes were closed and the witchfinder's dagger was pressed to his throat.

"The wand," Marcus said triumphantly. "Give me the wand."

I felt a gnawing in my guts.

"You want to test my resolve, Meg?" The knife pressed harder into Alejandro's neck; two drops of blood oozed out. "The wand is what I came for. A prize indeed. But it was left to you as a bequest and I cannot use it without your permission. You must give it to me freely." He smiled grimly, meeting my eyes. "A fair exchange. The Spaniard's life for your mother's wand. What do you say?"

I stared at Alejandro. A thrush sang nearby in the branches. The blade pressed deeper.

"Give me the wand and you shall have him." His smile made me shiver. "Why must you always defy me, Meg? For some women, my kiss has been a better prospect than the scaffold. I would offer you the same protection if you drop this defiance and kneel to me. I promise to be gentle."

I ignored his foul taunting. Richard had fallen near the house, blood on his temple. Beyond him, in the doorway, I could see the princess staring out, her ladies tugging frantically on her arms, stopping her from leaving the house.

Everywhere I went, I dragged my friends into danger and

left behind a trail of destruction. My hand wavered, then I lowered the wand.

"Don't you dare give up that wand, Meg Lytton!" Richard shouted hoarsely. "Alejandro would not want you to give it to him. He would rather die and you know it." He struggled up onto his elbow and cried out, "*Invictus!*"

"*Invictus?*" Marcus repeated, his blue eyes flashing sharply from Richard's face to mine. "What does he mean?"

I took a step back and stared down at my mother's ring. It glinted on my finger, a double ring of gold.

Invictus.

The hazel wand did not want to belong to him, I knew that much. Its power flowed as if coming from the earth itself, the good English dirt beneath my feet, strength tingling in my veins, along my arm, then out through my mother's wand.

The spell struck Alejandro in his face like a bucket of cold water, and in the same second I yelled, "*Excite!*" meaning "*Wake!*" in Latin.

The force of the spell knocked Marcus backwards, as he was taken unawares by my sudden attack. Released from the witchfinder's grasp, Alejandro fell clumsily to the ground.

Marcus roared. His face shifted back to the scarred visage I remembered from the year before, his white eye glaring at me fiercely.

"You will suffer for that, witch!" He sketched a gesture in the air, and I froze, half expecting to be blown away or turned to stone.

But nothing happened.

My wand hand lifted again and his hands were suddenly bound to his sides as though by invisible cords, his mouth full of horrible writhing things that began to pour out furiously, leaving me shocked and silent, staring at him.

I stood watching, amazed by my own power.

Marcus Dent was choking and retching, stones and frogs falling from his mouth, a spell I had certainly not intended. They littered the path, the vomited stones glossy, small and black, the green frogs hopping indignantly away to vanish into the grass as though they had never existed.

I was shocked. Not that I regretted what the wand had done. But it was disconcerting that it could make decisions for me.

"Hurry!" I urged Alejandro, who was scrambling to his feet, unsteady, his face dark with fury. "It's Marcus Dent. He put a spell on us all. We have to get back inside the house. I can protect us far better there."

But Alejandro was too quick for me. His eyes met mine and I saw an unspoken apology there. Then, in a flash, he grabbed up Marcus's dagger and turned, thrusting it deep into the witchfinder's side.

Marcus made a strange noise in his throat. He stared at me past Alejandro, wide-eyed, his mouth still bubbling with green frogs, then he collapsed, sagging against Alejandro. He grabbed Alejandro's shoulder, muttering a few words hoarsely into his ear. Then his eyes closed and his fair head fell back limply, the witchfinder's mouth open, empty at last now, his lips glistening with what looked like frothing green bile.

I stepped back, watching in horror as Alejandro tilted Marcus back onto the grass, then straightened, looking down at the blood on his hands.

The silence was terrible.

Alejandro turned to me, his expression agonised. "Get back inside, Meg. I will take care of this."

"Let me help you."

"Look, *la princesa* is at the door. She will come outside if you do not reassure her that it is over. That Marcus Dent is dead."

"Forgive me, Alejandro," I managed to say, my throat suddenly clogged with unshed tears. "This is my fault."

He held out his arms. "Come here, *mi querida*."

Not caring at that moment what anyone might think, I burrowed into his shoulder, and breathed in his heat, the masculine smell of his body. I felt no triumph. Just an intense weariness, and a nagging fear that the Lady Elizabeth would order me to leave her household again.

Marcus Dent was dead. Alejandro had killed him.

But could it really be that simple...?

As though sensing my mood, a cloud darkened the face of the sun. The shadows of the beech and oak trees around us seemed to grow longer, stretching cold black fingers towards us across the lawns.

"Alejandro," I murmured thankfully.

He drew back and looked down at me. His face was a bloodied mess, one of his eyes swollen. "Meg."

It was a measure of our topsy-turvy love that this struck me as one of the most significant exchanges we had ever had.

"The prophecy said Marcus Dent would die at the hands of a witch who had raised a dead King."

Alejandro nodded. He met my gaze thoughtfully. "Perhaps it was more of a curse than a prophecy."

"What now?" I asked simply.

"Now you go inside." Alejandro kissed my forehead. "I will say the last rites for Master Dent. Then Richard, William, and I will bury him together. Somewhere discreet in the woods. Not on consecrated ground. He does not deserve a holy burial."

I nodded my agreement. Turning, I glanced reluctantly towards the body—and froze in horror.

The dead, wide-splayed, motionless monster that had been Marcus Dent was stirring. A leg jerked, then an arm. Slowly the fingers of his right hand groped at the grass, as though searching for the bloodied dagger that had dealt his death-blow. Then his eyes opened, and the dead white eye swivelled round to stare at us, sinister and unearthly.

"Alejandro," I whispered, my fingers gripping his arm. "Look at Marcus."

Alejandro spun on his heel, staring back at the man we had both thought dead.

I heard a sudden thud of hooves and turned in search of the sound, my breathing constricted. The black stallion had reappeared, galloping swiftly out of the trees and back across the lawns towards us.

The horse circled Marcus, who had staggered to his feet now, his dagger in hand. The witchfinder's face was as white as his collar, and withered too, like that of a very old man, his one blue eye the only flare of colour left. His black doublet was horribly stained with blood; I could not bear to look at it.

Richard too was on his feet again, groping his way up the house wall. He called hoarsely, "Meg, don't let him escape!"

But it was too late.

Marcus had already gripped the horse's long mane, and with a muttered enchantment was transported onto the animal's back. His arms clutched the strong neck as the stallion reared, dangerous hooves flashing out, then the animal galloped away with him.

I raised my wand to strike Marcus down as he fled, but Alejandro was running after him. I lowered my arm slowly; I could not risk hurting Alejandro by mistake.

A moment later, the stallion had vaulted the boundary wall and disappeared from sight, thundering across the fields with Marcus on its back.

Alejandro gave a gesture of despair and came limping back to me, his chest heaving.

"Forgive me, Meg. This is my fault. I thought him dead."

"So did I."

"I don't understand it. The wound should have been fatal." He looked down at his bloodstained hands, a kind of horror on his face.

"Though I am glad, in a way."

I nodded, understanding what he meant. There was always a darkness out there, ready to swallow us if we made a mistake. It had taken the witchfinder long ago. To have killed Marcus might have driven Alejandro into the darkness too.

The Lady Elizabeth was outside, administering to Richard with Kat Ashley at her side. The conjuror's apprentice looked badly hurt, his face creased in pain, and I felt suddenly ashamed. I had not realized until that moment that he had been injured, not simply knocked down.

I ran across to my friend, who had sagged against the wall again, unable to walk. There was blood on his face, perhaps from a bump on the head, but otherwise I could see nothing.

"Where are you injured?"

He had closed his eyes, but opened them again. "My back. I had a rough landing when Dent threw me backwards."

"But you can walk? You can feel your legs?"

"Aye, a little."

William lifted Richard as though he weighed nothing. "I will carry Richard up to his room," he announced unsteadily, not meeting my eyes. I guessed he was a little afraid of my power. "If Alice could fetch hot water and cloths, we can make him comfortable at least."

When they had gone, the Lady Elizabeth rounded on me sharply.

Her face was pale, her small dark eyes fixed on my face. "Did you know Master Dent was coming here today?"

"No, my lady."

"Kat was right," she said abruptly. "You bring this house more trouble than I can afford."

"Forgive me—" I began wearily, guessing that she was about to dismiss me.

She held up a hand, interrupting me. "But you have done me good service too. And we Tudors do not forget loyal servants." She met my eyes, her look stern. "I will not send you away, Meg. You have caused a mess here, and it is only by remaining that you can protect me from it."

"My lady?"

"It is time you rid the world of this Master Dent. The man has become troublesome, and his testimony alone could damage my reputation a thousandfold." She shook her head in disgust. "Vomiting frogs? The whole sky turned black as night in the middle of the day? Our minds and bodies taken over by a spell? If my sister were to hear of these happenings, I would face torture at the hands of the Spanish Inquisition until I confessed myself a witch too."

"I will do my best to prevent that, my lady."

"See that you do. For I will give them your name first if I am arrested. And keep out of my way until the thing is done."

The Lady Elizabeth swept away into the house, her back very stiff, Kat Ashley and Blanche Parry following her with fierce looks thrown back at me.

I thought of what Marcus had said. *A virgin Queen.* Was that what lay ahead for Elizabeth, a reign without a husband? It seemed unlikely. I could not imagine such a passionate young woman welcoming a chaste existence. But then, none of us were privy to the secret workings of the Lady Elizabeth's heart. Perhaps she would rather be alone than marry a man for whom she had no love, as many noblewomen were forced to do.

And who was his "excellent informant"?

"Meg?"

I turned.

Alejandro was waiting, the cut on his face weeping blood again. Impatience, love, and frustration all surged inside me as I examined his battered face.

"You're so stubborn. Will you at least let me tend that cut before it gets infected?"

He nodded, his eyes were very dark. "But only if you let me come to your bedchamber first, *mi querida.*"

14

LIKE THE WORLD'S ABOUT TO END

Five minutes later, I closed the door to my bedchamber and turned, only to find Alejandro a few inches away, watching me, his face bloodied and raw.

"Alejandro?" I whispered, my eyes widening at his intent expression.

His hands came down either side of my hand, pressed flat against the wood of the door. I stared up into his face, astonished and a little afraid of this new Alejandro, so serious and determined.

"May I kiss you?" he asked.

"Th–that would hardly be right…or fair…to either of us," I stammered, taken aback by the intensity in his gaze. "I have already told you we will not be getting married. And the Lady Elizabeth…it is her househould…she forbade me to be alone with you…."

"I do not care about that. Well, I care. But not at this exact moment. Right now all I want to do is take you in my arms, *mi querida,* and kiss away the memory of what just happened."

His eyes flickered, and suddenly I saw the emotion raging inside him, emotion he had been struggling to suppress.

I was hardly breathing, as still as a mouse. Something in me had latched onto the emotion in him, and was driving us both forward, inexorably, towards the one thing we most certainly should never consider.

His finger brushed my cheek, feather-light, and I realized that he was trembling. Then his thumb dragged slowly along my lower lip, his dark gaze following the movement.

"Alejandro, what...what are you doing?"

"Something I should have done a year ago." His look was savagely hungry as he searched my face, hunting for some sign that I felt the same. It took every ounce of my strength not to kiss him there and then. But that would be madness. I still knew *that,* at least. "Meg, I love you. I would die for you. I hope you know that."

"I don't want you to die for me," I whispered. "Alejandro, please, we can't do this. It's not what you want. Not in your heart."

"Then order me to leave your bedchamber," he challenged me. "Slap my face. Throw me out. I will not argue with you, *mi alma.*"

I could not take my eyes off him. "Listen, this thing between us...you know it will not end well. It never could. That's why you must give up on me, Alejandro."

"I will," he promised, lowering his head with painstaking slowness. "But not yet."

His kiss burned me up from the inside, like setting a torch to stacked brushwood that had stood too long in the sun. Our mouths and bodies met at the same time, pressing intimately together, and then it was too late to stop.

I felt my heart take off, racing alongside his as we forgot sanity and discipline, and kissed like lovers.

Alejandro made a rough noise under his breath, then slammed his fist against the door as though suddenly furious with himself. *"Dios!"*

Yet he did not pull back as I expected.

"Si, mi amor," he muttered.

His mouth worked more hotly against mine now, tempting me like the Devil, persuading my lips to open. Utterly lost, I kissed him back, thrusting my hands into his short dark hair, forgetting everything except him.

Suddenly Alejandro groaned, then lifted me in his arms, turning to lay me on the narrow bed. He came down beside me on the mattress, throwing one possessive arm about my body, his gaze locked with mine as we stared at each other, both trying to read the other's secrets.

I could see from his face that he too felt dazed and off-balance, as though something between us had shifted, tilting us both into more dangerous territory. Had coming so perilously close to death done this?

"Meg." He bent to kiss my throat, his lips warm against my skin. "I must tell you something important."

"What?" I murmured, my face flushed with heat.

"What you saw of me today, I am sorry for it...."

I thought he meant being taken over by Marcus Dent, and tried to reassure him. "It was a spell. He controlled all of us, it was not your fault."

"No," he said hoarsely. "Not that. When I opened my eyes, and saw what was happening...I knew I had to finish him, or he was going to kill you."

"Hush," I reassured him, stroking my hands through his thick black hair. "I understand, you wanted to protect me."

"Back in Spain, we were taught to fight as young novices, permitted to wear a sword and dagger, even to ride into battle if the King ordered it," he told me, his voice muffled against my neck. "But we were still training to be priests, members of a holy order, and so the taking of a man's life must always be a last resort. What I did today, it was not easy for me. I have not trained to be a priest so that I can kill. That is not the man I want to be."

"I know," I whispered.

He lifted his head, and I was shocked to see tears in his eyes. I wanted to kiss them away, to make everything better. But I knew it would take more than kisses—more than my love—to heal whatever was hurting him so badly inside.

"Is there something you have not told me, Alejandro? Some secret you are keeping from me?"

He said nothing, shaking his head, but his smile was bitter. I was right; he was hiding something from me. But what? He would tell me when he was ready, I told myself feverishly, and hoped I was not mistaken.

I stroked his cut face, my heart aching to see him so hurt. "You are hurt. Let me clean this for you."

"It's nothing, leave it."

Alejandro bent, touching his lips to mine, and my heart began to thud again. He leaned above me, pressing close. I could feel the hard line of his body against mine and it lit a fire in me that I could not quite control.

His hands played with my hair, stroking through the pale strands, then he cupped my face, holding me still while he kissed me so deeply I thought I would faint.

There was no doubt in my mind that he wanted me, nor that I wanted him just as badly in return.

He rested his forehead against mine, the veins in his throat standing out with the effort of not kissing me. "Meg, Meg, I'm drowning."

Daringly I kissed his throat and heard his muffled protest. But we had nearly died out there today. How could it be wrong to want to love him, to celebrate with our bodies that we were alive, that we had survived Marcus Dent's assault?

Suddenly Alejandro pushed me back against the mattress and kissed me hard, pinning me down with his body. I was breathless and trembling by the time he raised his head again, shocked and more than a little excited by the raw emotion between us.

"Forgive me," he said hoarsely. "I should not have kissed you like that. But I've held back so long, it was hard to stop."

I was so breathless and dizzy, my lips still tingling from his kiss, it took me a moment to respond. "There's nothing to forgive. I was not unwilling."

His dark eyes glittered as he absorbed what I was saying. "How you tempt me, *mi querida*. If you knew what was in my mind…"

"I think it may be in mine too," I whispered.

"Ah, don't…please."

The muttered words sounded tortured. I touched him lightly, one hand brushing down his body, and his jaw clenched hard.

"Would it be so very wrong?" I asked quietly.

"You know it would. And why." His face was stiff. "You said it yourself when you allowed me in here."

Because I had refused to marry him. But did that mean we could not love each other? Bitterness and despair coiled inside me. Of course it did. It meant the end of everything between us. He was not the kind of man to take advantage of a woman like that.

And yet I still wanted him. "Alejandro…"

He rolled over onto his back, shaking his head, but stayed close beside me on the narrow bed, our bodies astonishingly hot where they touched.

He sounded almost furious. But not with me, I realized.

"There's plenty for you to forgive, Meg. You don't know the truth."

"Then tell me."

"Ay, Dios mio!" Alejandro fell silent for a moment, then replied unsteadily, "No, some things I cannot tell you. You must trust me to do what is right for you. My silence will keep you safe."

"I can keep myself safe."

He gave a short bark of laughter. "Is that so, my love? Because you did not look very safe, facing Marcus Dent out there with nothing but that crooked old wand in your hand. You looked about a hair's breadth from being annihilated."

My love.

I savoured the sound of those words in my head.

"My mother's wand may be old, but I can assure you it is not crooked," I corrected him, my voice dignified, but my hand wriggled down nonetheless to seek his and squeeze it. "Alejandro, will you always kiss me like that?"

"Like what?"

"Like the world is about to end."

He turned his head, smiling at me wryly. "It does feel that way, *mi amor.* And that is why we must take care never to be alone together again. Because *this*…this is rapidly becoming the thing I cannot live without."

He caught my wrist on that last word and pulled me slowly towards him, making his intention plain long before our lips met, as though giving me the opportunity to refuse this time. But of course I did not, knowing this intimacy must end, yet desperate at the same time for it to continue.

His mouth opened against mine in a long drugging kiss that left us both hot and breathless.

For a long while afterwards we lay together in drowsy silence, turned warmly into each other, my head on his chest, his arm loosely linked about my waist.

"Need to sleep," I mumbled, my eyelids so heavy I could not seem to keep them open.

"Then sleep."

"I have my duties...."

"You saved the princess's life today, Meg. I think you may be granted a few hours' respite from your duties."

Eventually I slept, my whole body weary and bruised from the long fight against Marcus.

When I woke, the room had darkened into twilight. I yawned, stretching out stiff limbs, and felt Alejandro shift away from me awkwardly.

It felt strange to be lying next to him on a bed. I could not quite believe what had happened.

"Hello," Alejandro murmured in my ear.

I turned my head to look at him. "Hello." There was an odd expression in his eyes that made me frown. "What is it? What is the matter now?"

"You snore," he said plaintively.

"I do not!"

"Just a little, when you are deep asleep. Through your nose." He pinched his nose shut and made a quiet droning noise through it. "But I am relieved you are awake at last. I feared I might have to stifle you with a pillow to get some rest."

"Beast!"

He smiled, and his gaze moved to my mouth. "Sometimes, yes, *mi alma*. But I am your beast."

I shivered at the intimacy in his eyes and voice, and sat up, tidying my dishevelled hair. "It's late, we should go downstairs."

What we had done—sleeping together on my bed while the household was quiet—was dangerous enough for our hearts.

But it was also strictly against the Lady Elizabeth's wishes. The room had grown dark, and I knew supper would soon be served downstairs in the Great Hall. If we did not make our way down there, we would be missed.

Then I saw that the door was slightly ajar, and realized someone must have peeped in and seen us lying together on the bed, then gone away again. My cheeks burnt.

"What is it?" Alejandro asked softly, taking my hand and kissing the inner skin of my wrist.

"I think someone may have seen us together."

He glanced back at the partially open door, then shrugged. "Do not concern yourself. We lay together, yes, but only to sleep." His voice deepened. "There is nothing to be ashamed of in that. At least, I am not ashamed of it. If you would marry me—"

"I have already said no."

He did not answer, but instead turned his head away, not moving. Then he sat up and swung his legs out of bed. But his shoulders were bowed, and I guessed from the way he fingered his cheek that his cut must still be painful.

There was some noise from below. I guessed from the clattering and the raised voices that supper was being laid out for us in the Great Hall. I fumbled with the tinderbox in the gloom until he came over and lit the candle for me, his expression shuttered.

"Thank you." I raised the candle to examine his face. He seemed to flinch at my touch, but at least the blood had dried, the cut crusting over. The edges were red, sore-looking. "Come down to the kitchen, I will bathe that cut for you in salt water. Else it will be infected by tomorrow, trust me."

He nodded, his eyes searching my face. His hand caught my wrist when I would have turned away.

"Meg," he began uncertainly.

Someone shouted up from the hall below: Blanche Parry calling my name. "Supper must be ready," I whispered, still waiting. "What do you want to say to me?"

"Another time, *mi querida*."

With obvious reluctance, Alejandro took the candle from me and we wandered down the stairs together in a thick silence, both a little drowsy and flushed after our long rest.

I had expected to hear the usual hubbub of voices from our small company as I descended. But though a fire was burning in the hearth, and supper was laid out on the long table, those gathered in the hall below were silent.

"Meg," the Lady Elizabeth spoke sharply, coming to the foot of the stairs. "You have a visitor. I sent Blanche to fetch you downstairs, but she came back and told me you were…" There was a flush in her cheeks as she glanced from me to Alejandro, her face stiff. "Asleep."

"Forgive me, my lady. I should not have slept so long."

I was hot-cheeked myself, hearing the open accusation in her voice. The princess had told me to stay away from Alejandro, to avoid being alone with him. Instead, I had curled up to sleep with him in my chamber.

Yet how could Elizabeth be angry with me when she felt every bit as lovesick about Robert Dudley? At least Alejandro was not *married!*

Then her words slowly sank in. "A…a visitor, did you say?"

I paused on the last stair, and looked across towards the hearth. A strange woman was standing in front of the fire, a wild look on her face. Her clothes were simple, her hood and cloak that of a country woman on a journey, but she had a striking face, lined with years but with such bright and intelligent eyes she looked almost young. The staff she carried was surely magickal, for those were astrological symbols carved into the wood.

And she was staring straight at me.

"Meg Lytton." She came forward, studying me as intently as I had just studied her. "I have come here to speak with you on a matter of great urgency."

I glanced at the Lady Elizabeth, but she had returned to the fireside with her ladies, clearly unwilling to speak with this wild-looking woman.

"Forgive me if I am discourteous," I said directly to our visitor, "but I do not know you. What is your name, mistress?"

"My name is Gilly Goodwife," she told me, unsmiling. "Once upon a time, when I was a girl and still unmarried, I lived in Oxfordshire and was friend to your mother, Catherine Canley."

We sat cross-legged under dark, broad-trunked trees, facing each other across the circle Gilly Goodwife had drawn in the dirt with her staff. In the centre burned a roughly made fire, damp stacked wood hissing, the air thickening with smoke. I watched Gilly through the leap of flames, and tried to imagine her and my mother and my aunt Jane together as powerful young women, the three of them sitting around a magickal fire just like this one.

I shivered, looking up at the whispering treetops, the black sky winking with stars, and hoped I had not made a mistake by agreeing to speak alone with her.

"No need to be afraid or guard your tongue, child. None can see or hear us within the sturdy protection of my circle," Gilly said, smiling across at me in a reassuring manner. "Here within the boundary we may speak freely."

"You knew my mother, Catherine Canley, and my aunt Jane too? Tell me about that."

"We used to meet in the woods when the moon was full, and there cast spells and practise our craft. Catherine kept a journal, and noted down all our spells, those which worked and those which didn't, and why. I have often wondered what became of her spell book, and hoped it would not fall into the wrong hands, for some of our work in the early days was quite dangerous. Catherine and Jane could both read and write, of course, being destined for the royal court. But I had not been schooled and only learned those skills after I married." She paused. "I was saddened to hear of your mother's death. It must have been hard to lose a mother so young."

"Not so hard perhaps as to lose Aunt Jane to the fire. I do not remember my mother properly. But my aunt…"

Watching my struggle against tears, her mouth tightened. "Master Dent is the Devil's servant."

I could not argue with that. "Why have you come to see me, Mistress Goodwife?"

"When I finally chose to marry, I abandoned the craft for a few years," she began. "One summer my youngest daughter grew sick, very sick, and I knew the spell that would heal her. I could not let my child die. So I cast the circle and gathered herbs at the new moon, preparing them in the prescribed manner for working magick. Bethany recovered from her sickness that summer, and I knew it was my craft that had healed her. Later it came to my attention that several other women in my village, and more in the villages around, were also engaged in the dark arts. We had to be very careful, but we began to meet secretly and hold sabats as a coven." She smiled proudly. "There are seven of us now, and that is a goodly number for working magick. Together we keep our villages free from the plague, and our children healthy, and those of us who have husbands manage to keep our menfolk biddable."

Her explanation fascinated me. I had always believed, like Aunt Jane, who had lived out her days as a spinster, that a witch must give up her craft on marrying. Yet Mistress Goodwife was both married and a mother. Her husband was the smith of their village, she told me, a tiny place not five miles from Hatfield.

"I am a witch born, just as you are," she explained calmly when I asked how it was possible to be married and still remain a witch.

"The witch born should not yield her craft for anything, not even the love of a good man."

I nodded, wondering what Alejandro would make of *that*. "The Lady Elizabeth said something like that once. But about her throne, not magick."

"She suffers, does she not?"

I held my breath, fearing I had been indiscreet. "What do you mean?"

"The princess...she is in love, and unhappily. I can tell the signs." Mistress Goodwife looked at me across the flames. "I can help her with that, if she wishes. There is a spell...."

"She wishes to know her future," I said bluntly.

Gilly nodded. "Harder, but I can help with that too."

I wished I could have known Gilly Goodwife sooner. She seemed so wise and calm: traits I badly needed to acquire myself. I always seemed to be lurching from one disastrous spell to another, no space to draw breath. Perhaps with an experienced witch like this to guide me...

But there was little time for learning new skills, I thought grimly. Marcus Dent would come back at us soon and I must be ready.

Curious to know more about my family, I asked, "What was my mother like?"

"Catherine was the cleverest among us, always reading books and learning new spells, and yet she was the boldest too. She loved to dance under the full moon, sky-clad, where Jane and I would refuse to shed our clothes. But she was very beautiful, you see. Even with dirt on her face and her hair be-draggled after a night in the woods. And so proud, she would have choked herself to death rather than accept help from any-one." Gilly smiled. "You have a strong look of her. I would have known you anywhere for her daughter."

I was pleased. "Truly?"

"You are very beautiful too." She raised her brows at my stunned look. "What, you do not know your own beauty? Ah, but the young never do. And powerful too. Though you shed some of your power when you cast Marcus Dent out of this world."

My mouth fell open and I gaped at her. "How do you know about that?"

"Cecilie told us."

"Cecilie?"

"One of our coven, and a gifted seer." Gilly smiled, though she seemed sad too. "A pretty girl. Her mother is French, her father Scottish. She came to us last year when her father in-herited property here, and brought his whole family down from Scotland. She is a little older than you, twenty years of age, but already a talented witch with great powers of divi-nation." She paused, looking at me oddly. "Cecilie foretold the rise of Marcus Dent. She knew a young witch would try to block his power, but not that it was you."

"Except I've ended up making him more powerful in-stead," I muttered.

"That is a problem, yes, but it can be reversed," she said coolly. "Perhaps with your mother's enchanted ring…"

"*My mother's ring?* Do you know *everything?*" I demanded, shocked by how much this woman seemed to know about me and my life.

"I remember the ring from when I knew your mother. Though she only rarely wore it, for safety's sake. Possessing the ring gives you a look, an air, a certain presence. I sensed it back there at the house." She met my gaze. "You have the ring with you now, don't you?"

I nodded, then realized too late that it might have been better to lie. After all, I only had this woman's word that she had known my aunt and mother as a girl. She could be working for Marcus Dent.

Though somehow I doubted it. Especially after the "Devil's servant" comment.

"Then I presume you understand the workings of the *Invictus*-spell?" she asked briskly.

"Of course. It's...erm..." Daunted by her knowledge and experience, I fumbled in my pouch for the ring and pushed it back onto my finger. The double coils gleamed there, red-gold, almost glowing with power. At once I felt the fatigue of the past day fall away. I straightened my slumped shoulders and met her gaze more confidently.

"*Invictus*. It means unconquered."

"*Invictus* is a powerful and dangerous spell cast upon an object like a ring or a dagger that renders the bearer invincible against magickal attack."

Invincible.

With a start, I remembered Marcus Dent throwing all his power at me—the darkness, the swirling winds, the repeated attacks on my psyche—and getting nowhere. I had suffered under that onslaught. But I had not broken.

"How can it be dangerous though?" I looked down at the double-coiled ring, then twisted it around my finger, for it was a little loose. "Surely if it makes me invincible—"

"When you carry such a powerful magickal object openly about with you, it's like holding up a candle against the dark and being surrounded by moths. You invite attack from every evil creature that sees its light. Those who are drawn to the ring may not be able to harm *you,* but they can harm those around you, or influence the innocent to attack you." Gilly looked at me sombrely. "So avoid putting it on until you need it."

Grimacing, I dragged the ring from my finger. Already the dark woods around us looked more threatening. It explained why Blanche had attacked us in the old shepherd's hut when the Lady Elizabeth had placed the ring upon her finger, and the odd feeling of menace in the shadows at Hatfield.

I had thought Alice's possession one of Marcus's cruel tricks. But perhaps he was simply another evil creature drawn to the ring's light. It had been in my mind at the time, my hand on the pouch I carried it in.

Gilly was watching me, a wry smile on her face. "Oh, you are safe enough here. I always cast spells of protection about me as I travel, to ward off unwanted attention, and when I arrived at Hatfield tonight, I put an enchantment about the house too, for I found it undefended. Why was that?"

"It's too long a story. But thank you for the protection. Tell me, what else did Cecilie say about Marcus Dent?"

"That her destiny was inextricably bound up with his. And indeed we fear it has been. That is why I have come to you for help."

Frowning, I hid the ring in my belt pouch. "Go on."

"Just before Christmas, a gang of men attacked the house where Cecilie lives. They came on horseback, wearing hoods and carrying torches. Her father told them to leave, but their leader demanded he hand over 'the witch,' or they would torch the house and everyone in it." Gilly looked grim. "It was Marcus Dent."

My chest hurt, it was so tight. I recalled how Dent and his men had crashed into our house at dawn one morning—and the horrors that had followed my aunt's arrest.

"He dragged Cecilie from the house, accusing her of witch-craft and claiming she would stand trial before the Spanish Inquisition in London. That was the last any of us heard of Cecilie. Her father wrote to the chief of the Spanish Inquisition at court, begging for his daughter's release. But there was no reply."

Miguel de Pero. I thought of the Chief Inquisitor's dark sneering face and was not surprised by his lack of response. He had probably been overjoyed to hear of another girl's arrest for witchcraft. He and his fellow torturers had probably laid on a feast to celebrate the occasion.

"Then a few days ago," Gilly continued, looking at me, "Cecilie appeared to me in a dream. She told me to travel to Hatfield and seek out Meg Lytton, servant to the Lady Elizabeth and the only woman in England who can defeat Marcus Dent."

"No, no." I felt sick, shaking my head instinctively at the terrible challenge being laid before me. "I have tried and failed many times to defeat him. He is too powerful."

"Then Marcus Dent will make it his business to find and send to their death every witch in England until he is the only person of power left. Is that what you want?"

I closed my eyes, wishing I was anyone but me. But in my heart I knew she was right. Marcus had some fantasy about playing Merlin to a Catholic King Arthur, and he would not rest until he had made it truth.

"Cecilie is being held prisoner by Dent. She could not tell me where. But in the dream, she showed me her hurts, which are terrible. Dent has been torturing her, making her scry for him, to foretell the future, determined to drain every last ounce of magickal power from her body. And when Dent has finished with her, she told me he will hand her over to his friends Bishop Bonner and the Spanish Inquisition. They will find her guilty of witchcraft, and execute her."

"*What?*"

I started up in surprise. His cruelty did not shock me. I could believe him capable of the worst kind of viciousness. But could Marcus truly have a connection with the great Bishop Bonner, a man whose burnings surpassed even his own?

I wondered if John Dee knew of their friendship. And if the black-robed priests of the Spanish Inquisition understood that Marcus was himself a creature of darkness.

Cecilie was his "excellent informant," I realized grimly, the one who had foreseen Elizabeth holding the throne alone. He must have tortured the visions out of her.

"That devil… But no one can stop him now," I muttered, shaking my head. "No one."

"Is that so? I think you have more power than you know, Meg Lytton. Do not turn your back on your own kind out of fear."

"But I wouldn't even know where to start!"

"I will help you find the path. No, look at me, Meg." Gilly Goodwife held my gaze across the fire, fierce and intent. "Will you allow yet *another* witch to die at the hands of Marcus Dent? Or are you ready to put the inheritance you have been squandering to its proper use at last?"

She was talking of Aunt Jane, of course. Last time I had tried to rescue one of the witchfinder's victims, I had arrived too late and the brushwood had already been lit. Anger flooded my heart as I remembered my aunt's dying cries, how she must have suffered at the end.

"Tell me what I must do," I said.

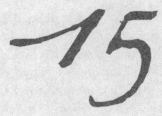

ASPICIO

Of course, if we were to stand any hope of rescuing Cecilie, we had to discover first where Marcus Dent was holding the seer. It seemed unlikely that he would have chosen his absurd tower, constructed last year a few miles from my father's house in Warwickshire, for he would have known that was too obvious. Also, if no one could work magick there, it would not be a great place to force a seer to have visions.

But perhaps he had some other secret place where he kept his victims locked up before hanging or burning them.

"The *Aspicio*-spell," Richard suggested on the following morning, eager to be in on this rescue attempt. Presumably he hoped there would be some opportunity for him to take his revenge on Dent for knocking him aside as easily as a fly. "Use it to find Cecilie, then we'll know where to attack him."

I glanced apprehensively at the princess, who was deep in conversation with Gilly Goodwife, but she gave her permission with a distracted wave of her hand.

We found a quiet side room off the kitchen corridor, then

moved aside the table and various chests we found there. Then out came a soft cushion for me to sit, and a small handbell—Richard had decided the ringing of a bell would make a good signal for me to return from the far-seeing-spell—and my mother's grimoire.

Alejandro unfolded his arms and went to the door as soon as we began our final preparations, his face strained, knowing me too well to bother arguing. Besides, we were supposed to be mere friends now, so he could hardly have demanded that I stop.

Friends that kiss, I thought drily, and avoided his gaze.

"Just bring her back safely," he muttered to Richard, then left the room.

"Whatever you say, sir," Richard replied under his breath, glaring at the closed door.

I laughed to myself. They were like two cockerels, each trying to outstrut the other to attract the attention of a hen. While the hen, I thought grimly, knew that there was a fox at the door. . . .

Taking a deep and calming breath, I took up my position on the sunny floor of the bright, east-facing room and closed my eyes.

"*Aspicio!*"

Almost at once it was broad daylight and I was flying so low I could almost have brushed the tops of the trees. Water flashed by below me, catching my eye. The River Thames, broadening with lush meadows on either side, dotted with skiffs and sculls, tiny boats insignificant against its deep rolling current.

Houses sprawled below me then, thatched roofs gathered tightly together in clearings and beside bright streams. Suddenly a high wall blocked the way, looming darkly ahead, and when I cleared it, my stomach lurching with a sickening flutter, I knew this to be the city of London. Narrow lanes, overhanging buildings, filth in the gutters, and people everywhere, ants filling the city, light and shadow following one another every few yards as the sun streamed down between buildings.

The air lifted my hair, and my body turned, shifting lower as my destination drew nearer. The world creaked and swung, bringing me gently to earth.

I was standing on the corner of a busy city street, facing a row of market stalls clustered about a high wooden cross, most ornately and beautifully carved. Beyond the stalls the way sloped down towards the river, where a great building stood on the bank, tall pennants fluttering in the warm breeze.

That must be Whitehall, a palace I had never visited but where the court often resided in the winter. To my left, an alley cut between cramped buildings, dropping into deep shadow, with coarse linen shirts and petticoats strung out of the casements to dry. People passed me like water flowing around a rock in the stream, blank-faced as though they could not see me—which was indeed the case, I reminded myself— and going about their business in the sunshine.

At that moment two men turned into the alley, talking quietly together, and I caught the name *Master Dent.*

I fell in behind the two men. Soon they led me to a narrow building propped precariously against its neighbours, its painted exterior peeling, foul-smelling mud shored up against the entrance.

Stepping over the mud, they pushed the door open, and I followed them inside the house, drifting silent as a ghost through the dark, high-ceilinged rooms.

Through another doorway, I found myself in a crowd of evil-looking men, sitting about playing dice or drinking from cracked tankards while two skinny boys entertained them on a pipe and tabor.

The men I had followed paused, looking about the smoky chamber.

"Where is Master Dent?" one of them, a tall man with thick red hair, asked.

"Downstairs. With the gentlemen."

The red-haired man looked at his friend. "Shall we go down?"

"I'm not going into that rats' nest." He spat on the floor. "Not with that Scottish heathen he keeps down there."

"She can't do you no harm. Not gagged like that."

But the man shook his head. "Freeze a man to death with her eyeballs, she could. And what about the other women?"

"Come on, damn you. This message won't keep."

Scottish heathen.

The red-haired man looked uncomfortable as he pushed between the tables and peered through a doorway. Floating behind him I could see dark narrow stairs leading down into candlelight.

So that was where he was holding Cecilie. There was a large cellar space below the house, murky and damp this close to the river, and thick with cobwebs.

"Master Dent?"

A door creaked open and a man looked out. It was the handsome Marcus, not the grim-faced man with the dead white eye and the terrible scars. The shock of seeing him again almost stopped my heart. I had tried to prepare myself for it, but I still felt sick. Even though I knew none of them could see me, it was still terrifying to be standing face-to-face with my enemy in that confined space.

Dent's eyes narrowed. "You have news?"

Nervously the man dragged a folded paper from his pouch. "One of the boys intercepted this on its way into Hatfield a few days ago, sir. The messenger got clean away."

Dent took the paper and straightened it out. His lips drew back in a snarl. "From Master John Dee. You see his mark there, the triangle?" He shook his head. "The rest is in code, like the others. Damn him."

"Aye, master, we could not make head nor tail of it."

"The games these traitors play... Well, I'll look at it later. I have not yet given up hope of deciphering their absurd codes." He stuffed the letter into his own pouch, then looked at the man. "You may go."

"Yes, Master Dent."

The man vanished the way he had come. I remained there, looking directly into Marcus's false face and loathing him with all my being.

"Who is it, Dent?" a man's voice, deep and impatient, called from within the room.

Marcus, who had hesitated on the threshold, frowned into the shadows, almost as though he could sense my presence as John Dee had done, and swung back into the room. "Nothing important, my lord." His cheerfulness sounded forced. "Come, drink up. Then I shall show you the witch as I promised."

Then he closed the door in my face. I smiled grimly. Plain wood could not keep me out, however thick.

In my ghostly form, I pressed against the closed door and was instantly inside the room. A candlelit table greeted me, with three men about it. Marcus was seating himself at the table again, reaching for his wine cup. I recognized Bishop Bonner at once, though he was out of place in such humble surroundings. The other man, I realized with a thudding heart, was none other than Miguel de Pero, head of the Spanish Inquisition here on English soil. They were priests notorious for their cruelty and merciless hunting down of heretics, sinners, and those who dabbled in the black arts.

I averted my eyes from that dark face with its hooded beak

of a nose, unable to forget how he had tortured me for hours at Hampton Court. I had hoped never to see him again. Yet here he was, in the company of my greatest enemy, Marcus Dent. Though there was a rightness about their association, for both men were steeped up to their necks in foulness.

The cellar room was dank, but some effort had been made to make it homelier. The walls had been covered with a dark patterned fabric, a small fire burned steadily in the grate, and a pewter dish of nuts had been set on the table. Alongside it I saw papers and maps they had been studying, and what looked like a list of names.

My back to the door, I tried to approach the table, but something held me back.

Had Dent enchanted the room so this meeting could not be spied upon? I struggled against the protective barrier in vain. No doubt he could not set an effective spell elsewhere in the house, for too many men were freely coming and going upstairs. But here, in his private chamber below the house, it seemed he was intent on keeping spies at bay.

But it seemed I was able to listen, even if their voices were muffled, as though coming from a great distance away.

Bonner turned to Marcus Dent, fingering the creased list of names. "How long before these men and women can be accused of witchcraft?"

"Allow me free rein, my lord, and I can have them marked for death within a few days of their arrests."

"I deal in heresy myself. Though I have known a few cases of witchcraft. But some of these heretics are very hard to pin down. They conceal their prayer books. They lie to my men when they are brought in for questioning. They go to Mass like everyone else."

"As do witches."

Bonner shrugged, his double chin quivering. "It is hard,

sometimes, to find a reason to arrest these scoundrels more than once. English law is too lax, I find. Though when a heretic has been rooted out and condemned, I make every effort to bring him back into the church before he burns—there is always time to save a man's soul."

He cracked a nut and scooped it out with his fingers. "Do you not feel the same about your witches, Dent?"

Dent was smiling thinly, his cold eyes flicking from de Pero to Bonner, assessing each man in turn. "My lord, I can assure you that a condemned witch never truly repents of her sins, whatever cries and prayers she may utter when she stands upon the gallows. Never. Such protestations of innocence are entirely false. It is not in a woman's nature to seek absolution."

De Pero shook his head at this. "A witch is a tool of the Devil. She should burn, not hang."

"I must agree with you there, *señor,*" Marcus said swiftly, turning to the Spaniard. "But it is not easy to change English law. Perhaps if his lordship were to approach the Queen on this matter...?" A witch in England had to be hanged, under the law. But Marcus always preferred to see his victims burn rather than hang, and if heresy could be asserted as well as witchcraft, then the sentence was death by burning.

Bishop Bonner looked doubtful. "The Queen would shrink from such a painful duty, ordering the burning of her own sex."

"Yet you have condemned women heretics to the bonfire before now, and the Queen has not refused *their* executions."

"Her Majesty quite rightly views heresy as the most grievous sin of all. The fire purifies the heretic and is a just punishment for those who deny the Catholic faith, both male and female. Nonetheless, you make a good point, Master Dent. I shall put it to the Queen next time I am at court. Witches to burn rather than hang!" Bonner laughed, reaching for another nut, and the other two joined in. "Yes, that has a righteous ring to it."

My stomach churned at their callous laughter. But I had learned something useful: Marcus was hoping to work secretly for Bonner and de Pero, drumming up victims for the hangman when they had escaped the bonfire.

I shuddered, recalling how Alejandro had accidentally caused the death of a Spanish woman in his father's employ, being a young child and unaware what an idle comment could do. Then the woman had cursed him as she died, swearing his wife would die in childbirth. It was hard, at that moment, not to sympathize with the poor woman.

"Well, I must say, Master Dent, I am glad you approached us." Bonner flicked the paper before him. "This is an impressive list of credentials. You claim to have hunted down every witch in Warwickshire, is that not so?"

"All but one, my lord," Dent said bitterly.

The bishop looked at him sharply. "You must give us the witch's name. De Pero here will order her arrest, I promise you."

"I..." Dent ran a finger under his collar as though it sat too tight about his neck. "I fear I cannot give you her name, my lord."

"Cannot?"

"It is on the tip of my tongue. Wait... No, no, it's gone. I cannot... In truth, I do not know it. Her name, that is." Dent downed his cup of wine, then sat drumming his fingers violently on the table, staring at nothing. His voice was clipped. "You must forgive these fits and starts, my lord. I will catch her one day...you can be certain of that."

I grinned in amazement as I realized that my silencing-spell on Marcus Dent—my hastily wrought, homespun spell last spring after our confrontation in Woodstock village—was still in place, providing an effective gag on the witchfinder's mouth and that of his men. He could not name me publicly as a witch. Nor denounce Elizabeth as my protector.

But my burst of triumph did not last long.

"You must come and meet my man Dee," Bonner exclaimed, clapping him on the back. "He is an astrologer. Knows things. He will get the name out of you soon as winking."

"John Dee?" Marcus repeated, a sly look on his face.

"That's the fellow." Bonner's eyes narrowed on his face. "You know him?"

"We were at university together."

"Oxford? Later than me, I expect. What college?"

"Trinity."

"Ah...you would know young Christopherson then, I'll be bound."

"Not well, though he and John Dee were very close in their first year."

Bonner glanced briefly at de Pero. "Christopherson went into the church like me. Very pious man. He'll go far under Queen Mary." He looked back at Marcus. "But you see, I already have a man in my employ who knows how to get at the truth—John Dee can crack a man open like one of these nuts, and all with words. Words and mathematics! I don't know how he does it."

Marcus seethed. "You do not suspect your tame conjuror of using the dark arts himself?"

"What, Dee?" Bonner shrugged, as if this were old news. "Well, even if he is, and I've seen no evidence of that, it was the Queen herself who placed him in my household. I would be a fool to question an appointment of Her Majesty's making."

Marcus looked thunderstruck. "*The Queen?*"

"She did it to keep the astrologer out of her sister's path, if you ask me. And why not? A dangerous association, that. John Dee is out of favour officially. Caught meddling where he should not. But privately, the Queen still sees him. Grants him funds for books, that kind of thing. He has some strange idea about setting up a library of scientific study." Bonner glanced about for a napkin, then wiped his mouth on his sleeve. "But John Dee is not my concern at the moment. No, I am determined to sweep this country clean of those who will not bow the knee to Rome, particularly recalcitrant priests of Cranmer's persuasion. If you can help me with my mission, Master Dent, we shall deal well enough together."

Marcus rolled up the list and slipped it inside his doublet. "I will help you and Señor de Pero condemn these heretics, my lord. That I swear."

The three men stood and drank a toast to their success.

Bonner shook Marcus's hand. "Well, I shall leave the rest to our Spanish friend here. I have much to do and must take my leave."

Marcus frowned. "But, my lord, will you not stay to admire my greatest prize? A true seer, not some mud-witted witch but a creature of Satan, with powers of divination that make your John Dee look like a child. And no danger to any of us, for she is kept chained and gagged day and night."

A look of horror crossed Bonner's face. "Merciful heavens, no. I could never stomach a witch, even in chains. Such fiends of Hell are best avoided by those who are obedient to God, except as judge and executioner. Though no doubt you have found some good use for her, Master Dent." He turned away, rejecting Marcus's protest. "No, I must bid you both good day, masters. Fare you well!"

When the bishop had gone, Marcus waited in silence for Miguel de Pero to speak.

The Chief Inquisitor looked at him a long while from under drooping lids. "Master Dent, this must remain a private arrangement. You will be paid—and handsomely—for every soul that is led to the bonfire on your account. But if you are caught inventing evidence for their judges, our association will be denied—and you too may face the executioner. So bear that in mind, and take caution in your dealings with evil creatures like the witch you keep here."

Marcus looked furious, but nodded curtly. "I shall be careful, *señor*. It is understood."

"Send the witch to Bishop Bonner—he will see her hanged without delay."

"Soon," Marcus promised him, but I could see he was lying. "When she has furnished me with the names of her other coven members."

De Pero smiled knowingly. "Of course." He finished his wine with an expression of mild distaste. "No need to show me out. I will send word when I am ready to receive your first report. Though duty calls me to leave London soon, alas, and I may not return for several weeks." His cold smile made my heart leap in fear. "You are not the only man who keeps a witch too close for his own good."

What had he meant by *that*?

The Spaniard passed through my body, opening the door, and headed for the stairs with his slow, chilling step.

Marcus bent his head and swore under his breath. Then he picked up a candle and trod heavily out through puddled water into the darkness of the main cellar. With me following, the witchfinder pushed past filthy curtains of gauze to where a pale female figure could just be seen in the candlelight, both arms raised as though chained to the wall.

Cecilie.

My stomach heaved in horror at how the young woman

was being kept, tied up like a dog in the black stench-pit of this cellar.

"Now, my dear," Marcus began silkily, and dropped the last gauze curtain, masking my view of his prisoner, "since you are awake again, I'll remove the gag and you can resume telling me about Meg Lytton and her priest. And don't lie this time. I always know when you're lying."

I pressed up against the gauze, desperate to see Cecilie for myself, to know for certain that she was alive, that Marcus had not hurt her too cruelly.

But at that moment the world tilted and rolled beneath me with a familiar sickening sensation. I screamed a silent, "No!" but my mute ghost was sucked from that dark house in London even as I protested, flailing and clawing at the air.

Then I was flying, tears in my eyes, having seen nothing but a haggard face raised towards her captor, gagged and marked with bruises, and a pair of tortured brown eyes.

When my senses finally returned, Richard was kneeling with my head in his lap, his frown concerned. "Meg, you little wretch. You've been gone nearly two hours."

"William, look, she's awake." Alice was kneeling on my other side, her cheeks flushed, her chestnut curls dishevelled, no cap in sight.

When had she arrived?

I stared up dizzily at William behind her, my brother peering over her head, his expression equally anxious.

"Quick, William, pass me that wine."

Then I noticed Alejandro standing by the door—looking furious, of course. I guessed that was because I had been gone so long. And was Elizabeth herself in the room? I caught a hint of perfume, then the swish of heavy silk skirts.

Good heavens, who else knew of our magickal business?

"I know where Dent is holding Cecilie," I croaked, my

head spinning worse than ever before, and I accepted a sip of wine from the cup Alice held to my lips. "But it's not going to be easy."

TORTURER

It was only a short while, yet somehow spring slipped into summer while we argued and planned how to rescue Cecilie from Marcus Dent. It only seemed like yesterday that we had celebrated the spring equinox, which was also the anniversary of my birth. Like most people, I had not marked my birthday in any special way, but noted its passing with interest. It was odd to think that I was now seventeen years of age, when I had once feared that I would not even reach sixteen. Would this next year see my death?

A night ride to London seemed wisest. But we had to wait for a full moon, for the roads would be lighter under a summer moon and we could travel more safely.

Richard sided with me on this. "It does make sense to wait for the next full moon before riding to London," he agreed, gathering herbs in the sunlit garden at Hatfield, though I could tell he was itching to be on the move. He seemed intent on revenge after the way Dent had brushed him aside, his pride hurt by his failure that day. "I only wish it could come sooner."

Alejandro wanted me to stay behind at Hatfield, of course. He had agreed that Cecilie must be rescued from Marcus at the earliest possible opportunity, but did not want me involved in this business.

"Why must you always be so hotheaded?" Alejandro demanded, leaning against the tall yew hedge that surrounded the formal gardens. "You will get yourself killed in this madness."

"Or save everyone else from death," I exclaimed, rounding on him. "I am hardly helpless against the witchfinder, Alejandro. You know my power."

His eyes clashed with mine, then he walked away. "Yes," he muttered. "I know it."

I watched him pace the sandy path in silence, his arms folded tightly, tension in every line of his body. My power would always be the thing between us, I thought sadly. The sword in the bed. It was too much for him. And he knew I would never give it up. Not for a man, anyway.

Will, sitting hand in hand with Alice on the wall as they listened to our conversation, jumped into this awkward moment.

"Alejandro is right to be concerned. It is madness for us to be charging into Dent's house and trying to get that witch out."

"Cecilie. She has a name."

My brother looked at me sternly. "I am sorry for her, Meg, truly I am. But I have no wish to die for a woman I have never even met."

"That's the spirit," Richard said drily, inhaling a fragrant handful of sweet marjoram.

"But we can't just leave the girl there to die, William," Alice exclaimed, frowning at him. "What if it was me?"

William shrugged, looking sideways at Alice, but I knew he would not refuse to come. He liked to bluster, and would often dig his heels in when he felt cornered, but he had a generous heart. I saw the way he and Alice were looking at each other, the message that passed silently between them, and could not help wondering how far things had gone there.

William might be good at heart, but he needed someone forthright like Alice to nudge him in the right direction and not let him wriggle out of his promises. That was something a woman would never need to worry about with Alejandro. His promises might be written in snow, carved on water, even blown away on the wind, yet he would keep them as solidly as though they had been etched in stone.

He would not be making any more promises to me though, I thought wretchedly. And that was a good thing, for Gilly Goodwife may have been able to live a married life with a blacksmith and still practise her craft, but I knew that if I married Alejandro—a nobleman from the country of the Inquisition—I would have to give up my power. And I had no wish to do that.

"Meg?"

I turned at the call to see Blanche in the doorway to the house, beckoning me inside.

"Forgive me," I murmured to the others, and hurried away across the grass, secretly relieved at the interruption.

Blanche was waiting for me in the cool, shady entrance. Since I had stopped wearing the *Invictus* ring, the place seemed less threatening. Hatfield House was almost pleasant now with summer upon us, always the scent of flowers drifting through the corridors and a harmonious drone of bees from the leaded windows that overlooked the garden.

"Her ladyship wishes to see you alone," Blanche said, her lips pursed disapprovingly. "Go up at once, she is waiting for you."

I climbed the stairs to Elizabeth's chamber and found her

by the window, staring out across the swaying treetops as though still a prisoner, as she had been when we first met at Woodstock Palace.

I paused on the threshold, my heart aching for her. This past year could not have been easy for Elizabeth, still living in fear of arrest—for everyone knew her acceptance of the Catholic faith was no more real than Archbishop Cranmer's had been, and he had been burnt for heresy—yet aware that at any moment a horseman might arrive and proclaim her Queen of England.

The princess turned, seeing me. "Meg, come in and close the door. I do not wish to be overheard."

There was a strange light in her face, and she was clutching the miniature portrait of Robert Dudley to her chest.

"When Mistress Goodwife was here, she offered to read my future," she said softly, "and I refused. The last time you scried for me, Meg, we misread the signs, and I thought it best not to meddle with the unknown again. But I have changed my mind."

"You wish me to tell the future for you, my lady?"

"Can you?"

I nodded. "I can try. There are a few things I need though. In my chamber."

"Fetch them," Elizabeth said abruptly. "And hurry. It must be done now, I feel. There is a great urgency in my heart."

I fetched what was required and cast the circle around us, all the time trying to calm my thudding heart. To tell the future of royalty was both dangerous and exciting. But I wanted to test my skill. And Gilly Goodwife had warned me not to squander my talent on petty spells. This was an opportunity to prove myself not only to the princess but also to myself.

Within the protection of the circle, the princess sank to her knees in a billow of green silk. The shutters had been closed and the door bolted against intruders. At my nod, the Lady Elizabeth kindled the black candle and spoke a few words in Latin over the flame. I turned to prepare the spell, suddenly light-headed, already half in a trance.

"What's that?" Elizabeth gasped when I unwrapped the mandragora root. "A homunculus?" She meant a tiny man.

"No, it is a mandrake root. Also called a mandragora. It belonged to my mother, and now is mine. Very dangerous, my lady, and to be handled with extreme care." Respectfully I bowed my head to the dark cloven root, then placed it before me in the circle. My voice sank to a whisper. "Powerful, especially when used in divination." Though indeed the mandrake root did resemble a shrivelled old man, I thought, having two legs where it was cloven and strange bulging knots for eyes and a mouth. It was a mystery of the Orient how these roots grew, and I had no wish to delve too deeply into how my mother had procured one, but under Richard's guidance I had lightly washed and dried the root, then wrapped it in a swathe of coarse black silk, keeping it concealed in my mother's chest.

Last time I had scried for the princess, I had used a black mirror. I no longer possessed one, for it had become cracked and useless for divination, so intended to use the mandragora instead, asking the man-root questions and letting it whisper the answers to me.

Gilly Goodwife had inspected the contents of my mother's chest before leaving Hatfield, and told me many useful things about how each item could be used in spellwork, including the mandrake root. I only wished she could have stayed longer. But the witch had clearly felt uncomfortable at Hatfield, perhaps because of the silent disapproval of the princess and her ladies—and their very real fears. One witch was the limit in Elizabeth's household. She had no wish to draw further attention to her household by allowing another to stay.

"What do you wish to know, my lady?"

"Will I ever marry?" she asked first, then frowned. "Will I rule England? And who will rule with me? I must know these things."

I bent over the mandrake root and breathed in the smoke from the black candle, letting it fill my senses. Chanting softly beneath my breath, I closed my eyes and touched my forehead to the root, as Gilly had described.

"Mandragora Man, Mandragora Man," I whispered, "spirit of darkness, sacred man of the soil, hear me, I beg you. By the red wine in which I bathed you, and the good earth in which you were nurtured, give me your wisdom. Will the Lady Elizabeth rule England?"

I waited, listening. The moments dragged by and I heard the princess draw in a harsh breath beside me, rocking to and fro, impatient to know her fate.

Then I heard the tiniest voice, like the breeze stirring a harp.

"*Yes…*"

I stared up at the princess, my heart thumping. "Yes," I gasped. "Yes, you will rule."

She put a hand to her mouth, shuddering. "And my husband? Ask him that too. Who will be my husband?"

I lowered my head back to the cloven mandrake, feeling a definite shock run through me as skin met root. My whole body was trembling now as the magick took hold of me, filling the room with strange power.

"Mandragora Man, Mandragora Man," I whispered again, "sacred spirit of the earth, what man will be the Lady Elizabeth's husband?"

The wait was awful this time. My neck was aching, my eyes itching and streaming as though I had touched onion to them.

After a long space, the root replied hoarsely, "*No man.*"

I jerked my head away, meeting the princess's wide gaze. "No man, he said. No man."

"Does that mean I will never marry? Is that what the spirit is saying? Or that I will die before I can marry?" Her face was hard.

"You must ask again, Meg. Say the answer was not clear, that we need him to tell us more plainly."

I swallowed, my fingernails pressing deep into my palms, for I was frightened, though I did not understand why. But this was dark magick, easily more powerful than anything Marcus Dent could have thrown at me, coming directly out of the spirit world. And spirits, as I knew, were very tricky to control.

"I do not know what it means, my lady, but we may not ask the same question twice, it is not permitted by the spirits." I was almost hissing at her, I realized too late, desperate for it to be over. My forehead was burning where it had touched the mandrake root, and I could feel a strange dark presence in the room with us. I sensed that meant the mandragora root was growing restless, unwilling to be questioned any further.

"But you must ask again," she insisted.

"His answer was *no man*. That is all I can tell you, my lady."

The candle suddenly flickered and went out. We knelt in silence, both frozen and listening. First a hiss came from the mandragora root, then a low rumble rolled threateningly about in the darkness like thunder.

Elizabeth gave a sharp cry and stumbled to her feet. "I will not be frightened by that…*thing.*"

"No, my lady," I warned her, but it was too late. She had

run to the window in her panic and thrown open the shutters on glorious sunshine, instantly breaking the spell.

Dazzled by the flood of light, I fumbled for the black silk and threw it over the exposed mandragora man. Thanking him in a hurried whisper, I wrapped him up again, protecting his withered root against the sunlight.

Elizabeth was trembling, standing against the window, her face white as she looked back at me. "What did it mean, Meg?"

"I am not sure."

"Never to be married!" She bit her lip so hard I saw blood beading there, then she gasped, "Because the man I love is already married? Or because no man...*no man will have me?*" Her eyes grew horribly wide. "Will I become sick? Disfigured, perhaps?"

She put her hands to her cheeks, staring at me in sudden bewildered consternation, and I did not know how to answer her.

Then she shook her head, struggling to slow her breathing. "No, no, that is a foolish thought. Once I am Queen of England, dozens of princes will come to offer me marriage, even if I am hunchbacked and at death's door. The question remains, is it marriage that I want, or only the thing that prompts it?"

She let her arms fall back to her sides, her emotions under control again. "Tell me, Meg," she asked softly, "what would you choose in my place? Freedom or marriage? To rule or be ruled?"

"What would a man's answer be, my lady?"

"Ah, very good."

I wanted to comfort her. "Perhaps the divination was incorrect."

"Or you misheard the spirit." Her eyes flashed. "Or perhaps heard nothing at all, and told a lie to cover your own failure."

My temper flared at that unjust accusation, but I gritted my teeth. Would she have spoken like this to John Dee if the famous astrologer had drawn up a chart and told her she would never marry? I doubted it, I thought savagely. But then I was a woman and this was women's magick. Not the scientific findings of an educated man.

"My lady, I promise you that is not true. I repeated the whisperings of the mandragora root exactly as I heard them. I have no wish to distress you."

"Well, all this is superstitious nonsense. I may marry one day, I may not. To own the truth, I am in no hurry to choose a husband—there is still plenty of time." Crossing to the table, she took up the miniature portrait of Robert Dudley and stared at it broodingly. "Go, leave me alone," she insisted, her face in shadow. "And burn that dreadful thing. It is an abomination."

I hurried away, my senses still raw and prickling from the brutal way the spell had ended, and found Richard skulking in the corridor, a knowing smile on his face.

"So the princess did not warm to the answers you gave her? No surprise there. It can be a double-edged sword, divination." Richard caught my arm as I tried to pass him without replying. "Don't burn it, Meg."

"I am not a fool," I replied, and shook my arm loose. "Besides, her temper will soon cool. She is only angry because she hoped to hear the name Robert Dudley."

The weather the next day was just as fine, a rising mist just after dawn, then a delicious balmy heat that made it hard to force myself into my heavy-skirted gown and woollen stockings. Since we had agreed to make no push to rescue Cecilie until the next full moon, after the ritual of prayers followed by breakfast we wandered out into the gardens instead, Alejandro playing the lute for us while I read my mother's grimoire out of sight of the hall windows and William played chess with

Alice. Richard hovered about on the edge of this hive of activity, ostensibly looking for insects to use as fish bait down in the pond, though several times I caught him looking at me with some dark intent in his eyes.

We were all as bad as each other, I thought achingly: Alejandro unable to let go of his love for me, me unable to make a clean break with *him,* and Richard following us silently about, burning inside for what he could never have.

Though in truth, I had found myself growing closer to the conjuror's apprentice this summer. Richard, at least, had no problem with who I was. And blunt straightforwardness was fast becoming a quality I prized.

Suddenly Richard gave a warning shout, pointing away to the road south. We all turned to look, and my heart stuttered at the sight of a dust cloud just visible above the treeline. As the dust cloud grew closer the sound of horses could be heard too, undoubtedly heading our way.

Alice stared, shielding her eyes. "What is it?"

"Horsemen, and a fair number of them by the sound of it," I said, suddenly afraid that news of my battle against Marcus had somehow reached the court.

Yet how could it have done?

I stood up, telling myself not to be so stupid. Simply because there were so many horsemen, it need not be a message from the Queen.

"Whoever it is, we had best go inside. Her ladyship will wish to prepare herself for their arrival."

But as we watched, the first outrider cleared the trees and turned down the track towards the house. The rider was in dark livery, carrying a white-and-gold pennant, and behind him rode half a dozen men, dressed with equal sobriety, with one man at the centre of the pack, richly cloaked and capped like a noble courtier.

"Goodness," Alice said blankly.

It was a deputation from the court, without any doubt.

I lifted my skirts and ran back to the house without waiting to see if the others were following, and met the Lady Elizabeth hurrying downstairs, her ladies tripping behind her, all three women breathless and unsure of themselves.

The princess stopped on the stairs, looking down at me, a flush in her cheeks. "Meg, who is it? Could you see?"

"Half a dozen horsemen, my lady. From their livery and the gold pennant they carry, I would say they come from the Queen."

Elizabeth made a tiny strangled noise under her breath. Kat hurried to her side at once, murmuring in her ear, her voice low and soothing.

"Yes, yes, you are right," Elizabeth whispered to Kat, then raised her chin with an effort.

Coming into the hall, she swept to the high-backed chair beside the hearth and seated herself there, arranging her full skirts to best advantage, careful to hide her scuffed slippers from sight, for she had no money for new shoes.

The others had trailed in behind me, and now stood about the hall, staring at each other nervously.

"Blanche, pass me the prayer book. I shall read aloud from the psalms." She glanced at the rest of us, then spoke briskly, "Meg, sit with Alice and attend to your embroidery. Blanche, take up the lute and play a few chords. Kat, you will remain with me."

"Of course, my lady," Kat agreed, and clicked her fingers at the rest of us so that we scurried into position.

Richard, having been given no task to perform, stood at the foot of the stairs with his arms folded, his gaze on the door. I was not fooled by his apparent nonchalance. His eyes glittered and his body was tense. Then I remembered that he had seen John Dee arrested once, for illegally drawing up the Queen's horoscope; no doubt he feared these men had come to take the princess to the Tower.

I was a little afraid of that myself.

Alejandro had disappeared upstairs, perhaps to change into his doublet and fetch his sword, for he had been wearing a simple white robe in the garden. If fighting were required, I knew he would prefer not to be wearing priestly garb.

Although unschooled in the instrument, Blanche took up his abandoned lute with trembling fingers and managed to strum a few awkward chords before there was a hammering at the door. She faltered and stared at the Lady Elizabeth, then at the door.

"*Veni!*" the princess called clearly in Latin, inviting the visitors to come in.

The door was thrown open and sunlight poured into the hall. A man stood on the threshold, booted and cloaked, his gaze flashing about the room at each one of us before he ducked his head to enter the house. He was tall, dark eyes gleaming in an olive-skinned face, and his bow to the princess was exaggerated to the point of insolence.

Miguel de Pero.

My hands clenched into fists as he came forward into the Great Hall, my nails digging into my palms at the very sight of him. I was trembling and felt as though my blood had turned to ice-water in my veins.

"My lady." The Chief Inquisitor addressed the princess smoothly, then straightened without waiting for her permission, replacing his black velvet skullcap.

There was an ironic smile on his face, for he was no doubt aware how much he was hated by our small company at Hatfield—and how little we could do to prevent his intrusion here.

"Pray forgive my unexpected arrival. I would have sent ahead to allow you to prepare for my visit, but alas, the urgency of my mission would not allow for any warning."

The Lady Elizabeth did not move, but closed the prayer book she had been pretending to read. "Sir?"

Alice nudged me to keep sewing, and I realized that I had been staring at the Spaniard like a madwoman. I ground my teeth and slowly set three crooked scarlet stitches into a country scene composed only of soft greens and browns. It was hard to sit there and pretend disinterest while he explained his errand.

Then I remembered who was *not* here. Alejandro.

Staring at the stairs in sudden apprehension, I gripped the edge of the embroidery frame, wondering whether Alejandro knew who had arrived. Richard caught my eye, and with some difficulty I forced myself to relax. It would not do to give away my vulnerability to this man.

De Pero's smile showed his appreciation of the princess's icy dislike. "I bring you most cordial greetings from Her Royal Majesty, Queen Mary of England, and humbly beg a private audience with your ladyship at your earliest convenience."

Elizabeth glanced at Kat Ashley, but said nothing.

Alice tugged at my sleeve, her whisper terrified. "Wh-what does that mean?"

"It means he wants to speak to her alone," I replied shortly, and bit my embroidery thread in two, setting aside the work as the Lady Elizabeth waved us all to leave her.

Alice and I rose from our bench, ready to follow the other women from the hall.

"And if Señor de Castillo could also join us?" he added sharply.

My hand flailed in shock at this unexpected request, and I knocked the embroidery frame to the floor. It clattered nois-

ily to the floor, and de Pero's head swung round at the sound,
dark eyes narrowing as he recognized me, his lips thinning,
his aquiline nose flaring.

He knew.

He knew about me and Alejandro. About my magick.
About our secret betrothal. I doubted though that he knew
it was over between us. For not even the others here at Hatfield knew that for sure.

Under the Spaniard's cold stare, I experienced a terror such
as I had never known before.

No threat to my own life had ever felt so acute as the fear
that burned through me as I saw into the Inquisitor's heart
and knew that he had come here for Alejandro.

MEG LYTTON IS A WITCH

I paced my chamber, pausing before the window to stare down at the men waiting beside their horses outside. Then I returned aimlessly to the book beside my bed.

My mother's grimoire.

I turned a few pages restlessly, not reading the words but viewing them in a daze. I was alone with Richard, and glad of his company. Kat and Blanche had scurried anxiously away to talk when we were all sent upstairs, and Alice had sidled into William's room, leaving me and Richard alone on the upstairs landing.

From the Great Hall we could hear the rumble of male voices, and occasionally her ladyship interrupting. Richard had been lying on my bed, watching me with expressionless eyes as I paced back and forth.

But when I abruptly turned and made for the door, he leaped up to stop me.

"No," Richard insisted, pinning my arms effortlessly to my

sides when I struggled. "Don't be a fool, Meg. You are not wanted down there. Let this play out."

"They won't see me. I can make myself invisible."

Richard cocked his head to one side, regarding me steadily.

"Eavesdroppers hear no good of themselves. Besides, I know you. You won't be able to enter a room unseen and not make your presence felt. A whisper in de Pero's ear, a soft breath across Alejandro's cheek, perhaps rustling a few pages of a book…"

I pushed him away. "Don't be ridiculous."

"I'm perfectly serious. You have to let this happen, Meg. It's for the best, you will see that in time."

"How is it for the best?"

"This man, this Spanish Inquisitor…he's come to take Alejandro away, hasn't he?"

Nausea gripped me as he voiced the very fear I had been trying to avoid looking at, though it had been mocking me all the time from the corner. This damn heat. I could not think, could not concentrate. Distractedly I dragged off my white cap and shoved a hand through my straggly fair hair. It needed taming, but I could not be bothered to find my comb. "We don't know that for sure."

"Yes, we do." Richard's face was hard, unyielding. His voice was like a knife, stabbing at my heart. "Alejandro has been playing a dangerous game with you, but it ends today. I saw de Pero's face, the way he looked at you. He has come to finish it. Alejandro does not belong here."

"He does not belong in one of their stinking prisons either."

Richard gave a disdainful laugh. "They won't put your pet Spaniard in prison."

I glared at him. "You have no idea what they may know. About us. About *me*."

"Nor do you," he said flatly. "But the fact remains, Alejandro is a nobleman. And an only son now his brother is dead, so he must be the heir to his father's estate, yes? Unless that priest down there has sworn testimony that Alejandro has been making midnight sacrifices to the Devil, he won't dare touch him. Not over this."

"*This?* You mean, over me?" I felt as though he had hit me.

"Listen, Alejandro is not the right man for you."

"You think I don't know that?"

Richard drew me close and whispered urgently in my ear, "It's not just that you're a witch and a heretic. Those are faults that can be fixed if a man wants a woman badly enough. Look at King Henry, the lengths he went to when it came to his marriage bed. No, the real problem for Alejandro is that you're a *commoner*. Not good enough for his proud Spanish bloodline. His family would never allow the match. So give it up before you get too badly hurt. Let the priest take him back to court."

I threw back my head, meeting his gaze. "What, so you can try your luck with me instead?"

Richard's smile was grim. "Luck. Ah yes, my old enemy. I would need more than luck with you, Meg Lytton."

"Well, you're wrong, anyway. It doesn't matter that I'm a commoner."

"Why's that?"

"Because I'm no longer betrothed to Alejandro." I swallowed, not looking at him. "We are not to be wed."

His head turned and he looked down into my face. "Oh, Meg, I'm sorry," Richard said huskily, then carefully stroked the errant hair out of my eyes. "No, I'm not sorry. You know how I feel about you."

I smiled bitterly. "I would have done better falling in love with you, that's for sure."

His breath seemed to catch in his throat, dark eyes narrowing on my face. "You mean that?"

I nodded, too hurt and confused by my feelings and the general horror of what was happening to see clearly what was going on between us.

"If I married Alejandro, he would expect me to give up my power. To be simply his wife." I shook my head. "I could never...well, you know."

"Is the man a fool?" Richard demanded, staring at me through narrowed eyes. "No, don't answer that. Just hear me out. If you were mine, Meg, I would never ask you to give up magick. You are a witch, and a powerful one. That is why you are special, but he can't see that. He wants to take you away from magick, make you...I don't know, *better*. Cure you with marriage." His mouth tightened. "I wish you had fallen in love with me instead. Then I would not be crawling about the place like a dog that's been whipped, I can assure you. I'd be spending my time far more pleasurably...."

Richard bent and kissed me, his mouth hard, punishing, almost angry. It felt more like hate than love, so topsy-turvy I could not begin to understand it. But for some reason my body responded, even if my heart was in shreds, and I did not push him away. Perhaps something in me craved the shock of this kind of desire, so very different from the way Alejandro kissed me. His hand tangled in my hair, dragging me closer. Slowly his mouth softened, persuading me, cajoling. Ah yes, he knew how to kiss.

I did not want to feel anything. In fact, I did not want to feel anything about a man ever again.

But I liked Richard. He had not been born into wealth and privilege like Alejandro but had fought for every scrap as a child. His father had been a brute and a drunkard, almost killing him on one occasion; Richard had only survived by a miracle. Now he could only show his interest by being unkind.

By attacking rather than protecting. By kissing me roughly instead of with love.

Something in me sympathized with his wounds. My life had been easy compared to his, but I too had suffered. Heat flickered inside me, and I tugged on his dark hair, drawing him nearer, kissing him back. Richard groaned in the back of his throat, then his body shifted, his knee pushing against my skirts, and suddenly we were kissing in earnest. Our bodies pressed together as Richard cupped my face in his hands, kissing me hungrily, his eyes closed.

I shivered, bewildered by my feelings, and Richard stepped carefully back, his hands dropping away, palms open, indicating that I was free to choose.

"I will always be here if you need me," he said huskily. "Just remember that."

Raking my fingers through dishevelled hair, I moved to the window, trying to get myself back under control. What was wrong with me? I was in love with Alejandro. Yes, all that is finished, I reminded myself bitterly. What difference does it make?

The men were mounting again below. I stared, relief sweeping through me as I heard their shouts and saw the last of their horses being led out from the stables where they had been fed and watered.

"What is it?" Richard asked, coming up behind me.

"I think they're leaving."

Someone knocked at my door, which was not closed. Alice looked round it at me, her eyes frightened. "The Lady Elizabeth says you are to come down to the hall at once. And do you know that Alejandro is packing?"

"*What?*"

The whole world seemed to stop. My lungs would not seem to fill, my chest impossibly tight. Richard looked at me sharply, but I pushed past him and stumbled along the narrow landing to the room William shared with Alejandro and Richard. Sure enough Alejandro was there, throwing his possessions into a dusty bag, his expression set and determined.

My brother had been leaning against the wall, talking quietly to Alejandro. He straightened as I came into the room, assessed the look on my face, then slipped past me.

"I'll be outside if you want me," William murmured, and pulled the door closed behind him.

Alejandro had turned, his dark eyes registering a blow as he saw me. Then he turned back to his packing, but moving more slowly, carefully.

"Is it true?" I demanded, my throat raw with pain. "Are you leaving with de Pero?"

"If you already know, why did you come to my room? Are you trying to make us look like lovers?"

I reeled at the harshness of his reply. He could not have shocked me more if he had struck me.

"Alejandro, I don't understand. I know I refused your offer of marriage, but this... What did Señor de Pero say to make you leave Hatfield?" My gaze narrowed on the back of his dark head. "Has he threatened you? I know a spell that could—"

"No spells!"

He sounded as though he hated me. Suddenly dizzy, I put out a hand, supporting myself against the wall. My palms were clammy and my heart was thudding violently.

"Señor de Pero reminded me where my true loyalties lie, that is all," he said, turning to face me at last.

I could not believe how remote Alejandro looked, head bent, not meeting my eyes, his face tight with some suppressed emotion.

"Alejandro..."

I took a faltering step towards him, then stopped when he

raised his head and fixed me with a desolate look. He did not speak, but I knew he did not want me to touch him. He did not even want me in the room with him.

My stomach churned as I saw the rejection in his face and the hard lines of his body.

"I was born under the planet Mars," I whispered, trying to explain myself, hoping it was not too late to make amends. "I cannot speak without fighting. I lose my temper easily, I make mistakes, I...I cannot bear to be told what to do. Especially by a man. But none of that means I do not have feelings for you, Alejandro, even if I know we can never marry."

He flinched.

Taking that as a good sign, I rushed on, desperate now. "If I have driven you away with my reckless behaviour, Alejandro, I beg you to forgive me and stay."

His voice was low and ragged. "Do not lower yourself by begging. I am leaving Hatfield. There is nothing more to say. You should go back to your room. Let me finish here. De Pero awaits me below and he is not a patient man."

The floor seemed to tilt beneath my feet.

"Go, get out, do you hear me?" he repeated harshly. "It's over."

"But I thought we were friends." My words sounded so hollow.

"A childish dream. We were both mad if we thought such a friendship could be possible in a world like this. There is one absolute good and one absolute evil, and we both know on which side of that line *you* stand." His eyes met mine, scorching me with dark fire.

"Take my advice. Burn your spell book and go home to your father. Marry an Englishman. Marry Richard and raise a family. The path you are on can only lead to damnation."

Abruptly he returned to his packing. "You can start by leaving my room."

My heart was beating sickly, as though it might stop at any moment. Without another word, I stumbled out onto the landing to find Alice and William locked in each other's arms, Richard nowhere to be seen.

The pair sprang apart guilty as I closed the door behind me, but I had nothing to say to them. I needed to be alone, to curl up in a ball and weep until my eyes were raw.

Alice said uneasily, "The Lady Elizabeth wishes to see you, do not forget."

"Yes, in a minute."

I stopped, my back to them, and rubbed a hand across my wet face. I did not want to speak to anyone. But I could not defy my mistress. I had already lost Alejandro's friendship. I could not lose my position in the Lady Elizabeth's household too.

Unless that was why she wanted to speak with me, to tell me that I was dismissed. I could imagine the tales Miguel de Pero must have spun about me while they were talking below.

What did it matter what Elizabeth said to me? In service or dismissed, here or at home, from now on I would be for ever empty.

My head in a fog, I descended to the Great Hall and found the Lady Elizabeth standing in front of the fire, her face pale but composed, chin raised in what I had come to recognize as a gesture of defiance. Miguel de Pero was seated at the table, a hurried meal having been set before him by a tight-lipped Bessie. He was pushing dripping meat into his mouth, speared on the point of his dagger, his sharp gaze examining the hall while he chewed as though hoping to spot some incriminating detail.

When he saw me, the Spaniard finished his mouthful and dragged his sleeve across his wet mouth, gesturing me forward.

"Mistress Lytton," he said with heavy irony, "I was surprised to find you still in the Lady Elizabeth's household. But I had been told the Queen's sister has a soft heart. Now I see it is true. For most ladies of her elevated rank would have dismissed a suspected witch from her employ as soon as any whisper against her was heard, rather than have her good name mired by such a creature."

"Suspected," the Lady Elizabeth reminded him coldly. "Not proven."

"But even suspicion may leave its mark, madam. And when the crime is witchcraft, an inquisitor cannot be too thorough in his examination." De Pero stabbed at his last slice of meat, then bent to devour it. He spoke with the food in his mouth, staring at me, gravy running down his bearded chin, his words muffled but still sinister.

"Come here, Meg Lytton." He pushed his empty platter away and held out both hands to me.

I had little choice, glancing at my mistress for permission, but to put my hands in his.

The Inquisitor turned my hands over, examining my palms, then my fingers. He paused over the discoloured fingernail, but did not mention our last meeting.

I shivered, remembering how he had chained me to a wall at Hampton Court Palace, then cruelly torn off one of my fingernails as he questioned me, his aim to prove that Elizabeth was in some way implicated in the practice of witchcraft.

He had failed, of course, for I had denied everything. But that night had been one of the longest of my life.

"You wear no ring, Mistress Lytton?"

"As you see, *señor.*"

"Nor is there any mark to show that you have worn one in the past."

"*Señor?*"

The only people beyond this house who knew of my mother's ring were John Dee, the astrologer, and Marcus Dent. I had seen no indication during the *Aspicio*-spell that de Pero knew how deeply Marcus was involved in the black arts. And I knew Marcus could never implicate me or Elizabeth in witchcraft, under the terms of the spell with which I had bound him to eternal silence. Still, they were both clever men, and I could not entirely trust that Marcus had not found some way to circumvent my spell.

My suspicious gaze narrowed on his face, and at once he dropped my hands, sitting back.

"Her ladyship has assured me that no indiscretion could have occurred between members of her household, and therefore I do not talk in terms of punishment." He looked me up and down, his mouth tight, making it obvious that he did not believe a word Elizabeth had told him. "But I think it best to remove an inexperienced young novice from a source of temptation before he can be led into…sin."

He lingered over the final word, his gaze insulting.

For a moment I indulged the image of Miguel de Pero running about the Great Hall on four trotters, oinking and with a curly tail sprouting from his vile hairy backside. Then I reminded myself of his men outside, armed and loyal to the Queen. I would endanger the princess and every member of her household by working magick so openly. I had just admitted to Alejandro that my temper was unsteady and my nature reckless. I might be born under Mars, but it was time to stop excusing myself and exercise some discipline.

"You will be unaware of this, but Alejandro's father has summoned young Alejandro back to Spain, and I have agreed to escort him back. We must leave today, for a ship already awaits us at Plymouth, ready to sail."

Plymouth.

A boat to Spain.

Alejandro was not just leaving Hatfield. He was leaving England and going home to Spain.

I had assumed that Alejandro had been recalled to court, that he would not be so very far away, and whatever had made him so cold to me upstairs could be fixed in time.

But Spain could not be fixed. Spain was an eternity away. Spain was for ever.

"I asked you once if you had any dealings with the Devil," de Pero remarked, getting to his feet. "Now I must ask you again, Meg Lytton, for it is my duty as Inquisitor to know the hidden truth of things. Are those who have suspected you of evil practices correct?"

"No, sir," I muttered.

"Look at me, girl! Are you a witch, and in thrall to the Devil?"

My hair had fallen forward to hide my face. I lifted my head now and stared at him. "No, sir," I repeated coldly.

"Señor," Elizabeth said with dangerous quietness, "I must ask you to seek permission of Her Majesty the Queen if you wish to interrogate my servants further. I am sure my sister would not have sent you here on such an unpleasant mission without first informing me in writing of your intent."

Miguel de Pero looked at her in silence, a muscle twitching in his cheek. Then he forced his thin lips into a smile. *"Muy bien,"* he murmured, and bowed. "Forgive me if I was too zealous, my lady. I am so used to finding guilt in those I question, it is sometimes hard to accept innocence. I beg your pardon for this intrusion." His head swung sharply as footsteps sounded on the stairs, and I thought there was a note of relief in his voice. "Ah, here is Señor de Castillo now. We shall be on our way at once, my lady, and trouble you no more."

Alejandro did not look at me as he descended the stairs. His beautiful dark eyes were shuttered, long eyelashes hiding their light, his face grim, the skin drawn taut over his cheekbones. It hurt to look on him for the last time, yet I was unable to drag my gaze away from his face, feeding my hunger, memorizing every graceful line of his body before he disappeared from my life for good.

He was dressed for travelling, in his most sombre black doublet and hose, cloak thrown back to reveal the ornate Spanish sword belted about his waist. There was no sign of the silver crucifix that had always hung about his neck as long as I had known him.

My breath almost stopped. Yes, I could see the Spanish nobleman in him now. It was quite plain to me, looking at Alejandro de Castillo, that he was high-born, and far above a commoner like me.

Then Alejandro's head turned, seeking me out, and our eyes met at last. I took a step back, physically recoiling from what I saw there. There was a darkness in his face that I had never seen before, his whole being possessed by shadow. Devoured by it, almost.

Still Alejandro did not speak to me. "My lady Elizabeth," he murmured, and sank onto one knee before the princess.

She gave him her slender white-fingered hand to kiss, and his dark head bent over it.

"Forgive me for taking my leave so abruptly, my lady," he said. "But my father demands that I return home to Spain."

"And one must always bow to a father's demands," Elizabeth murmured.

I felt there was a note of irony behind her words. But then

her father had been King Henry, and a greater tyrant I could not envisage.

"Will you return to us in due course, *señor?*" the princess asked, gesturing him to rise.

Alejandro stood, his face still averted from me. "I fear that will prove impossible, my lady."

She frowned, looking from him to me in obvious surprise. Elizabeth had never condoned our relationship, nor approved of it. She had even tried to prevent us from becoming too close under her roof, such was her sense of duty to her women. But she was no doubt taken aback by this sudden departure.

"Must your business in Spain take so long to conclude?"

"Indeed it must, my lady." De Pero stepped forward before Alejandro could answer, dropping a hand on his shoulder as though to congratulate him. "Young de Castillo here has finally agreed to take up his place at the Spanish court by his father's side. Before that though, Alejandro is to return home for his marriage. It was all arranged months ago."

Marriage? Arranged months ago?

My heart withered and died.

De Pero's laugh was an obscene jeering that echoed about the hall; it made me feel sick.

"I am quite envious of de Castillo's luck in procuring her father's agreement to this union," he added. "For I have seen the young lady myself, back in Spain, and she is most beautiful. She will make Alejandro an excellent wife."

I stared at Alejandro's averted profile, willing him to deny this lie, to give me a sign that his return to Spain was in some way being forced upon him.

But he made no sign, and his head did not turn.

For the next few minutes, as Alejandro courteously took his leave of the Lady Elizabeth and her household, embracing William and a tearful Alice, even inconceivably shaking hands with Richard, I stood motionless and unspeaking in the Great Hall, my body numb, my face cold.

At last it was my turn.

"Meg," he began hoarsely, then stopped, staring at me as though he had forgotten how to say goodbye.

A terrible silence descended between us, where I could hear nothing but the painful lurch of my heart and the rasp of my own breath. I said nothing, looking at a point on his black doublet mid-way between his chest and his chin, my heart frozen inside the icy hell that had been building around it since de Pero's arrival.

What was there to say, after all?

Alejandro suddenly bowed his dark head, not looking at me again, his farewell a husky "Go with God."

Then he was gone, bustled away to the waiting horsemen by Miguel de Pero, whose look told me he knew perfectly well what agonies I was suffering.

For several days after Alejandro had left, I wanted nothing more than to die. I became a coward. I begged Alice to tell the princess I was sick. I spent all my waking hours alone in the dark, curled up in my nightgown, refusing food, my hair oily and unkempt, my body shivering.

At last the Lady Elizabeth came to see me, dismissing Alice and her women to speak with me alone.

"Who are you?" she demanded coldly.

I sat up weakly, combing down my hair with my fingers. "Forgive me, my lady. I do not understand."

"Your name, girl?"

"M-Meg Lytton," I stammered, frowning.

"Good. Now do not forget it again." She lowered her voice. "The full moon approaches. This woman Dent holds against her will. Is she indeed a seeress?"

"So Mistress Goodwife said."

I saw a restless excitement in her face. I had seen it there before, and always it presaged danger.

"I may be Queen of England one day," she said softly, "and with a witch by my side, I could reign over this turbulent land for many years in peace. Yes, there would be danger in such an association, but how much stronger would I be with both a witch and a seer in my household?

"But if a woman wants power, Meg," she continued, "there can be no place in her heart for this weakness we call love. Not in a world where man still holds sway." Her eyes darkened. "My sister may be Queen, but she has given her power away to her husband, Philip. By marrying, she weakened herself. To yield to a man, to become obedient to him, a mere possession…that is a weakness I cannot afford, not if I would be Queen, and stay Queen."

There was bitter hurt in her voice as she added, "Besides, Robert is already married and can never be mine. Do not think this decision has not given me many nights of pain and anguish. But if I am to be Queen, and a Queen worthy of this great land of ours, I must play by rules so hard they would break another woman's heart."

Gently she touched my shoulder, her gaze sympathetic. It struck me that she had looked at Alejandro in the same way when he knelt before her in the Great Hall, begging her forgiveness for leaving.

"Señor de Castillo has gone back to Spain. I know you and he still had an understanding, even though I asked you to sever that connection, and that his absence must be painful. But it is time to put away this long face and rise. Do what you were born to do, Meg. Unless you believe your case to be crueller than that of the seeress Marcus Dent holds captive," Elizabeth murmured, watching me, "and whose salvation may yet depend on you alone.

"Besides," she said, pausing at the door, "I have decided to ride with you to London. I have a plan. Now get up and wash yourself, girl. You look like a beggar maid."

After the princess had left my room, I lay in shocked silence for a while, thinking over what she had said.

Then I stumbled out of bed and jerked open the wooden shutters to let in the light. The room flooded with sunshine, seeming to mock my long misery. Dazzled, I poured a little chilly water from the pitcher into the wash bowl and splashed my tears away with it.

Meg Lytton, I told myself, staring down at my hands as I dipped them in the bowl and watched my reflection shiver. That is my name. That is who I am.

And Meg Lytton is a witch.

Part THREE

LONDON

THE LADY ELIZABETH'S PLAN

When the Lady Elizabeth made up her mind to do a thing, it was done swiftly and with great style. No moonlit ride cross-country, as we had planned amongst ourselves, but a bold cavalcade of horses leaving Hatfield House in full daylight, waved off by Kat Ashley and the servants, with sturdy-looking outriders hired from neighbouring villages, and William and Richard fully armed in case of attack by highway robbers. Elizabeth brought both Blanche and Alice along to attend her, and insisted the ladies all rode side-saddle, which slowed our pace. But it was still early on our second day of riding when we reached the outskirts of London, having stopped at a roadside inn the night before.

Elizabeth's plan was to arrive unannounced at the Palace of Whitehall, where she believed the Queen to be in residence. There she would throw herself on her sister's mercy, claiming an illness at Hatfield that had forced her to flee the country, bringing almost all her household with her.

It was a bold plan, and terrifying. For if the Queen proved

to be angry with her sister for arriving without warning, no one could safely predict what would happen next.

"Mary suggested in her letter that I visit her this autumn for a state occasion," Elizabeth had insisted, trying to reassure Blanche, who was convinced we would end our journey in the Tower of London.

"Clearly my sister hopes for another reconciliation after our bitter parting last year. Her Majesty may be surprised to see me earlier than invited, but when she hears of my sorrows, I am sure we will be made welcome. All of us."

The next part of her plan was less clear. But I soon discovered it involved the princess being able to spend time with Master Robert Dudley. Who just happened to be back at court again. Without his wife.

I eyed her speculatively when this fact was revealed, but Elizabeth did not even blush.

"I have been thinking of your strange divination, Meg, the words the mandragora man whispered in your ear. That I would marry *no man*." She raised her frank eyes to mine. "If virginity will keep England in my hands, I am at peace with my destiny. But that does not mean I must never see Robert Dudley again, nor speak with that gentleman, nor...nor let him kiss my hand. His loyalty may yet prove useful. To me, and to England."

I said nothing, for it was not for me to interpret the obscure whisperings of the mandragora root.

"It is arranged that once I am settled at my sister's palace, we will all meet with John Dee in London at a discreet lodging place owned by one of his friends," Elizabeth continued briskly, seemingly relieved that I had not challenged her decision—as though I would ever dare. "There we shall discuss how best to remove the seeress from her prison."

Entering the narrow gates of the city of London was an

unsettling experience. Strangers jostled us in the sunlit streets around the gate, frightening the horses, women and children selling their wares in shrill voices, men staring after us as though they had never seen a retinue so fine before, beggars kneeling in the dirt or leaning against the filthy walls. An open ditch ran down one of the larger streets, stinking like a midden, clouds of tiny black flies dancing above it.

I covered my mouth and nose with my mantle, and rode past as swiftly as I could, given the unrelenting crowds and traffic of the city.

We came to a crossroads marked with a broad-trunked oak, mossed with age, its leafy crown providing shade for the beggars beneath, some of them terribly deformed and crying out for bread. Horrified, I fumbled at my pouch and tossed a few coins to the beggars as we waited for a cart to clear the crossroads.

After there we turned onto a narrow cobbled street, heading downhill towards the river. I was weary by the time we reached the Palace of Whitehall, standing flagged and turreted along the river bank, with towering walls that blocked out the sun as our horses clattered through the cobbled and well-guarded entrance.

I was a little apprehensive as the pikes flashed down to block our way. But then the captain of the guard recognized the princess, and a shout went up among his men.

The captain dropped to one knee on the cobbles and bent his helmeted head. Elizabeth, gracious and smiling, bid him rise and send for an escort, for she had come to visit the Queen, her sister.

A moment later, everyone in the narrow courtyard seemed to be kneeling, and cheers echoed about the high walls as we rode slowly forward.

"Long live the Lady Elizabeth!" one man shouted, and was soon joined by other voices.

A servingwoman near the palace entrance crossed herself, gazing up with admiration at Elizabeth's pale face and long, unbound hair, glinting reddish-gold in the sunlight. "May God bless you, Princess Elizabeth!" she called out, and was rewarded with a smile.

The warmth in their voices reassured me that, even if her sister was unhappy to see Elizabeth arriving at court uninvited, she could hardly send her away again without incurring the wrath of her people. For it was clear that they loved Elizabeth. No doubt beside the dark-featured, often miserable Catholic Queen who had married a Spaniard and brought the bonfires of the Inquisition to our shores, this young Tudor princess looked like an angel.

Inside the palace, her reception was less warm. The steward who led us, with a disapproving expression, towards chambers fit for a princess and her entourage, explained that there had been no warning of her visit, and therefore the bedchambers would not be ready for habitation for several hours. But we could wait in an antechamber while the Queen was informed of her arrival. Elizabeth, courteous as ever, thanked the man as though he had handed her the keys to the palace itself, and said she would be content with whatever was available.

The antechamber turned out to be quite spacious and well-provided with comfortable seats, much to our relief, for we had ridden a long way. Soon after we were installed there, a whole team of impassive servants appeared through a side door, bearing generous trays of drinks and platters of both hot and cold food, and soon we were licking our fingers, enjoying a feast.

Elizabeth even went so far as to joke that she did not know why she had not come back to court before, when the hospitality was so good....

At that moment the steward returned. He opened the large double entrance doors and bowed, his face stiff when he found us all convulsed with laughter.

"If you would follow me, my lady, Her Majesty the Queen will be pleased to admit you to her royal presence," he announced coldly.

An awkward silence fell in the room.

Alice chewed on one of her fingernails, staring at the steward with wide eyes, and William slapped her hand.

With his back to the steward, Richard carefully tightened up the gold doorknob he had been unscrewing.

"Shall I come with you, my lady?" Blanche whispered, but Elizabeth shook her head.

"I will not need you, Blanche. Stay and see that the rest of my household is properly housed."

"Yes, my lady."

Cool, unhurried, Elizabeth cleaned her fingers in the water bowl provided, dried her hands carefully on a white damask napkin, then followed the steward from the room without a backward glance, her bearing erect.

"That's the last we'll see of her," William muttered.

Alice tutted at him. "Hush, bad boy."

"Mistress Alice, you *like* me bad…." he teased.

Blanche's eyes widened in horror and she turned at once, separating the two and remonstrating with William for being coarse-tongued in the Queen's own palace.

I looked across at Richard, his doublet and hose stained with dust from the road, meeting his intent gaze. He smiled, winking at me over the absurdity of it all, and I suddenly wanted to rush over and embrace him. For still being there, for putting up with my moods, for not leaving…

But I did not, of course. It would not be fair on Richard, and would only serve to confuse my own heart further. For much as I found Richard clever and handsome and funny and as curiously dark-souled as I was, he was not—and never could be—Alejandro de Castillo.

The princess did not return to our apartments until quite late that evening, having dined with her sister and been "forgiven," she claimed, for her arrival when Queen Mary heard the totally untrue tale of a sickness in the village that had necessitated our speedy removal to court.

I thought Elizabeth looked quite white with fatigue when she came back, but her eyes were glowing with triumph.

"Things will begin to change now," she muttered as we dressed her for bed, smiling about herself at the gilt walls and lavish furnishings, our lodgings far more suited to royalty than the cramped rooms we had shared at Hampton Court. "They have to change."

The next day I saw Queen Mary again myself, and was shocked by the change in her since last summer. I remembered well the proud, slightly plump lady in the sweeping Spanish gowns who had presided over the court, handsome husband by her side, and even argued passionately with him before us all.

Now the Queen seemed almost shrunken, her skin grey, her thin mouth unsmiling as Elizabeth knelt before the throne, the rest of us kneeling several paces behind her.

"Rise," she said briefly, then looked away at the high windows of the Great Hall.

There was an air of desolation about the Queen now. I watched her with pity, for this was undoubtedly a woman who believed she had been abandoned by her husband.

"I have to meet with the Privy Council again today, but the palace gardens are open to you, sister, or you may ride out if the sun is not too hot. I remember that you enjoy riding. You have brought ladies with you? Yes, good. There are games to be played in the gardens at this season, croquet and bowls, and tonight you will join me in dining with the Spanish lords who have come with news from my husband's camp. He still disputes against the French. It goes on and on." Her gaze wandered back to us, frowning now. The Queen looked almost suspiciously at me, then back at her sister. "But where is Señor de Castillo? Was he not among your household?"

"He was recalled to Spain, Your Majesty," Elizabeth replied with quiet respect, her head bowed. "His father has arranged an advantageous marriage there for him, and he is to attend King Philip's court."

"Yes, I remember now. Señor de Pero came to me, seeking permission for his return to Spain. No doubt young de Castillo will make a good husband, he was always most loyal. Though one can never tell."

Queen Mary seemed to lose interest, though her words had been bitter, and when her eyes lighted on her sister, there was a curious hardness in them. She tapped her hand on the velvet arm of her throne, a huge jewel flashing on her finger.

Glancing surreptitiously about the Great Hall, I noticed a courtier all in black standing beneath a wall tapestry depicting an ancient hunting scene—a pack of hounds chasing a stag across a deep river, with horsemen watching from the bank. The man was watching us with equal fascination, arms folded across a broad chest, his dark gaze narrowed on the princess's bent head. I recognized him at once.

Robert Dudley.

He was lean and undeniably handsome, exactly as I had seen him in my *Aspicio* vision—except that his beard had since been trimmed to a neat strip down the centre of his chin.

"Well, I must speak with the Council," the Queen was saying. "It is a dreary business but necessary."

She rose and the courtiers fell back, all of us kneeling in a great whispering rustle of silk and taffeta as the Queen made her way heavily to the great doors, followed by her ladies-in-waiting.

The Lady Elizabeth stood and watched her sister leave the Great Hall, her dark eyes intent. As her head turned, I saw her gaze meet Robert Dudley's, then move on after only the tiniest hesitation. A moment later, she turned to us with complete composure as if she had not even noticed him in the crowd.

"Today I shall ride out and pay a visit to an old friend," she remarked calmly.

No one watching the princess would ever have guessed that there was love between those two, I thought, and marvelled at her control.

Once again, we attracted attention throughout the city, and the princess made sure she did, smiling and waving to those men and women who knelt at the roadside as she passed, stopping once to accept a posy of flowers from a young boy.

"She will make a good Queen," Alice whispered, nudging me as we rode together behind the princess.

"The Lady Elizabeth has the love of the common people," I agreed, watching the princess as we turned our horses down a narrow side street, and people stared from open casements above, their looks of astonishment and pleasure obvious even through the swathes of clothes hung out to dry between the houses. "She only has to wave, and they cheer."

Alice met my gaze. "I have not liked this breach between them. Sisters should be friends, not enemies. Perhaps things will become better now that her ladyship is reconciled with the Queen again."

"Perhaps," I said dubiously.

But Queen Mary had not looked pleased this morning, despite Elizabeth's claims of her warm welcome yesterday. But then, I suspected it would only take a little poison in a lonely woman's ear to turn her against her only surviving flesh and blood, especially when Elizabeth was so much younger and more beautiful.

The house where John Dee was lodging was narrow but tall, and its second storey overhung the front step to provide more room on the upper floor. As Richard dismounted, the door opened, and several servants hurried out to hold the princess's horse while William helped her dismount.

We were hurried inside while the horses were led away for water. Removing my riding gloves, I walked down the short dark corridor and found myself in an open courtyard within the house, watching the play of water in a sunlit fountain beside an ancient oak. A door flew open and I recognized John Dee, the Queen's astrologer, as he came out to greet us, his hair slightly unkempt, long robe brushing the dirt.

"My lady," he said, bowing low to the princess. "You honour me with this visit."

Elizabeth nodded, unsmiling. "Let us hope it does not reach the ears of the Queen. I am glad your friend was able to open his lodgings to us, but of course we cannot stay long. It would draw suspicion."

She looked about the place, a little breathless, her eyes darting into every corner. Her cheeks were unnaturally flushed. "Is Master Dudley here?"

"He awaits you within, my lady."

"Show me the way, sir, if you please. Time is short."

I watched as the princess followed John Dee through the doorway and into shadow. So she had indeed come here to visit Master Robert Dudley without the eyes of the court on her. I had been left unsure after the way she failed to acknowledge him in the Great Hall. But I had reckoned without her natural caution, for of course she would not wish anyone at court to suspect their relationship.

Yet did she mean to bid Robert Dudley a last farewell today, or encourage the courtier to pursue her in greater secrecy?

With the princess, it was never easy to guess her mind. Elizabeth had lived too long under the shadow of disgrace to risk being open about her motives or emotions.

The rest of us stood about the courtyard in silence, uncertain what to do. The place was beautiful though, the fountain splashing delightfully into its shadowy green pool beneath the oak, and it was no hardship to take our ease there a while.

"Whose house is this?" I asked Richard in a low voice.

He made a face. "No one of significance. A bookseller. A friend of a friend."

Cunning of Elizabeth, I thought, to choose a place to meet unconnected with either man. But our visit here was still doubly dangerous. The Queen would suspect at once that Elizabeth was plotting against her if she discovered we had come here to visit both Dee—a man already imprisoned once for his activities, however much he might have redeemed himself by agreeing to join Bishop Bonner's household—and Robert Dudley, the son of an executed traitor.

John Dee came back into the sunlit courtyard a few minutes later, a knowing smile on his lips. I guessed that Elizabeth's reunion with Master Dudley had been a passionate one, despite her protest that she had accepted her fate as a lifelong virgin.

I could hardly blame the princess for being in love though. Not when I had made so many foolish decisions myself in the name of that dangerous emotion.

"Richard!" John Dee embraced his apprentice with genuine pleasure, then looked at him closely. "Come inside. How was your journey? You look remarkably well. Is there a Venusian transit to your sun, perhaps?"

Richard grinned. "You could say that."

"You are welcome too, Meg Lytton." John Dee turned to me, smiling. His strange pale eyes searched my face, then he nodded as though I had spoken. "Did you get my message when you came to Bonner's table?"

I nodded, no longer surprised by the conjuror's amazing gift for understanding the dark arts. "*Invictus.*"

"Excellent. And now we meet again in corporeal form. I have calculated the stars' positions, and the auspices are good for what you intend. But if you wish to remove the seer unharmed, as Richard's letter suggested, then it must be tonight."

William, who had been talking head to head with Alice, turned to stare, shocked. "Tonight?"

"Mars in the eighth house inclines to an afflicted moon tonight, suggesting a plan to deceive and attack a hidden enemy, with Jupiter on the Medium Coeli granting you good hopes of success. But only between the hours of midnight and two in the morning." John Dee gestured us inside the house, supremely unmoved by our horrified expressions. "By dawn, the Great Corrector Saturn will have clashed with Mars the warrior, and then the struggle could be won by either party."

"Oh, pay no attention to Master Dee," a deep, amused voice said from the doorway. "My old tutor has been predicting rain these past three nights, and not a drop has fallen from the sky. Though he may have something there about the Great Corrector, for Saturn was a tutor like himself."

I looked up to see Master Robert Dudley himself, handsome, dark-haired, and dark-eyed. He must have ridden straight here from the court after this morning's audience with the Queen, I thought, then wondered what he and Elizabeth had been discussing in private. Not Marcus Dent, I suspected.

"See? The ground hereabouts is dry as a bone, save for that stinking ditch where they throw out the ordure." Robert Dudley smiled, bowing so courteously that it disarmed me.

I could not help smiling back, and saw Richard's frown. But Robert Dudley was very charming—I could perfectly understand Elizabeth's attraction to him.

"Come inside, friends," Robert Dudley said, and beckoned us into the house. "Let us sit round a table together and talk. Our time here must be of short duration, which I regret, so we will have to forget the civilities and speak swiftly. But for the Lady Elizabeth to stay too long under this roof would cause tongues to wag."

He smiled, leading us into a narrow room that contained nothing but a long table set about with chairs, at the head of which sat Elizabeth, head bent, already studying a document with apparent fascination. The princess looked a little flushed, and did not look up when Dudley bowed, murmuring, "My lady."

I wondered if they had argued. No doubt Robert Dudley was not a man who would easily give up the chase, however many times Elizabeth tried to throw him off the scent.

The table was covered with astrological charts, loose papers and books, many opened to a particular page as though for reference, an untidy jumble that reminded me of my father's study when I was a child.

"So," Robert Dudley prompted me softly, not looking at the princess again but leaning his arms on top of a large red leather-bound book, "do you have a plan, Meg Lytton?"

"We attack," I told him, instinctively seating myself at the far end of the table opposite Elizabeth. "I cause a diversion, cast a spell, anything to draw the witchfinder's men outside. Then we fight them, hopefully get inside his house and down into the cellar where he keeps his prisoners." I paused, a little disconcerted by the silence.

"And rescue Cecilie."

William was shaking his head. His tone was impatient. "Fire will distract them, Meg. Not a spell. Two of us could sneak in round the back, set a fire and smoke them out. A spell could too easily go wrong."

"And a fire won't go wrong?" Dee questioned him mildly.

Robert Dudley was looking down the length of the table at me, his dark eyes thoughtful. "And what of Marcus Dent?"

Everyone stopped talking and looked at me. My brother was frowning, Alice watching me with a scared expression, John Dee seemingly distracted by the play of sunlight reflected on the white plasterwork. Only Richard was smiling, arms folded as he leaned back in his chair, his confidence in me almost terrifying.

I looked down at the table, intimidated by so many eyes on me at once. There was an odd trail of salt on the table, left over from a recent meal by the look of it.

Slowly I drew a circle in the salt, then a cross within it, thinking out loud. "Marcus is not a fool. He is holding a powerful seer in that house and probably already knows we'll be paying him a visit. The house will be ringed with defensive spells, designed to keep us out and her in. And the only quick way past a protective-ring-spell is to be invited inside."

Robert Dudley glanced sideways at Elizabeth. Their eyes met and I saw her smile, my breath catching at the look in her eyes. They were in love. So deeply in love they might as well have been alone in the room for that instant. And my heart squeezed in pain for the princess. For it was a love that could only lead to unhappiness, the kind that lasts a lifetime.

"My lady?" he murmured.

Elizabeth nodded, then stood up, looking at each of us in turn.

"I have a suggestion for that. But I will need magickal help to make it work." She raised her brows at me. "Meg?"

19

FREAKISH HORRORS

The two men on guard at the front entrance to Marcus Dent's house had been leaning against the wall, one with his arms folded and eyes closed, the other talking to him conspiratorially.

Both men straightened and turned to stare at the sound of approaching horses, then glanced at each other uncertainly. The younger one disappeared into the house; the other lifted the flaming torch from the wall and held it high above his head, no doubt hoping to illuminate the street.

"Who goes there?" he called out, though it was clear from his frightened expression that he had a good idea who it was.

Just ahead of me, Richard dismounted. With Robert Dudley two steps behind him, he adjusted the long sword at his belt, then swaggered towards the man on the door.

"Have you no eyes in your head, sirrah?" Richard demanded, his tone arrogant. "Can you not see who this is?"

The man stared past him at me, still seated on my horse. His eyes widened slightly, then he crossed himself and stepped back into the doorway. "I see, yes. But what…what do you want?" he demanded, but there was no longer any threat in his voice. Only fear.

Behind him, several men emerged, pressing forwards in that dark narrow space, all staring towards me. They had come to see if it were true.

I sat straight-backed in the saddle, waiting as news of my arrival raced round the place, whispered at first, denied, confirmed, then called back inside the house, the younger man running back inside with a horrified exclamation.

"Fools!" A bearded man studied me through narrowed eyes, then spat over the threshold. "That is not the Queen."

"Then you are the fool, for it is Her Majesty," the younger man insisted in a hoarse whisper, pushing past this doubter to stare at me again. "I have seen that face before, and I tell you it is the Queen!"

A roar came from deep within the house—Marcus Dent, roused from whatever hellish pursuits went on in the grim bowels of that house. The men scattered, and suddenly he was there in the doorway, staring like all the rest.

My enemy.

"It will not work for long," Robert Dudley had warned me when Elizabeth first outlined her plan. "And the magick must be strong. Even in the dark, there is no chance you could pass for Her Majesty. Not without a spell."

I had glanced at John Dee for assurance. "Sir, you know my power. It is possible for me to disguise myself as Queen Mary, is it not? Though if Master Dudley were to come too, as himself, he would lend credence to our play."

"Too dangerous," Elizabeth had said at once.

"My lady, I do not think we need to fear reprisals," I had told her. "After this night I very much doubt any will dare name Master Dudley as one of this party. Nor any of us, indeed. For who would believe the Queen of England herself to be involved in such a venture? Marcus Dent will not wish his failure to be known by his allies, I am sure, and his men will keep quiet for fear of looking like fools."

Dee had raised his pale hand. "If Meg Lytton says she can do this, then she can do this. The girl has great power, skill beyond even Richard's reckoning. I have known her to speak with spirits and journey in the celestial realm with only the barest knowledge of such high magick." His strangely intent gaze moved about the table, then returned to my face. "Let me know how I can assist you, and it shall be done. For I am eager to speak to this seeress myself and discover if her powers are true."

Late in the afternoon, having returned to Dee's lodgings under cover of dark, I had adapted a complicated spell from my mother's grimoire—with the disconcerting message, "Beware, not long-lasting" scribbled in the margin—darkening my hair and altering my features to match what I remembered of the Queen's appearance.

Then I had knelt in the circle and worked the same magick on Richard, John Dee, and a small handful of Dudley's loyal servants who had been chosen to accompany us, turning them into a company of Spanish priests and guardsmen.

Once night had fallen, and Elizabeth was safely at dinner with the Queen at Whitehall—her alibi, in case the attack went badly—we had ridden across the city to Marcus Dent's house, following John Dee's directions.

Robert Dudley was alone unchanged, for even John Dee had asked to be disguised as a Spanish priest, lest word of this got back to his master, Bishop Bonner.

"But I am still myself," John Dee had exclaimed on seeing himself in a looking glass, in a tone of such severe disappointment that I had to smile.

"You have not changed. To us, we will look like ourselves, for we are outside the enchantment. But everyone else will see Queen Mary, her priests and attendants, and allow us entry into Marcus Dent's house without argument."

Now Marcus Dent himself came forward, almost to my horse, and I saw his face grow pale, staring up at me.

I said nothing but gazed down at him with my most icily regal expression, borrowed from the Lady Elizabeth along with the gown I was wearing.

Then he dropped, his head bowed in obeisance. Marcus Dent, down on his knees to me in the filth of the road. If I had not been so on edge, my gloved hands clutching tightly at the reins, I might almost have laughed.

"Your Majesty," he said hoarsely, not quite daring to lift his gaze to my face again. "Forgive my rough welcome. My name is Master Dent of Oxfordshire, and I am witchfinder to that shire. But perhaps you have been shown sundry of my letters, for I have always been careful to record all my successes and relay them to Your Majesty's council."

"Not all your successes, Master Dent," Richard said coldly, putting on a Spanish accent.

"*Señor?*"

"I have heard from Señor Miguel de Pero that you shelter a witch within your walls, Master Dent. If this is true, your life will be forfeit."

There was a deathly silence, and I wondered if Richard had gone too far, naming one of Marcus's own allies.

Robert's eyes met mine, his hand on his sword hilt. We had arranged a signal—the drawing of my hazel wand, secretly tucked up the sleeve of my gown—should a fight look inevitable.

But Marcus still seemed deceived by his unexpected visitors. "I hold this girl merely to question her about the Devil before she hangs, *señor*. That is my business as witchfinder and I do it well. How can it offend?"

"In that case, Master Dent, you will not object to allowing us entrance," I said coldly, "so we may satisfy ourselves of the veracity of your claims."

Now Marcus could smell the lie outright. I saw a flash in his eyes, hurriedly veiled as he glanced about at Dudley's men, all heavily armed.

"You wish to look inside my humble dwelling, Your Majesty?" My skin crawled under his dangerous gaze. "But if the *señor* here wishes to question this girl, he is welcome to enter. There is no need for you to sully your feet with the filth on these cobbles, Your Majesty."

We were outnumbered, I thought, and saw the same thought in Robert's face. At that moment John Dee, disguised as a Spanish priest, stumbled as he edged closer to the house. Marcus's head swung and he studied Dee for a long moment, narrow-eyed, his nostrils flaring.

I stiffened, suddenly fearful that he could see through the disguise. Marcus and John had been friends at university, after all. But there was no flicker of recognition in his eyes, only a growing fury at this humiliation.

"Bring her out!" a man shouted hoarsely from the crowd, which had been steadily growing since our arrival.

"Yes," another yelled from an upstairs window in one of the houses opposite. "Let's see this witch you've been keeping hidden in there."

Robert Dudley folded his arms and looked at Marcus, his brows raised. I felt my hands curl into fists, suddenly excited, the hairs rising on the back of my neck. This was even better than I could have hoped for. We might not even have to trick our way inside the house to rescue Cecilie.

Reluctantly Marcus nodded to his men. "Bring up the

witch. But keep her gagged and restrained. There are decent folk here."

I raised my brows. "You keep the girl in chains?"

"She is *dangerous*," Marcus said angrily, glancing about at the crowd. "Forgive my blunt speech, Your Majesty, but in my experience the need for such harsh measures when dealing with a witch is beyond a woman's comprehension."

The insult robbed me of breath. I almost drew my wand there and then. Then I saw Richard's tiny shake of the head and said nothing. But I glared back at Marcus with such venom that it seemed impossible he did not recognize Meg Lytton in the Queen before him.

A stir at the door to his house distracted me. I looked up and drew a sharp breath. In the same instant I saw Richard's instinctive recoil, and heard Dudley curse under his breath.

Cecilie was a tiny creature, thin-faced, her brown eyes huge, her hair so fair it was almost white and shorn close to the head—just as mine had been when Marcus Dent had me arraigned for witchcraft. She looked half a child, and her pale skin marked with cuts and bruises, exposed by the torn shift they had dressed her in.

The watching crowd rumbled with disgust and outrage as they strained closer for a better look at the "witch."

"For shame!" a woman called out roughly. "What have you done to that poor child?"

But one of the men shouted her down with a crude yell of "Look at the shameless witch! Hang her from the nearest tree before she can curse us!"

Then the calls drowned each other out, and a scuffle began somewhere behind us, the fight swiftly put down by our men at a signal from Dudley.

Richard came to me at once, grasping the horse's bridle. His hand was shaking. I could see a savage fury in his dark eyes. "Let us take the seer now," he hissed, "and cut this villain down where he stands."

"No, there are too many witnesses, we must be patient," I muttered, hoping Marcus could not hear us.

"I am sick of being patient," Richard spat out, and before I knew what he was about, Dee's apprentice had reached up and dragged the hazel wand from its hiding place in my sleeve.

Richard spun, a viciously sibilant curse on his lips, using the wand to flatten the two ruffians on either side of the seer.

Taken aback, Robert Dudley had frozen, his hand still on his sword hilt. This was madness. Half the street was watching. His eyes sought mine.

But it was too late to contain the fight.

I cried, "Take them!" and tried to slide down from the saddle, but failed miserably, landing on my knees, tangled up in the folds of my cloak.

Fighting to be free I heard a shout that terrified me, then the whole street was lit up by a flash of red light.

Richard was thrown violently backwards as though by a lightning strike, arms splayed wide, the wand falling from his open hand.

He did not move again.

Richard.

I felt sick, staring at him. It would be my fault if he was dead. I had sworn that I could do this and get us away before anyone was hurt. Instead, there was now a good chance none of us would make it out alive. Including Cecilie herself.

There was pure, terrifying chaos in the crowded alleyway. Women were screaming, men yelling for weapons or for the men of the Watch. And above it all, cool and clear, I could hear Robert Dudley issuing orders, no doubt well-used to the confusion of a battlefield.

I crawled on hands and knees towards Richard's still and

silent body, frantically whispering, "Don't be dead, Richard, please don't be dead."

Before I could reach him, Marcus Dent was there too, tall, gliding, wrapped in a shroud of black smoke, moving unseen—except by me, it seemed—through the chaos.

I twisted round, scrabbling for the fallen wand.

His booted foot came down hard on the back of my neck, shoving me into filth, closing my mouth on mud.

Ignoring my struggles, he reached down, seized my hand, and dragged off my riding glove.

The ring!

I thought he would snap my neck while I lay helpless and thrashing under his boot, the hazel wand lying just out of my reach in the mud. Had he seen it? He had wanted it before....

But he could not have noticed the wand. For he was after a greater prize. He drew my mother's ring from my finger, then let my hand fall back.

"Now I am invincible," he said unsteadily.

Groaning out my horror into foul-tasting mud, I clawed at the filth and wished it was his face. I could hear screams, a horse neighing in terror, and the clash of swords.

I had to get up.

"Be still," he commanded me in Latin, and my body obeyed against my will, paralysed by the spell.

"I warned you that you would suffer for your disobedience," he said. "Did you think I meant your death? Oh, no, this is far sweeter. Do you know why I allow you to live? Shall I tell you, Meg Lytton?" Marcus bent closer, his breath hot on my cheek. "Because you will suffer more as you watch me destroy your friends one by one. The apprentice is just the first. And at the end, when all the others are dead, I will come for you."

His boot was crushing the life out of me. I had failed.

The thought was terrifying. In my head I fought to be free,

reaching wildly for a spell, any spell that would allow me to strike Marcus down without speech or gesture.

"Surrender, miscreant, or die!"

Relief flooded me. Then despair. It was Robert Dudley, somewhere behind me, challenging the witchfinder. Cold steel against magick. I knew which would win. Again I struggled in vain against the binding-spell. Was it Robert's time to die now, while I lay like a landed fish in the mud?

Marcus gave a laugh and turned to face his challenger. The appalling pressure on my neck eased as his foot lifted, but now I could feel the pain. The sense of my failure was a deeper hurt though.

Paralysed, my body useless, my mind burning in torment, I listened to their brief scuffle at my back, then heard Dudley curse.

Suddenly there was an inky blackness all around me, muffling the sound of fighting, its tendrils spreading like smoke about the street. I heard running feet, people crying out in fear as they fled the alley, shouting, "Fire, fire!" then "Witchcraft!" and "Flee for your lives, the Devil is come to London!"

With all my will, I battled against the paralysing-spell. My friends needed me whole. If I could just find the strength…

Wake, wake!

Wrenching myself onto my back with a gasped incantation, I stared up into darkness as a cloud cleared the face of the moon.

I had lost my mother's *Invictus* ring. Now Marcus was invincible. Richard was dead. Possibly Robert Dudley too, and the others. It was a disaster.

A disaster.

The word meant star-crossed. And surely we had been crossed by the stars tonight, for all John Dee's blithe assurances of an "auspicious hour" in the heavens.

Richard, I thought abruptly.

I turned my head. He was still not moving, a pale figure on the cobbles, face upturned to the moon. I scrambled to my feet, snatched the wand out of filth, and fell to my knees beside his prone body.

"Richard," I moaned, and cradled his head. It was dark and wet, and not with gutter mud. I stared at my hand, shock leaving me numb and stupid. There was blood on my fingers. Was his skull split?

"Richard, speak to me."

The black smoke tendrils had dissipated almost as quickly as they had appeared, no doubt a screen to allow Marcus to escape. I glanced over my shoulder, and saw to my relief that we had not been entirely defeated. Dent's men were being rounded up, some already kneeling sullenly before the house, hands linked behind their heads, watched over by our own people. The seer had been led to one side by John Dee, still disguised as a Spanish priest, his gaze intent on the girl's face as they spoke.

But I could not see my brother or Robert Dudley. Of Marcus, there was no sign either. But then I had not expected the witchfinder to be captured so easily.

He has taken my mother's ring, I reminded myself dully. He will be invulnerable against magickal attack now.

A shadow fell over me. I tensed, my fingers tightening on the hazel wand. But it was only John Dee.

The Queen's astrologer stared down at Richard, his face suddenly white as the moon framed between buildings behind his head. "Is he dead?"

My brain shifted, idiotically slow to grasp what he had just asked, and I realized that in my horror and fear I had not checked.

"Wait." My fingers fumbled for a pulse at his neck. Richard's skin was cold and clammy, but to my astonishment I caught a feeble beat. "No, he lives."

"Thank God," John Dee breathed, and crossed himself. Kneeling beside Richard, he examined his head wound with gentle, expert hands.

"But we need to get him back to the house. I can care for him properly there."

I was staring across at the seer, standing alone, none of the men wishing to approach her. She looked scared and very far from being a powerful witch. But then, I could not begin to imagine the horrors she must have suffered at Marcus's hands.

"Where is my brother?" I asked suddenly, forcing my mind to focus on essentials.

"He followed Robbie. They went in pursuit of Marcus Dent."

Cold panic filled me. I stared about, frantic. My horse had vanished, scared away by the fighting.

"Which way did they go?"

"Down towards the Thames, I think. Cecilie says Dent keeps a boat moored on the river." Frowning, the astrologer raised his head as I picked up my skirts and began to run, calling after me, "Meg Lytton, you cannot leave now. I need help with Richard and the girl."

I did not want to leave Richard, but there was no time to stay and help with the wounded, not if I was to save my brother—he did not truly know what he was going up against. If I had failed to hold Marcus Dent, William would be brushed aside as easily as a fly. Besides, John Dee was the one with the healing arts. I was a witch, not a healer.

I turned left at the head of the alley, turning downhill towards the Thames, which I could not see in the dark cramped streets but could smell.

I had lost Aunt Jane to the witchfinder. I would not lose my brother too. But what would I do when I found Marcus?

Wearing the ring, Marcus was proof against magickal attack.

But I had to try. Kill or be killed.

As soon as I had seen Richard lying there on the cobbles, motionless, white-faced, blood running down from his temple, I had known Marcus Dent must be stopped. Even if it meant my own death.

I had a stitch in my side from running. I stopped and bent over, panting, my long hair dishevelled. I had lost my hood and must have seemed quite wild to any onlookers, my disguise as the Queen falling away with every step.

The river was ahead, a dark rolling mass at the end of the street, just visible between buildings under the light of the moon. I could hear faint shouts from the riverfront.

I straightened and staggered on at a walk, still breathless but thinking hard. To my right rose the high towers of Whitehall, guards on the side gates, the empty courtyard beyond illuminated by flaming torches. The palace guardsmen stared as I passed, one shouting an insult that I ignored. No doubt they thought me a woman of the streets, selling her body for a few meagre shillings, struggling to survive in this city.

Gritting my teeth, I began to run.

I tracked Marcus down on the dark waterfront, just where Cecilie had told John Dee he would be. A small river craft bobbed at anchor behind him, its sail already hoisted, torches in brackets lighting the deck, no one on board. I guessed that Marcus planned to sail it himself, using the powerful outgoing tide to sweep him swiftly away from London.

I was surprised that he would leave his prize so readily, the seer he had tortured for so many months. But the witchfinder's

mind was a maze with many vile, convoluted twists and turns.
I did not understand him, nor did I seek to.

I just had to stop him.

But what I found at the dockside was Robert Dudley also
on foot, threatening Marcus with a sword, and my terrified brother, suspended in mid-air above the dark water by a
magickal spell.

"Marcus!" I yelled, stumbling along the wooden dock towards them. "Let him go!"

Marcus whipped round at the sound of my voice. Fury
chased hatred across the falsely handsome face.

"A fine trick you played on us up there at the house, Meg,"
he sneered. "Queen Mary, indeed! But I do not begrudge you
the seeress. I had already taken everything she had to give.
The slattern is nothing to me now, you may keep her."

"Thank you," I said drily.

"And this ring is a curious object. Many hundreds of years
old, by the look of it." His gaze flicked cautiously to Robert
Dudley. Then the witchfinder held up the ring to show me,
glinting between thumb and forefinger. "*Invictus*. As deadly
to the wearer as it is protective, according to the seer."

In the torchlight his magickal visage looked almost young
again, intelligent blue eyes, fair hair shining sleekly. I wondered what he might have been without the hatred, without
the dark centre that had destroyed him as a man and made
him into this monster.

"An interesting dilemma, is it not?" Marcus mused, smiling at me. "For every prize there must be a price."

I had been wearing the ring outside his house, I realized,
when he had pushed me down with his foul boot. The ring
had brought that upon me. For if he had tried to use a spell,
it would have failed.

With clenched fists, I watched my enemy admire my

mother's legacy, and wondered if the ring itself had betrayed me.

"When I have killed your brother, and this gallant fool here, there will only be the Lady Elizabeth left to destroy. Oh, and your little friend, the Spaniard." Marcus lowered the ring, and looked at me gloatingly. "Though Señor de Castillo has returned to Spain for his wedding, I believe. Such a shame. I thought you two would make a match of it."

He was laughing at me. Mocking my agony, my loss, my failure.

"But you need not die," he said, his voice sharpening. "Leave these fools and come with me. I will teach you more than your mother's spell book will ever do."

My mother's grimoire. So he knew about that too?

He read my thought. "Yes, Cecilie saw everything at Hat-field, which means I know everything too. She is—or rather, was—a very talented seer. But sadly broken now. Past her prime. I would not want you to share her fate, Meg." His voice dropped to a whisper, barely audible over the lapping of water against the jetty. "Come with me and share my power instead. You will find me a generous and attentive master." He was almost hissing now, his eyes flickering with venom. "I shall not abandon you as *he* did."

I understood at once what he was offering me, and the bile rose in my throat. My hand tightened on my wand and I saw his sharp blue gaze drawn to it, suddenly greedy, intent.

"If you will not come with me, then you must give me your mother's wand. I have the ring, now I want the wand. Come, Meg, don't tempt me to drown your brother. The Thames runs deep and fast here. He would not stand a chance."

He was still holding the ring: the ring that had belonged to my mother, and ought by rights to belong to me.

"Last time of asking, Meg. You will not join me in power?"

I shook my head, contempt in my face.

His mouth tightened, and I caught a flicker of frustration in his eyes. Not as confident as he wished to appear, perhaps. "Then it is time for me to kill your brother, just as I killed your aunt. I expect he will die screaming too."

Bitter fury exploded in me at this mockery, laughing at my aunt's cruel death. How dared he?

"*Desiste!*" I shouted, putting all my anger and hatred and despair behind the spell.

To my astonishment, a crack of lightning seemed to leap from my wand, striking Marcus Dent full in the chest. Abruptly the spell was broken and William plunged with a hoarse cry into the river.

"No!" I spun, wand in hand, and used magick to drag him out of the rolling current, then flew him—dripping wet and gasping—onto the wooden jetty, where he collapsed, Robert Dudley kneeling swiftly beside him.

"I will tend your brother," Robert said grimly, shaking his head when I ran forward, frantic to help. "You take care of the witchfinder. Look!"

I turned, following his gaze. On the very edge of the jetty Marcus was swaying, a dark figure against a dark river. For a moment he just stared at me, blue eyes stretched wide with pain.

"Meg," he mouthed, his expression almost plaintive. Then his face shifted, rapidly changing, his skin pale and coarse, and suddenly it was as though a cover had been pulled away to reveal a cage of freakish horrors within. As his control slipped, the blind eye grew white and dead again, and the scars once more gleamed cruelly in the moonlight.

His lips drew back in a grimace of surprise and Marcus fell backwards into the river, the *Invictus* ring tumbling from his relaxed fingers. His body hit the water with a loud splash, then there was no sound but the river rolling by.

He was gone. And so was my mother's ring.

Robert Dudley ran forward at once, staring down into the black current.

William was still lying face down on the jetty. Throwing myself to my knees beside him, I shook him. None too gently either, for I was terrified of losing him too.

"Speak to me, Will!"

My brother started to choke as I shook him, then suddenly rolled over, still spluttering, a trail of green weed on his face, his eyes bloodshot. Foul river water drained out of the corner of his mouth. He coughed, trying to spit out the last of it. "M-Meg?" He struggled to sit up, still coughing, but I restrained him. "Where is Dent?"

"Half a mile or so downstream by now, I would say." Robert Dudley had come up behind us. He sheathed his sword, his voice calm.

"The current is flowing quickly tonight, and when a man is dead, he travels fast."

"Dead?" I stared up at Robert Dudley, feeling numb.

"I saw his face as he fell. Whatever you did to him, his heart had stopped beating before he went into the river, I would swear it." Robert raised his brows at my expression. "That was your intention, was it not?"

I took William's hand and squeezed it, so thankful that he was still alive I could not get everything clear in my head. Had I intended to kill Marcus Dent tonight? I had yelled "*Desiste!*" which meant "Stop!" in Latin, and hit my enemy in the chest.

And his heart had stopped.

"But he had the ring," I whispered.

"Holding it, not wearing it." Dudley crouched beside us.

"Perhaps the witchfinder did not understand that it would only protect him when it was on his finger."

"Perhaps." I stared dully at the river. "And now my mother's ring lies at the bottom of the Thames."

William spat out a thin strand of green weed, a look of disgust on his face, and struggled to sit up. His wet hair was plastered across his forehead, almost in his eyes. He thrust it back impatiently. "Who cares?" my brother demanded hoarsely. "He's dead, it's over. Did we save the girl?"

"I...I think so."

"Good, then let's go home." William looked about himself at the darkness, the river, the wet jetty. His lip curled up. "I do not like London."

20

BLADDERWRACK

"*Take the juice* of two dead toads—" I made a face. "Disgusting. Why does it always have to be *toads?*"

"Read on and stop complaining," Richard muttered from under the brim of his floppy straw hat.

I sighed, finding the place again in my mother's grimoire. "Take the juice of two dead toads that have been dried three days on a hot brick…. Wait, that's wrong. *Powdered toad.* Yes, sorry, wrong spell. That was for stopping a wound from bleeding."

"Huh, that could have proved useful when Alejandro was wounded." He sounded impatient. "Have you not studied all the spells in that book? I told you, there's little point finding a remedy *after* you needed it."

I said nothing, holding my breath for a count of ten, then letting it go slowly. I had frozen at the name Alejandro.

Very carefully, no one had mentioned Alejandro since we returned from London a bare month ago, though now and then Elizabeth spoke warmly of the "sacrifices" that made us better people. But it was ludicrous to shrivel up inside every time I thought of a certain Spaniard. Alejandro was gone from my life, and so was Marcus Dent. I was free of all past ties, good and bad.

I had to admit, it was odd to think that Marcus Dent would never trouble me again. Of course, Richard had his doubts about that, and despite being confined to his bed for many days after Dent's attack he had quizzed me at length over the circumstances of the witchfinder's death.

But I was the one who had struck him, and knew my spell had connected. Marcus Dent was dead. And it was time I began to live again. Even if that meant learning to smile even after hearing Alejandro's name.

So I forced my lips into a mimicry of a curve. It felt hard. But worth the effort if it concealed my broken heart.

"I've been too busy," I explained huskily, pretending to leaf through the pages, "for I still wish to learn more natural magick from Cecilie while she is still with us. She must return home soon, of course, now she is feeling stronger."

I glanced at him curiously, for Richard and Cecile had grown close over the past weeks. Though that was not surprising, for both had power and had spent long hours together as their hurts healed.

"Will you miss her when she goes?" I asked softly.

Richard pushed back the brim of his straw hat to stare at me.

His eyes were hard but ironic. "Hoping to push my affections onto some other woman, Meg?"

"I thought perhaps it had happened already."

He shrugged, closing his eyes again, his arms folded loosely across his chest. "I like Cecilie, I will not deny it. But I have promised Master Dee that I will return to his service as soon as Bishop Bonner releases him from his duties. I cannot be in two places at once, so to tie myself to another person would be foolish. Besides," he added calmly, "you forget I am not a free man. I am still Dee's apprentice and bound to him under law."

"John Dee would let you go if you asked," I murmured, but did not pursue the matter. I knew his affection for Dee to be as strong as mine for the Lady Elizabeth, and that was a bond I too would find hard to break.

"Spells to repel evil spirits," he reminded me.

Turning back to the grimoire, I searched through the pages. "Oh, here's one. Burn two small coals in a copper dish when the moon has been new three days. When the coals have cooled, take nine pinches of ash and scatter them across the threshold at noon. This will attract friendship and good luck to your house, and repel ill will."

"That's a love-spell," he said contemptuously, and sat up, holding out his hand. "Give me the book. I will find the spell."

"No, it's mine," I insisted childishly, and jumped to my feet, clutching the grimoire to my chest. "Anyway, why do we need to repel evil spirits? Marcus is dead. The Queen has lost interest in persecuting her sister now that King Philip may be coming back to England, and we have added to Mistress Goodwife's protective ring around the house. We are safe from all threats here."

Glaring up at me, Richard made the sign to avert bad luck. "You never learn, do you? Have you forgotten that small thing called tempting fate? It is not possible to defend a place completely. There is always a counter-spell for those determined enough to find it."

I heard laughter, and looked up in relief to see Cecilie and Alice slowly crossing the lawns towards us, my brother in tow. I did not like arguing with Richard, so seized on this excuse not to answer him. William was looking sheepish, I noticed, perhaps because he had an armful of cushions.

"Here," Alice instructed him, pointing. "And you can sit there. By your sister."

"Thanks," I said drily, and made a rude face at William, who stuck out his tongue in turn.

William had returned from London a changed man, more ready to laugh at himself, and less quick to take offence. Perhaps his encounter with Marcus Dent had proved the making of him.

"But I thought you two were hanging that new tapestry this afternoon. Is it done?" I asked them.

Alice smiled, settling herself demurely on the cushion and pulling Cecilie down beside her. "Not quite. We came out because…" She glanced shyly at William. "Your brother has some news he wishes to share with you, Meg."

I stared. "William?"

My brother grinned. "Wish me happy, Meg. I have asked Alice to marry me, and she has said she will speak to her father. If he gives his consent—"

"Which he will," Alice interrupted quickly, "or there will be trouble about it!"

Everyone laughed, even Richard from under the brim of his hat.

"Then we will marry next summer. I wrote to Father last week and received his reply today. He has agreed to let us rent the small cottage from him, up near Home Farm. The farm will be mine when he dies, of course, but until then the cottage will make a cosy home for the two of us."

I hurried to embrace him, tears in my eyes. "I do wish you happy, William. With all my heart."

"And I wish you happy too." Richard pushed back his hat and held out a hand for William to shake, without rising, for although he had recovered from his injuries, he was still meant to be convalescing. The two shook hands, Richard's smile lopsided. "One day you must show me how to do that."

"Do what?"

"Persuade a woman to take you on. And such a man. I fear Alice will have a hard task ahead, smoothing off your rough corners."

William pretended to curse, but was laughing all the same.

"Well," he said awkwardly, "there is always Meg. She would make you a good wife, though perhaps not a biddable one."

Richard stilled, as did I.

No, I thought, and winced inwardly.

Alice looked aghast at her new betrothed, then covered her face with her hands, shaking her head.

"I thank you for that kind recommendation, sir, and will take it into consideration when I am ready to lose my liberty," Richard said lightly, a smile on his face, but his gaze had moved past me to where Cecilie sat listening to our lively conversation, her fair head bent.

Since being brought back from London with us, Cecilie had settled into Hatfield with gratitude after her imprisonment, but it was obvious to me why she had remained here so long after her hurts had healed. She was hoping for some sign from Richard that he was interested in more than just friendship.

She would have a long wait, I thought sadly. Richard was not easy. Not easy at all.

William was frowning. "Forgive me if I spoke out of turn," he said, looking at me.

"You are forgiven." I closed the grimoire. "Enough reading for one day. Does the Lady Elizabeth need me?"

Alice shook her head. "No, she is reading with Kat and Blanche. Some great dusty tome on the government of nations."

Richard crooked a brow. "Sounds delightful."

"Well, it's better than love poetry, the way she suffers. Poor Lady Elizabeth, I caught her crying this morning. She was very cold with me afterwards." Alice sighed, shaking her head. "She is taking it hard."

"Master Dudley, you mean?" I asked quietly, for it was plain now that her ladyship had dissolved the knot between them in London. It was a pain I could perfectly understand, though I had only noticed how the princess had drawn away from us all since returning from her brief visit to court. It was almost as though Elizabeth had finally seen the crown within her reach, and was now determined to think of nothing else—not even the man she loved but could never have. "At least she will see him again one day. He has not *left the country.*"

I had intended to go inside and sit in my bedchamber for a while. It was something I did most afternoons if I was not needed for my duties. Sitting alone in my room, not thinking about... Well, just sitting alone.

But to my surprise, Cecilie was looking up at me. "Shall we take a walk? I was hoping to talk to you, Meg."

My mother's grimoire still clutched to my chest, I followed her slowly across the lawns and into the well-kept herb garden. The fragrance was intense there in the afternoon sun, almost dizzying. I stopped to break off some delicately scented thyme, handing it to her.

"Good for speaking with spirits," I said, as she bent her head to sniff at the dark green spikes. "Dried, ground into powder, then burnt in small pinches in a censer."

"Not bad in rabbit stew either."

I grinned.

"What did you want to talk about, Cecilie?" I asked, pausing beside the sweet marjoram to drag out a thin straggling weed from near its base.

"I have enjoyed our talks about magick," she said lightly,

"but it is time I went home. My mother is not strong, and she has no daughters at home now."

"Of course." I linked my arm with hers, suddenly wishing she could stay at Hatfield a little longer. Not since Aunt Jane had I been able to speak at length with another woman about the magickal arts. "I knew the day would come, but I shall miss our late-night discussions on the proper use of the Devil's turnip."

"Or how to counter a curse with human blood and bladderwrack!"

We both snorted with laughter.

"When you have returned home, may I come to visit you sometimes? If her ladyship gives permission, that is."

Cecilie smiled. "I insist upon it."

"Maybe on the night of a full moon?" I teased her.

"I think that would be an excellent time, yes. I expect Gilly Goodwife will be glad to see you too. And share news of our craft." She glanced at the heavy grimoire under my arm. "Bring your mother's spell book. Unless you would prefer not to share it?"

"No, I am happy to share my mother's spells," I insisted, and in truth I was, for I had never before belonged to a coven, a group of witches with one common purpose and belief. It seemed a rare and beautiful thing to enjoy the fellowship of wise women under a full moon.

We had reached the bounds of the gardens, and woodlands lay ahead. Sensing that Cecilie was tired, I suggested we turn back and, walking slowly, we returned to the narrow stretch of grass before the house. To my surprise the lawn was empty except for Richard, asleep now under his wide-brimmed hat.

"The others must have gone into the house. Perhaps her ladyship has summoned them." I hesitated, then thought she might wish to speak with Richard alone too. "I am probably needed inside too. I shall see you at supper."

Cecilie smiled, a warm autumn sunshine lighting up her face. The seer bore little resemblance now to the thin, wide-eyed creature we had rescued from Marcus Dent's cellar, looking more like a skinned cat than a young woman. Her hair was still short, her skin pale, but her face was beginning to fill out. She would always be slender though, small-boned, her wrists still cruelly scored from the manacles Dent had used to restrain her. "Yes," she whispered.

Suddenly I felt like a gooseberry. The odd one out. Again. I turned away, thinking drearily of the chores I had left undone, and trailed back to the house.

As I reached the door, I heard a wild cry behind me and spun, staring. What I saw was beyond any horror I could have dreamed in one of my nightmares.

It was Marcus Dent.

Alive.

Walking across the lawns towards me in a swathe of smoky black tendrils, his arms upraised, chanting steadily as he came.

The bright sky darkened with his approach, turning day to night.

It was not possible.

Time had never moved more slowly. Even as I took a step back towards my friends, I saw my mother's ring on his finger, glinting proudly there, and knew he had fooled us at the river. I should have known it would not be easy to kill the witchfinder. But my relief at his death had drowned all my suspicions along with the man himself. Now he had walked straight in here, brushing aside our protective spells with an ease only one wearing the ring could have managed. And it was easy to guess what he wanted.

Cecilie was staring, white-faced and shaking, at the sight of her captor, still alive and walking freely among us.

"No, no…"

"You devil!" Richard threw aside his hat, hauling himself up from the grass in the same movement. "Get away from her!"

Marcus flicked his gaze that way, and at once both Richard and Cecilie were thrown backwards by a violent wind, cut off from me and Marcus by a ring of fire that sprang up from the grass itself, burning waist-high with a fierce and very real heat. I thought at first he meant to burn me himself, since I had evaded his damn bonfire every other way. But then Marcus turned, sweeping his hand up to the sky, then down to the earth in a graceful age-old gesture, and I realized what he was doing.

Casting the circle in fire. An ancient trick from the days when they still worshipped the sun and moon. I had heard of such a thing, but never believed it possible.

A thousand times more powerful than the hand-drawn circle, the fire ring was impenetrable by any magic, however strong, however determined the witch behind it.

Nonetheless I saw Richard struggle to his knees in the shivering darkness beyond the flames, sweat on his forehead, his eyes wild, pushing against the spell, spitting out word after word and still failing.

Marcus looked at me, his smile an insult, his one good blue eye piercing straight through to my soul.

"You could not kill me at the river, Meg Lytton, just as you cannot kill me now. I took your mother's ring at the river, and now I shall take her spell book, then the lives of your friends, and there is nothing you can do about it." I tried to run, and his spell cracked like a whip across my back, flogging me with pain. "Be grateful I do not take your life too.

But where would be the pleasure in that? This way you will feel your loss more bitterly."

I stumbled, backing away, shaking my head.

"The book, Meg, protect the book!" Cecilie was shouting above the crackle of flames.

He was almost within reach. I did not have my mother's wand with me, but I was inside the circle of fire, which meant I could still use magick against him.

"Leave this place!" I shouted, willing the ground itself to rise up and devour him, or the birds in the air to strike him, any weapon I could find.

He threw back his head to laugh, clearly amused. "Weak. Very weak. Is that the best defence you have? I expected something rather spectacular after your efforts last time. But you had the *Invictus* ring then. Now..." The witchfinder held up his hand, showing off the ring on his finger. "Now it seems I have the advantage."

Then he spoke a single word and I was flung backwards, my face burning like it was alight, my scalp prickling as though I had been struck by magickal lightning again, unable to see anything but his shadow growing taller and taller.

Soon his shadow had filled the entire sky, a vast column of blackness whirling about him like a wind whipped up out of nowhere, spiralling up his body until he was nearly consumed by it, only his scarred white face showing.

As I lay helpless, a long thin arm come down out of the blackness, with hairy spiderlike fingers, and plucked at the book I was clutching tightly to my chest.

I struggled and shouted and clung on desperately. My body bowed with the force of his grip, but the book was being prised away, loosened inch by inch, unable to resist his insistent fingers. Then suddenly the book flew free, and my arms were empty.

I wanted to rip his face off. But I had neither wand nor ring, and at any moment I could be reduced to cinders. My body already felt as though it were burning up from the inside, heat bubbling under my skin. Flame danced across my eyes as I stared up into whirling darkness, hating Marcus Dent for having defeated me. But all the hate and loathing in the world could not prevent him from taking my mother's grimoire.

"So now I have the book too. And I still have your friends to kill. I would make it quick, but I owe them a painful death for daring to take away my little pet." His triumphant smile flickered out the black cloud. "Next time you stop a magician's heart, Meg, check he had one in the first place."

The black column of wind rushed higher, blowing the fire this way and that, great swathes of red-hot flame lurching towards me in a sudden fireball, then being sucked away into darkness. Abruptly the circle of flames was extinguished, now that he had got the book, and its massive, deadening pall of smoke seemed to conceal him entirely, turning the whole world black. All I could hear above the rising whine of the wind was his laughter.

He would go for Cecilie and Richard first. Then the house and the Lady Elizabeth. My brother and Alice…

I gritted my teeth. I could die, but I would be damned if he would touch even one hair on my friends' heads.

"I'm not done yet, Marcus," I growled into the darkness after him, still lying on my back, the wind tearing at me.

I did not have a wand or a ring, but I had never truly needed them. And my voice alone had sufficed to send him from this world in Woodstock. It was time I reminded Marcus Dent why I was a witch born, and his powers merely borrowed robes.

My hand swept round in my own protective charm circle, throwing out every ounce of power to cover Cecilie and Richard, and the house beyond.

The darkness shook, threatening me with fury. And as the wind rose, so did my voice.

"By the fire you conjured, by the wind in the trees, by the good earth I lie upon, by the magickal blood in my veins, by the ninefold charm, by the knotted rope, by candle and bell, by the clapping of hands, by the four great directions, by the high road and the dark road, by those you have killed, *I bid thee depart!*"

I could hear him thrashing violently in the darkness above me, resisting the spell even as it tore at him. He was counter-cursing, throwing everything at me, but my protective circle was holding...just.

"By heath and by hollow," I continued doggedly, though it felt like my head was cracking asunder, "by the book in your hand, by the green spirits and the red spirits, by the ghost of my mother, by the death of my aunt, by breath and by bread, by the tongue in my head—" I raised both arms, shuddering under the strength of the spell "—*I bid thee depart this place, Marcus Dent, and never return!*"

For five or six beats of my heart, I could see nothing. I lay there in despair, thinking the spell had not worked. Could I do nothing right?

Then I heard his furious roar, thundering at first, shaking the ground under my back, but growing fainter and fainter as the witchfinder was whirled away by my banishing-spell. Almost at once the blackness began to fade, clearing within seconds to show a cloudless blue sky—and a lawn charred black where he had cast the circle in flame.

Richard, released from Dent's spell, got slowly to his feet. "How is that demon still alive?"

I rolled over, then managed to get onto all fours, my legs not quite obedient enough yet to stand. "I don't know. But look to Cecilie. Is she hurt?"

He bent over the witch, who was kneeling on the grass, her face buried in her hands. "I'm sorry," she cried, "I'm so sorry. I couldn't help. He stopped my tongue. I could feel his power. Oh, God, I wish I were dead."

"We should all be dead," Richard said, his hand on her shoulder. He looked across at me, and for the first time I saw awe in his face. Awe, and perhaps a tiny sliver of fear. "That was a powerful exorcism, Meg Lytton. Your mother would have been proud."

Alice was running towards us from the house, clutching something in her hand. Her voice was a squeak. "What in the name of all that's holy was that?"

Richard raised his brows at her. "You need ask?"

"But…" Alice stared from him to me, bewildered and scared. "Marcus Dent? I thought he was *dead*."

"You were not alone in that."

I ignored Richard's jibing tone. "Alice, is the Lady Elizabeth safe?"

"Yes, of course. Though the whole house was shaking as if the windows would come in. But no one is hurt." Alice looked about herself, wide-eyed. "Is he…? Has he gone?"

I nodded wearily, slowly picking myself up off the grass. "Go back and tell her ladyship to stay in her bedchamber until I come though. Just in case."

"No, no." Cecilie shook her head, her voice husky and admiring.

"No, your banishing-spell worked. It was magnificent, Meg. It was so powerful, like being struck with a sword. I felt it myself. Marcus Dent won't be coming back from that for a long time. Not to Hatfield, anyway. You have forbidden it to him for ever."

"A pity I couldn't have found that spell before he stole my mother's book," I said heavily, and wiped my hands on my gown. They were damp and grimy, and smelt strongly of smoke. "I've done nothing but fail this year. I've lost the ring and the book, I've lost Alejandro. What's next, I wonder? My brother?"

"Oh, no, not William!" Alice embraced me, trying to smile. "And at least you are alive. We are all alive."

I heard William call, "Alice!" from inside the house. He sounded urgent, though Alice merely glanced that way but did not move. The Lady Elizabeth would be waiting too. There would need to be explanations, discussions....

"Without me, there would be no attacks by Marcus Dent. It's my presence that brings him here," I pointed out bitterly.

"True power attracts the hatred of the weak...." Cecilie began, then suddenly stopped, her voice drying up, her eyes wide.

We both looked at her, surprised.

Cecilie made a horrible choking noise, clutching her chest as though she could not breathe. Her eyes suddenly blurred, mouth twisting sideways in an odd grimace. Her face was grey, spittle on her lips as she turned to me.

Was the seer having some kind of fit?

Her voice came from somewhere deep inside her body, the Scottish accent pronounced, hoarse and rasping. *"He is in a desolate place. There is a darkness inside him, and it will devour him and all around him unless you stop it. Only you can destroy the darkness."*

"Cecilie?"

"Go to him, Meg Lytton." Her hand was a claw on my arm, her eyes narrowed to shining brown slits. *"Lift the darkness from his soul. It is your destiny."*

I was horrified, trying to push her away. "You want me to...to give myself to Marcus Dent?"

"*Not Marcus.*" Cecilie was shaking violently now as though in the grip of an ague. "*Not Marcus. Alejandro.*"

"What?"

I could not breathe. I could not take my eyes off her.

Nor could Alice, it seemed, both of us staring at the seer with our mouths open.

Cecilie slumped down onto the grass, waving me away as I bent instinctively to help her. "No, no," she managed to say, struggling for breath. "I'll be myself again in a moment. Forgive me…if I frightened you. The visions come and I…I cannot hold them back."

William called insistently again from inside the house. Alice shook herself and turned away, mumbling, "I must go and tell them about Marcus Dent…." then stopped abruptly, coming back to me with a shaky smile. "Forgive me, I almost forgot. Talking of Alejandro, Lucy found this down the side of his mattress after he had gone. It's a letter from his father in Spain. You remember, it arrived while he was with you at Lytton Park and I gave it to him on your return? Well, I…I'm afraid I took it to the Lady Elizabeth, since the seal was already broken, and she wrote a translation on the other side, and…" She looked so pityingly at me, I was suddenly struck with terror. What did the letter contain? "I think you should read it."

Frowning, I took the letter she was holding out to me, unsure whether it would be a betrayal of trust to read his father's letter when he was not there. But Alice was already walking away, and if the Lady Elizabeth had thought this letter important enough to translate for me…

To my son, the Most Noble Alejandro Carlos Fernandez de Castillo. In my last letter I asked you to return to Spain at once, to take up your rightful place at my side. You did not reply, nor have you

returned. My mind is greatly troubled by this disobedience. It is imperative that you return home.
Do not think that you can escape your duty to
your family and to Spain.

To add to these concerns, I have received a worrying letter from one Miguel de Pero, a priest of
the Inquisition who serves the Queen of England
on our King's behalf. He tells me you have become
entangled with a young English commoner, a girl
not only suspected of the terrible sin of witchcraft
but who serves the Princess Elizabeth, known for
her heretical denial of the Catholic faith.

You must cut yourself off from this witch and
her mistress immediately. If you do not, I shall
myself write to His Majesty, King Philip, and
request that you be removed from that heretical
household.

You bring great shame upon our name with this
evil association, and also upon the Holy Order of
Santiago de Compostela. I must warn you that
de Pero has suggested you could be removed from
the Holy Order of Santiago if you have comported
yourself in any irregular way with this girl. He
has also indicated his willingness to have the girl
arrested and condemned if you refuse to comply
with our wishes. I do not need to remind you of the
treatment this girl can expect at the hands of our
Inquisition if found guilty of witchcraft. For you
have seen such executions with your own eyes.

I advise you to consider your future seriously,
Alejandro, and write as soon as possible so we can
arrange your voyage home. I have not forgotten
the heat of youth, nor its desires, but you are not

free to seek a wife in England. Remember you have
been promised since childhood to Lady Juana, and
will be expected to marry her when she comes of age.
  Your father, Carlos de Castillo

Oh, Alejandro, I thought, closing my eyes in pain as I imagined his reaction to such a letter. What kind of ludicrous, noble idea have you got in your head now?

And who is Lady Juana?

Part FOUR

SPAIN

21

CASTLE DE CASTILLO

I turned, my skin prickling. Somewhere across the valley I could hear a great thunder of horses' hooves, a cavalcade riding steadily towards me in the shimmering afternoon haze. A moment later I could see them too, sunlight glinting off helmets and flashing armour, so impossibly bright I had to shield my eyes: Carlos de Castillo and his knights returning home from the Spanish court for his son's wedding.

I closed my eyes and leaned my head against the doorway of the rough stable where I had slept the night before. Why had I come all this way, across the sea, across the land, through the hot dusty mountains, after the way Alejandro had spoken to me when he left Hatfield?

Because he had lied.

"Please, please, please let it have been a lie," I whispered, my sunburnt cheeks even hotter as I considered the horror and humiliation ahead if he had meant every word when he told me I should burn my spell book and marry Richard, that our love had been "a childish dream."

Do not lower yourself by begging.

But that was precisely what I was doing here in Spain. A country so alien, and yet so beautiful in its harshness and majesty, I did not understand how Alejandro could ever have left it for the plain green fields of England.

"No, not begging," I whispered to myself, then knelt in the warm dirt of the stable floor to make an oath. "Even if Alejandro lied to protect me and truly loves me, if he will not allow me to keep my magick after we are wed, then I shall go back to England without him. That is a solemn promise I make to myself." I drew the symbol for Saturn in the dirt with my finger, to bind myself to the oath, then stared out into the aching heat of the afternoon and added softly, "And to the memory of my mother."

A moment later there were footsteps on the winding path down to the stable. I jumped up, my dagger at the ready. But it was only Richard.

"Did you see him?" I searched Richard's face as he hurried inside and bent over, hands on knees, breathing hard. "Did you find out which room is his?"

"Incredibly, yes," he gasped. "That place is *vast*."

I waited for him to get his breath back. "No one suspected you?"

"No, your spell worked. I might as well have been a rat scuttling in the shadows for all the notice they took of me. I walked straight through the main gate, expecting at any moment to be stopped and questioned, and into the castle. And when I finally dared open my mouth and try out my magickal Spanish, I was word-perfect. Even Alejandro himself would have sworn I was born and bred half a mile down the road from here. At least you were able to commit a few of your mother's spells to memory before that devil snatched it."

Richard held out his hand for the flask, then drank deep.

He was flushed and sweating, for it was a steep walk up to the castle where Alejandro was living.

His father's castle! No wonder Carlos de Castillo had been willing to go to such trouble to prevent his son and heir from marrying a common English girl. In England, only the Queen or her highest nobles would live in such a fortress. Here, it belonged to Alejandro's family—and would become his on his father's death.

"Your Spaniard's at the top of the tower," Richard said, wiping a hand across his mouth. He nodded towards the formidable castle, which bristled with bone-white turrets and battlements and sinister arrow slits like eye-holes in the stone. "The tallest one, there, with the red-and-gold pennant. That's the de Castillo flag, by the way. Yes, they have their own flag."

I stared, not understanding. "Why is he in the tower? That doesn't sound very comfortable."

"I think that's the idea. Apparently Alejandro has refused to go through with the wedding. Sworn off women for life, given up his inheritance to some distant cousin, and is planning to join the local monastery after he's seen his father tomorrow."

"*What?*"

"I know. Madness." Richard looked at me broodingly. "And all over you."

It sounded like something only Alejandro at his most stubborn would do. He had come all the way back to Spain, to his father's home here in the mountains, to prevent me being arrested by de Pero. Only now he was refusing to marry the girl of their choice.

And become a monk.

No, no, no. Alejandro would make the worst monk in the world. He was far too passionate for a life of prayer and silence.

"But how could they lock him up in a tower?" I demanded. "He's their only son!"

"They didn't. Alejandro took himself up there a few days ago. Won't speak to anyone except the monks and some old priest. The man who trained him."

"Father Vasco?"

Richard shook his head. "No, that wasn't the name. Father Pietro, I think."

"Come on, I have to see him," I said violently, grabbing up my travelling bag.

"Wait, not yet. Sundown. That's when we'll go." Richard shook his head, staring at me. "So in love with him, you would rush straight into danger to be with him again. I thought there was hope for me once. But after that letter…"

"I'm sorry, I truly am," I whispered. "I thought so too. And I do love you, Richard. But as a friend. You know?"

"I know," he said heavily.

I bit my lip. "Maybe you and Cecilie…"

"Match-making now? Leave it alone for once, Meg." He shook his head, but I could see that he was not angry. "Let's just get you safely up into that tower, so you can have your argument with Alejandro, the one you've been rehearsing in your head ever since you read that letter. The sooner that happens, the sooner we can both go home. It's a long way back to England, and quite frankly, I'm thirsty and exhausted, and not happy about this heat. Not happy at all."

I grinned. "I would never have made it here without you, Richard. Thank you."

"You may be less grateful when you see what I did to your hair."

I dragged off my Spanish cap, put a hand to my hair, then laughed at his mocking expression. Since my rough-and-ready "disguise"-spell could only keep us inconspicuous for an hour or so at a time, Richard had cut my hair short on the long voyage from England, then dressed me in men's clothing so

we would not draw too much attention to ourselves as we
travelled arduously through Spain.

"I had forgotten that I am a boy now." I tugged my doublet
down over my tight hose, enjoying the freedom of such clothes
after my heavy skirts. Though riding astride had taken some
getting used to, and I was still a little saddle-weary after days
on a horse. "Do you think Alejandro will mind?"

Looking me up and down with a wry smile, Richard murmured, "Not if he is anything like me."

It was almost dusk when we finally crept out of our hiding
place and climbed the steep winding path towards the castle.
A bell was tolling somewhere, a deep melancholy sound, and
the foregate was crowded with dark-eyed, dark-haired Span-
iards gathered for the lord's wedding—it seemed most were
still unsure if it was going ahead or not. The rasp of Spanish
could be heard everywhere, making me nervous as we kept
our heads down and hoped not to be noticed.

It had been easy enough to blind the guards to our presence, my muttered incantation turning their heads to admire
the sunset as we slipped through the drawbridge gate and into
the narrow courtyard beyond. But now we were inside the
castle, I was growing less confident by the second.

What if Alejandro took one scathing look at me in doublet
and hose, and told me to go home again?

He was to join a monastery, Richard had said. What if he
had chosen God over women, and no longer cared if I lived
or died?

"This way," Richard whispered, and I followed him round
towards the tower entrance, keeping to the wall.

There was a guard at the base of the tower, but he was easy
to distract with a wave of my hand. I had to admit, I was getting rather good at this. If all else failed, I could always become an English spy....

"How many steps, would you think?" I asked Richard, peering up dubiously into darkness.

"Too many," he said gloomily, then prodded me in the back. "You first. And draw your dagger. We may not meet a merry welcome at the top."

My heart was beating hard as I climbed, and not merely at the steepness of the winding stair. At each corner I stared out through the arrow slits at an alien landscape, Spain lit by the dying sun, dark mountains and vast sweeping plains below, green and gold stretching towards the black-rimmed haze of the horizon. The bell was still tolling, like a death knell, and my breath sounded impossibly small and human beside all this magnificence, the great fortress built into the living rock of the hillside, an impossibly hot sun beating down on it all day like an anvil, and the milky light of the moon rising to bathe it at night.

Dagger in hand, I reached the top and stared through an open doorway hewn into the stone, at a man on his knees. He was robed like a monk, his head bowed, and was praying in Spanish.

"Alejandro," I said softly, and the word echoed about the stone walls, startling even me.

His head whipped round, then he was on his feet, staring. "Who is there?" he demanded in Spanish, and thanks to the spell Cecilie had shared with me before I left, I was able to understand him. "Stand forward and reveal yourself."

I took a step into the chamber, holding my breath. The place was dark and bare, a monk's cell already, his bed a heap of straw on the stone floor, a great wooden crucifix on the wall facing the door, a single candle burning on the table.

He did not recognize me at first, striding towards me with a hostile expression. "I will not marry her. So you can save your breath, *señor*. Go back to my father and tell him you failed to persuade me. As they have all failed." He saw the dagger then, and his lip curled in contempt. "What, you think I would fear death? Get out, I tell you." And he grabbed me by the shoulders, no doubt meaning to cast me physically from the room.

My cap tumbled off and I gave a muffled cry, dropping the dagger.

He swore under his breath, then dragged me to the window, staring down into my face by the dying light. "Meg? I don't believe it. You, here in Spain? Alone?" He looked down at my doublet and hose, his expression stunned. "Like this?"

"Not quite alone," Richard murmured, and slipped into the room behind me. "Greetings, priest. Or should I say, monk? How does one address a friar? Should I call you Brother Alejandro now?"

Alejandro looked at Richard over my head as though he wanted to kill him. "You allowed this madness?"

"I could not stop her, so I thought it best to come along."

I was staring at Alejandro, entranced by how beautiful he was—even now, dark-eyed with anger, bristling, one hand still clenched like a vice on my shoulder.

"You fool," I whispered, and touched his face, still marked by a cruel red scar where Marcus Dent had cut him from his jaw to his forehead.

His eyes closed in pain. "Don't."

"You came to Spain to save me from de Pero, didn't you? Your father threatened me. I saw the letter you left behind."

"Dios!" He groaned, then shook his head. "But it was in Spanish."

"Oh, we speak Spanish now. Like natives." Richard folded his arms, leaning against the wall. "Magick."

"The Lady Elizabeth translated it into English for me," I said patiently, then turned my head. "Would you wait below for me, Richard? There is something I need to discuss with Alejandro."

"I should think so too, after having come all this way, and been as sick as a dog at sea," Richard said sharply, but grinned when I glared at him, bowing before disappearing through the darkened doorway again. "I will not be far. Call me if you need me."

There was a brief silence while Alejandro stroked a hand over my shorn locks. "Did you have to cut it?"

"Richard did it. So I could pass for a boy."

His eyebrows rose as he studied me in the tight-fitting doublet, which strained awkwardly across my chest. I had not realized how much I had grown over the past year, but by the look in his eye my figure was not displeasing to him. "You could never pass for a boy," he assured me. "But you should not have come. Yes, my father threatened your life if I did not come home. But on my return I found him at the Spanish court and made him promise never to pursue you, whatever happened. In return I agreed to come home and at least discuss my marriage with Juana." His mouth tightened. "My father is a man of power, and like most such men, he can be cruel and harsh in his methods. But he is also a man of honour. He has given me his word not to seek your death, and he will keep it."

"Juana?" I could not keep the note of jealousy out of my voice.

"We were betrothed from childhood. These arranged marriages are perfectly ordinary here in Spain, and I thought nothing of it for many years. I did not know her well, of course, nor did we meet often. I remembered her as a shy girl, not very pretty. But she has blossomed into the most beautiful creature," he said, a wry smile playing on his lips, "a bride any man would be proud to have."

I stared and could not breathe, my heart clenched like a fist. "Wh-what?"

He looked down at me, then grinned, his smile making it even harder for me to breathe. "Oh, no, I have no wish to marry her. But she will have no difficulty finding another husband. Though I do not think she liked her side of the bargain. She was ecstatic when she heard I had been removed from the Holy Order of Santiago—"

"Oh, no, I'm so sorry!" I exclaimed.

"It was inevitable, *mi alma*. Do not distress yourself. I had gone too far into the darkness to be redeemable in their eyes. But Juana was not pleased when I announced that I still intended to renounce my title and devote my life to God. It seems she has little time for men in robes," he said drily, indicating his brown monk's habit, "being a woman of deep passions."

"Deep passions?" Offended, I grabbed the back of his head and dragged him down to meet my mouth. Did he think I lacked passion?

But if he had been fooled by my repeated refusals to marry him into thinking me cold and uninterested in him, he soon realized his mistake. As our mouths met, he gave a protesting groan. Then the groan deepened. His arms came round me, and he pushed me backwards against the stone wall, kissing me as though we were about to be torn apart for ever. Which we would be, I thought grimly, if he insisted on joining a monastery.

"Meg," he gasped, staring down at me with glittering eyes. "We cannot…I love you. I would marry you tonight if I could. But it is impossible. Even if my father should allow it, there is still the curse. I do not want you to die in childbirth."

I shook my head, eager to share what I knew with him. "That curse has been lifted."

"*What?*"

"Cecilie had a vision of us together in the future," I told him briefly, spreading a hand against his warm chest to hear the slightly too-fast beat of his heart. "Well, she had several visions before I left. And in one of them, she saw our children."

He was frowning, his eyes narrowed on my face. "The seer?"

"Yes, we rescued her from Marcus Dent. Did I not say? Well, we can talk later—there is plenty to tell you." Laughing, I shook my head when he pressed me. "No, let me finish. I told Cecilie it could not be a true vision. I explained about the curse, why we could never be together. But then she reminded me of an old country witch's spell I already knew. Highly effective against curses. We did it together and lifted the curse. Blood and bladderwrack, that was all it took. Plus three days' fermenting."

"Bla-bla… What is that?" he demanded, shaking his head at the unfamiliar word.

"Dried seaweed."

He was silenced. "You stopped that woman's curse with seaweed?"

I nodded, adding lightly, "And human blood. That was the difficult part. It had to be mine, you see. Because the curse had been partly laid on me. As your future wife."

He was smiling, but his eyes searched mine anxiously. "You idiot. How much blood?"

"A pint."

He was aghast. "A whole pint of your blood? You could have died."

"We took it out very carefully—Richard knew how to do so. I was weak for a few days afterwards, it's true. But I recovered."

"*Dios mio!*" he exclaimed hoarsely, slamming his fist against the stone wall. "This woman will be the death of me, God!"

I bit my lip, waiting for the storm in his eyes to pass. It did not take long.

"But now you will marry me, yes?" He caught me up in his arms, saying huskily, "Say yes, *mi querida*. I could never have lived without you anyway. Not as a whole man. That was why I was preparing to enter the monastery. I spoke with my father today. He arrived from court, insisted I must marry Juana. But I refused. He was furious! I have rejected my title, my family, everything that makes me Alejandro de Castillo. I was just about to spend my night in waking vigil when you—"

"Burst in on you dressed as a boy?"

His smile was lopsided. *"Si."*

"I love you, Alejandro. Even if you do want to be a monk."

"I don't," he insisted. "Want to be a monk, that is. I want to be your husband, and live in England with you, and leave this place behind if it means I can be with you."

We kissed, then I drew back, still hesitant. "There's only one thing…"

"You must keep your power after we are married," he said bluntly, then nodded, seeing my shock. "Yes, I have had many long days to think since returning to Spain, and I see now how unjust it would be to demand such a sacrifice from you. Besides, I fell in love with you *because* you are a witch, Meg Lytton. It is who you are, not merely a dangerous game you like to play, as I once supposed. Why would I wish you to relinquish who you are at heart? I was a fool to ask it of you. And I beg you to forgive me."

"I do forgive you, I do. But you are not afraid of what may happen if I am ever discovered to be a witch?"

"You have been interrogated by the Spanish Inquisition, tortured by Miguel de Pero, discovered in the midst of magick who knows how many times…. My love, I have faith in you.

You could cast a circle in the great court of Spain itself and I swear you would escape unscathed."

We held each other for a long while, our mouths meeting passionately, until there was a discreet cough from the doorway.

"I was getting cold down there in the dark," Richard complained. "And there's a fat man coming up the stairs."

"Father Pietro!" Alejandro exclaimed, then grasped my hand. "He is a priest. And one of the finest men I have ever known." To my bewilderment, he dropped to one knee and took my hand, gazing up earnestly into my face. "I have thought of this moment a thousand times," he said intently, "and had all my lines rehearsed. But time is short, and we may never get another opportunity to settle this between us. Not if my father has his way." He kissed my hand, my skin tingling under his lips. "If Richard will consent to act as our witness, will you do me the very great honour of becoming my wife, Meg Lytton?"

"Here? Tonight?"

His face was tense, watching me. *"Si, mi querida."*

I looked about the bare cell-like room of the tower, where a cool wind was now whistling through the windows after the heat of the day. No flowers, no gown, no friends and family, no feast or dancing afterwards: just me and Alejandro speaking our vows, Richard as witness, and a priest to join us together.

Ours had never been an ordinary friendship. It seemed right that we should not marry in an ordinary way either.

"Yes," I said simply.

I woke in the night with a gasp, thinking a spider had run over my leg. But it was only a piece of straw sticking through the blankets Alejandro had laid down for us on the floor when the wine was finished and night had fallen.

His arms came round me at once, warm and protective, our

bodies spooned together under his cloak. "What's wrong?" he asked, instantly alert to danger, though I knew Alejandro had been asleep like me, both of us too tired to keep our eyes open a moment longer.

"Nothing. The straw…"

"Not a very comfortable bed for a wedding night, I know," he admitted with a chuckle. "We'll leave at first light, which should not be far off now. And we'll stop for the night on the road. Somewhere with a proper bed. And shutters over the windows. So I can demonstrate to my new bride just how very much in love with her I am."

"Oh, I think you demonstrated that quite well without a comfortable bed," I replied, and blushed as his hand crept lower, caressing me in a way that made my toes curl up with sheer pleasure.

"Yes, I was not very controlled. The servants are going to wonder how I broke that table," he muttered in my ear.

"And the stool."

"I broke the stool too?"

I nodded, and wriggled against him so that he gave a quiet laugh.

"Ah, so eager."

I smiled secretly. "I'm just making sure you don't decide to go off in the morning and become a monk after all."

"It is almost morning now. And you will not get rid of me that easily, my love." Sleepily he rubbed his cheek against my shoulder.

"But I still have not thanked you, *mi alma*."

"For what?"

"For forgiving me. I left you so cruelly at Hatfield. I thought it best to make you hate me."

"I very nearly did."

His voice was husky. "I thank God you changed your mind,

then. And came so far to find me. Without you, I would still be cursed. And alone."

My hand crept down between our bodies, and I heard him catch his breath.

"My love," he said deeply, "we have a long journey ahead. And a difficult interview with my mother and father before we leave. We need to sleep."

I turned in his arms, nestling against his bare chest. I could feel his heart beat now, strong and steady, and longed to make it speed up again, to race as it had done last night while we were learning every inch of each other's bodies.

"Husbands and wives do not sleep on their wedding night," I informed him primly. "Not in England anyway."

"But we are in Spain, *mi querida*."

"Enlighten me, then. What do chaste Spanish brides and grooms do on their wedding night?" I asked innocently, rolling my hips against him, and was rewarded when his heart began to beat more swiftly.

"Oh, I imagine they pray," Alejandro muttered against my mouth, then kissed down my throat, leaving fire wherever his lips touched.

"Even when the bride is a witch?" I teased him, gasping a little as his mouth slipped lower.

"Especially then."

Lying in the warmth of his arms, I worked the oldest magick of all while the stars faded behind his head and the sun began to rise over Spain.

★ ★ ★ ★ ★

Acknowledgements

As always, my grateful thanks to my agent Luigi Bonomi and his wife, Alison, at LBA, and to everyone at Random House Children's Books, especially my lovely editor Lauren Buckland, Harriet Venn, Natalie Doherty, Bronwen Bennie, Clare Hall-Craggs and Annie Eaton. Many thanks also to Natashya Wilson and the whole team at Harlequin Teen, who have worked so hard for my Tudor Witch Trilogy in the States. You are all total stars!

Big hugs to my husband Steve and of course my kids Kate, Becki, Bethany, Dylan, Morris, and Indigo. Keep those cups of tea coming....

Thanks also to the veritable army of bloggers, posters and tweeps who nudge me along every day on social media, and without whom I would probably go mad. Or madder. Plus a big thank-you to blogger Azahara Arenas for checking my Spanish. The friends I've made along this journey from first idea to final publication are all the more special for having helped shape the fictional world of my Tudor Witch Trilogy, chatting with me about my characters and ideas, often long into the night.

And lastly, thanks to Meg and Alejandro, without whom none of this would have been possible. I will miss them terribly now the trilogy is at an end. *Adiós!*

   Victoria x

THE TUDOR WITCH TRILOGY

VICTORIA LAMB

Enter Tudor England in 1554, when there has never
been a more dangerous time to be a witch.
The punishment for anyone branded a witch is to be
hanged or burned at the stake.

Don't miss the first two books of this magical and intense trilogy

SHE CANNOT
DENY HER POWER

HER POWER IS
HER DESTINY

THE TIME HAS COME
TO CLAIM HER DESTINY

AVAILABLE WHEREVER BOOKS ARE SOLD!

HARLEQUIN®TEEN
™ www.HarlequinTEEN.com